New York Times bestselling author and MWA Grandmaster Ed McBain has gathered ten masters of modern fiction and had them each write a novella for this one-of-a-kind series. Look for more *Transgressions* featuring new tales from these bestselling authors.

Lawrence Block

Jeffery Deaver

John Farris

Stephen King

Ed McBain

Sharyn McCrumb

Walter Mosley

Joyce Carol Oates

Anne Perry

Donald E. Westlake

TRANSGRESSIONS

Edited by Ed McBain

WALKING AROUND MONEY

Donald E. Westlake

WALKING THE LINE

Walter Mosley

MERELY HATE

Ed McBain

A TOM DOHERTY ASSOCIATES BOOK
NEW YORK

TRANSGRESSIONS

The novellas collected in this volume and the three companion volumes of *Transgressions* were previously published in 2005 as a single-volume hardcover edition under the title *Transgressions*.

A Forge Book
Published by Tom Doherty Associates, LLC
175 Fifth Avenue
New York, NY 10010

www.tor-forge.com

Forge® is a registered trademark of Tom Doherty Associates, LLC.

ISBN 978-0-7653-4752-7

First Mass Market Edition: October 2006

Printed in the United States of America

0 9 8 7 6 5 4 3 2

Contents

Introduction

When I was writing novellas for the pulp magazines back in the 1950s, we still called them "novelettes," and all I knew about the form was that it was long and it paid half a cent a word. This meant that if I wrote 10,000 words, the average length of a novelette back then, I would sooner or later get a check for five hundred dollars. This was not bad pay for a struggling young writer.

A novella today can run anywhere from 10,000 to 40,000 words. Longer than a short story (5,000 words) but much shorter than a novel (at least 60,000 words), it combines the immediacy of the former with the depth of the latter, and it ain't easy to write. In fact, given the difficulty of the form, and the scarcity of markets for novellas, it is surprising that any writers today are writing them at all.

But here was the brilliant idea.

Round up the best writers of mystery, crime, and suspense novels, and ask them to write a brand-new novella for a collection of similarly superb novellas to be published anywhere in the world for the very first time. Does that sound keen, or what? In a perfect world, *yes,* it *is* a wonderful idea, and here is your novella, sir, thank you very much for asking me to contribute.

But many of the bestselling novelists I approached had never written a novella in their lives. (Some of them had never even written a short story!) Up went the hands in mock horror. "What! A novella? I wouldn't even know how to *begin* one." Others thought that writing a novella ("*How* long did you say it had to be?") would constitute a wonderful challenge, but bestselling novelists are busy people with publishing contracts to fulfill and deadlines to meet, and however intriguing the invitation may have seemed at first, stark reality reared its ugly head, and so . . .

"Gee, thanks for thinking of me, but I'm already three months behind deadline," or . . .

"My publisher would *kill* me if I even dreamed of writing something for another house," or . . .

"Try me again a year from now," or . . .

"Have you asked X? Or Y? Or Z?"

What it got down to in the end was a matter of timing and luck. In some cases, a writer I desperately wanted was happily between novels and just happened to have some free time on his/her hands. In other cases, a writer had an idea that was too short for a novel but too long for a short story, so yes, what a wonderful opportunity! In yet other cases, a writer wanted to introduce a new character he or she had been thinking about for some time. In each and every case, the formidable task of writing fiction that fell somewhere between 10,000 and 40,000 words seemed an exciting challenge, and the response was enthusiastic.

Except for length and a loose adherence to crime, mystery, or suspense, I placed no restrictions upon the writers who agreed to contribute. The results are as astonishing as they are brilliant. The novellas that follow are as varied as the writers who concocted them, but they all exhibit the same devoted passion and the same extraordinary writing. More than that, there is an underlying sense here that the writer is attempting something new and unexpected, and willing to share his or her own surprises with us. Just as their names are in alphabetical order on the book cover, so do their stories follow in reverse alphabetical order: I have no favorites among them. I love them all equally.

Enjoy!

Ed McBain
Weston, Connecticut
August 2004

TRANSGRESSIONS

DONALD E. WESTLAKE

It's an accepted fact that **Donald E. Westlake** has excelled at every single subgenre the mystery field has to offer. Humorous books such as *Sacred Monster* and the John Dortmunder series; terrifying books like *The Ax*, about a man who wants vengeance on the company that downsized him out of a job, and probably Westlake's most accomplished novel; and hard-boiled books that include the Parker series, a benchmark in the noir world of professional thieves and to which he recently returned to great acclaim; and insider books like *The Hook*, a twisty thriller about the perils and pitfalls of being a writer. One learns from his novels and short stories that he is possessed of a remarkable intelligence, and that he can translate that intelligence into plot, character, and realistic prose with what appears to be astonishing ease. He is the sort of writer other writers study endlessly; every Westlake novel has something to teach authors, no matter how long they've been at the word processor. And he seems to have been discovered—at last and long overdue—by a mass audience. His recent books include *Ask the Parrot* and *What's So Funny?*, the latest featuring Dortmunder.

WALKING AROUND MONEY

Donald E. Westlake

1

"Ever since I reformed," the man called Querk said, "I been havin' trouble to sleep at night."

This was a symptom Dortmunder had never heard of before; on the other hand, he didn't know that many people who'd reformed. "Huh," he said. He really didn't know this man called Querk, so he didn't have a lot to say so far.

But Querk did. "It's my nerves," he explained, and he looked as though it was his nerves. A skinny little guy, maybe fifty, with a long face, heavy black eyebrows over banana nose over thin-lipped mouth over long bony chin, he fidgeted constantly on that wire-mesh chair in Paley Park, a vest-pocket park on East 53rd Street in Manhattan, between Fifth and Madison Avenues.

It's a very nice park, Paley Park, right in the middle of midtown, just forty-two feet wide and not quite a block deep, up several steps from the level of 53rd Street. The building walls on both sides are covered in ivy, and tall honey locust trees form a kind of leafy roof in the summer, which is what at this moment it was.

But the best thing about Paley Park is the wall of water at the back, a constant flow down the rear wall, splashing into a trough to be recycled, making a very nice kind of *shooshing* sound that almost completely covers the roar of the traffic, which makes for a peaceful retreat right there in the middle of everything and also makes it possible for two or three people—John Dortmunder, say, and his friend Andy Kelp, and the man called Querk, for instance—to sit near the wall of water and have a nice conversation that nobody, no matter what kind of microphone they've got, is going to record. It's amazing, really, that every criminal enterprise in the city of New York isn't plotted in Paley Park; or maybe they are.

"You see how it is," the man called Querk said, and lifted both hands out of his lap to hold them in front of himself, where they trembled like a paint-mixing machine. "It's a good thing," he said, "I wasn't a pick-pocket before I reformed."

"Huh," Dortmunder commented.

"Or a safecracker," Kelp said.

"Well, I was," Querk told him. "But I was one of your liquid nitro persuasion, you know. Drill your hole next to the combination, pour in your jelly, stuff the detonator in there, stand back. No nerves involved at all."

"Huh," Dortmunder said.

Querk frowned at him. "You got asthma?"

"No," Dortmunder said. "I was just agreeing with you."

"If you say so." Querk frowned at the curtain of water, which just kept *shooshing* down that wall in front of them, splashing in the trough, never stopping for a second. You wouldn't want to stay in Paley Park *too* long.

"The point is," Querk said, "before I reformed, I'd always get a good night's sleep, because I knew I was careful and everything was in its place, so I could relax. But then, the last time I went up, I decided I was too old for jail. You know, there comes a point, you say, jail is a job for the young." He gave a sidelong look at Dortmunder. "You gonna do that *huh* thing again?"

"Only if you want me to."

"We'll skip it, then," Querk said, and said, "This last time in, I learned another trade, you know how you always learn these trades on the inside. Air-conditioner repair, dry cleaning. This last time, I learned to be a printer."

"Huh," Dortmunder said. "I mean, that's good, you're a printer."

"Except," Querk said, "I'm not. I get out, I go to this printing plant upstate, up near where my cousin lives, I figure I'll stay with him, he's always been your straight arrow, I can get a look at an honest person up close, see how it's done, but when I go to the printer to say look at this skill the State of New York gave me, they said, we don't do it like that any more, we use computers now." Querk shook his head. "Is that the criminal justice system for you, right there?" he wanted to know. "They spend all this time and money, they teach me an obsolete trade."

Kelp said, "What you wanted to learn was computers."

"Well, what I got," Querk said, "I got a job

at the printing plant, only not a printer. I'm a loader, when the different papers come in, I drive around in this forklift, put the papers where they go, different papers for different jobs. But because I'm reformed," Querk went on, "and this isn't the trade I learned, this is just going back and forth on a forklift truck, I don't ever feel like I *done* anything. No planning, no preparation, nothing to be careful about. I get uneasy, I got no structure in my life, and the result is, I sleep lousy. Then, no sleep, I'm on the forklift, half the time I almost drive it into a wall."

Dortmunder could see how that might happen. People are creatures of habit, and if you lose a habit that's important to you—being on the run, for instance—it could throw off your whatayacallit. Biorhythm. Can't sleep. Could happen.

Dortmunder and Andy Kelp and the man called Querk sat in silence (*shoosh*) a while, contemplating the position Querk found himself in, sitting here together on these nice wire-mesh chairs in the middle of New York in August, which of course meant it wasn't New York at all, not the real New York, but the other New York, the August New York.

In August, the shrinks are all out of town, so the rest of the city population looks calmer, less stressed. Also, a lot of *those* are out of town, as well, replaced by American tourists in pastel polyester and foreign tourists in vinyl and corduroy. August among the tourists is like all at once living in a big herd of cows; slow, fat, dumb, and no idea where they're going.

What Dortmunder had no idea was where *Querk* was going. All he knew was, Kelp had phoned him this morning to say there was a guy they might talk to who might have something to say and the name the guy was using as a password was Harry Matlock. Well, Harry Matlock was a guy Dortmunder had worked with in the past, with Matlock's partner Ralph Demrovsky, but it seemed to him the last time he'd seen Ralph, during a little exercise in Las Vegas, Harry wasn't there. So how good a passport *was* that, after all this time? That's why Dortmunder's part of the conversation so far, and on into the unforeseeable future, consisted primarily of *huh.*

"So finally," the man called Querk said, breaking a long *shoosh,* "I couldn't take it anymore. I'm imitating my cousin, walkin' the straight and narrow, and that's what it feels like, I'm *imitating* my cousin. Once a month I drive up to this town called Hudson, see my lady parole officer, I *got nothin' to hide.* How can you talk to a parole officer in a circumstance like that? She keeps giving me these suspicious looks, and I know why. I got nothin' to tell her but the truth."

"Jeez, that's tough," Kelp said.

"You know it." Querk shook his head. "And all along," he said, "I've got a caper right there, right at the printing plant, staring me in the face, I don't want to see it, I don't want to know about it, I gotta act like I'm deaf and dumb and blind."

Dortmunder couldn't help himself; he said, "At the printing plant?"

"Oh, sure, I know," Querk said. "Your inside job, I'm first in line to get my old cell back. But that isn't the way it works." Querk seemed very earnest about this. "The only way this scheme works," he said, "is if the plant never knows it happened. If they find out, we don't make a thing."

Dortmunder said, "It's a heist."

"A *quiet* heist," Querk told him. "No hostages, no explosions, no standoffs. In, out, nobody ever knows it happened. Believe me, the only way this scores for us is if nobody ever knows anything went missing."

"Huh," Dortmunder said.

"You oughta try cough drops," Querk suggested. "But the point here is, this is a beautiful job, and I'm sick of getting no sleep, so maybe I'll leave reform alone for a while. But."

"Sure," Kelp said, because there was always a "but."

"I can't do it alone," Querk told them. "This is not a one-man job. So I was on the inside for six and a half years, and I'm both reformed *and* upstate for almost eighteen months, so I'm well and truly out of the picture. I try calling around, everybody's inside or dead or disappeared, and finally I reach Harry Matlock, that I knew years ago, when he first partnered up with Ralph Demrovsky, and now *Harry's* retired."

"I thought he maybe was," Dortmunder said.

Querk nodded. "He told me," he said, "*he's* not reformed, he's retired. It's a different thing. 'I didn't reform,' he told me, 'I just lost my nerve. So I retired.' "

"Pretty much the same thing," Kelp suggested.

"But with more dignity," Querk told him. "So he gave me your name, Andy Kelp, and now here we are, and we look each other over."

"Right," Kelp said. "So what next?"

"Well," Querk said, "I check you guys out, and if you seem—"

Dortmunder said, "What? *You* check *us* out?" He'd thought the interview was supposed to go in the other direction.

"Naturally," Querk said. "I don't want us goin' along and goin' along, everything's fine, and all of a sudden you yell *surprise* and pull out a badge."

"That would surprise the hell out of *me*," Dortmunder told him.

"We're strangers to each other," Querk pointed out. "I gave Kelp a few names, he could check on me, and he gave me a few names, I could check on him and you both—"

"Huh," Dortmunder said.

"So after we all meet here now," Querk said, "and we check each other out, and we think it's gonna be okay, I'll call Andy here, same as this time, and if you two are satisfied, we can make another meet."

Dortmunder said, "You didn't tell us what the heist is."

"That's right," Querk said. Looking around, he said, "Okay with you guys if I go first? You'll wanna talk about me behind my back anyway."

"Sure," Kelp agreed. "Nice to meet you, Kirby," because, Querk had said, that was his first name.

"You, too," Querk said, and nodded at Dortmunder. "I like the way you keep your own counsel."

"Uh huh," Dortmunder said.

2

If you walk far enough into the west side, even in August, you can find a bar without tourists, ferns, or menus, and where the lights won't offend your eyes. In such a place, a little later that afternoon, Dortmunder and Kelp hunched over beers in a black Formica booth and muttered together, while the bartender behind his bar some distance away leaned his elbows on the *Daily News*, and the three other customers, here and there around the place, muttered to themselves in lieu of company.

"I'm not sure what I think about this guy," Dortmunder muttered.

"He *seems* okay." Kelp shrugged. "I mean, I could buy his story. Reforming and all."

"But he's pretty cagy," Dortmunder muttered.

"Well, sure. He don't know us."

"He doesn't tell us the caper."

"That's sensible, John."

"He's living upstate." Dortmunder spread his hands. "*Where* upstate? Where's this printing plant? All he says is he goes to some place called Hudson to see his parole officer."

Kelp nodded, being open-minded. "Look at it from his point of view," he muttered. "If things don't work out between him and us, and he's gonna go ahead with some other guys, why does he wanna have to worry we're somewhere in the background, lookin' to cut in?"

"I mean, what kind of heist is this?" Dortmunder complained. "You steal something from this plant, and the plant isn't supposed to *notice*? 'Hey, didn't we use to have a whatchacallit over here?' You take something, especially you take something with some value on it, people notice."

"Well, that's an intriguing part of it," Kelp muttered.

"Intriguing."

"Also," Kelp muttered, leaning closer, "August is a good time to get out of town. Go upstate, up into the mountains, a little cool air, how bad could it be?"

"I've been upstate," Dortmunder reminded him. "I *know* how bad it could be."

"Not that bad, John. And you were up there in the winter."

"*And* the fall," Dortmunder muttered. "Two different times."

"They both worked out okay."

"Okay? Every time I leave the five boroughs," Dortmunder insisted, "I regret it."

"Still," Kelp muttered, "we shouldn't just say no to this, without giving it a chance."

Dortmunder made an irritable shrug. He'd had his say.

"I don't know about *your* finances, John," Kelp went on (although he did), "but mine are pretty shaky. A nice little upstate heist might be just the ticket."

Dortmunder frowned at his beer.

"I tell you what we should do," Kelp said.

"We should find old Harry Matlock, get the skinny on this guy Querk, *then* make up our minds. Whadaya say?"

"Mutter," Dortmunder muttered.

3

Where do you find a retired guy, sometime in August? Try a golf course; a municipal golf course.

"There he is, over there," Kelp said, pointing. "Tossing the ball out of that sand trap."

Dortmunder said, "Is that in the rules?"

"Well, remember," Kelp said. "He's retired, not reformed."

This particular municipal golf course was in Brooklyn, not far enough from the Atlantic to keep you from smelling what the ocean offers for sea air these days. Duffers speckled the greensward as Dortmunder and Kelp strolled over the fairway toward where Harry Matlock, who was fatter than he used to be and who'd always been thought of by everybody who knew him as fat, was struggling out of the sand trap, looking as though he needed an assistant to toss *him* up onto the grass. He was also probably as bald as ever, but you couldn't tell because he was wearing a big pillowy maroon tam-o'-shanter with a woolly black ball on top and a little paisley spitcurl coming out the back. The rest of his garb was a pale blue polo shirt under an open white cashmere cardigan, red plaid pants very wide in the seat and leg, and bright toad-green golf shoes with little cleats like chipmunk teeth. This was a man in retirement.

"Hey, Harry!" Kelp shouted, and a guy off to his left sliced his shot then glared at Kelp, who didn't notice.

Harry looked over, recognized them, and waved with a big smile, but didn't shout. When they got closer, he said, "Hi, Andy, hi, John, you're here about Kirby Querk."

"Sure," Kelp said.

Harry waved his golf club in a direction, saying, "Walk with me, my foursome's up there somewhere, we can talk." Then, pausing to kick his golf ball toward the far-distant flag, he picked up his big bulky leather golf bag by its strap, and started to stroll, dragging the pretty full golf bag behind him, leaving a crease in the fairway.

As they walked, Dortmunder said, "These your own rules?"

"When only God can see you, John," Harry told him, "there are no rules. And when it comes to Querk, I wouldn't say I know what the rules are."

Sounding alarmed, Kelp said, "You mean, you wouldn't recommend him? But you sent him to me."

"No, that's not exactly what I— Hold on." Harry kicked the ball again, then said, "Andy, would you do me a favor? Drag this bag around for a while? This arm's gettin' longer than that arm."

Kelp said, "I think you're supposed to carry it on your shoulder."

"I tried that," Harry said, "and it winds up, one shoulder lower than the other." He extended the strap toward Kelp, with a little pleading gesture. "Just till we get to the green," he said.

Kelp had not known his visit to the golf course today would end with his being a caddy, but he shrugged and said, "Okay. Till the green."

"Thanks, Andy."

Kelp hefted the bag up onto his shoulder, and he *looked* like a caddy. All he needed was the big-billed cloth cap and the tee stuck behind his ear. He did have the right put-upon expression.

Harry ambled on, in the direction he'd kicked the ball, and said, "About Querk, I don't know anything bad about the guy, it's only I don't know that much good about him either."

Dortmunder said, "You worked with him?"

"A few times. Me and Ralph— He didn't retire when I did." Harry Matlock and Ralph Demrovsky had been a burglary team so quick and so greedy they used to travel in a van, just in case they came across anything large.

Kelp said, "Ralph's still working?"

"No, he's in Sing Sing," Harry said. "He should of retired when I did. Hold on." He stopped, just behind his ball, and squinted toward the green, where three guys dressed from the same grab bag stood around waiting, all of them looking this way.

"I think I gotta hit it now," Harry said. "Stand back a ways, I'm still kinda wild at this."

They stood well back, and Harry addressed the ball. Then he addressed the ball some more. When he'd addressed the ball long enough for an entire post office, he took a whack at it and it went somewhere. Not toward the flag down there, exactly, but at least not behind them.

"Well, the point of it is the walk," Harry said. As he sauntered off in the direction the ball had gone, trailed by Dortmunder and Kelp, he said, "Ralph and me used to team up with Querk, maybe four, five times over the years. He's never the first choice, you know."

"No?"

"No. He's competent," Harry allowed, "he'll get you in where you want to get in, but there are guys that are better. Wally Whistler. Herman Jones."

"They're good," Kelp agreed.

"They are," Harry said. "But if some time the guy we wanted was sick or on the lam or put away, there was nothing wrong with Querk."

Kelp said, "Harry, you sent him to me, but you don't sound enthusiastic."

"I'm not *not* enthusiastic," Harry said. He stopped to look at his ball, sitting there in the middle of an ocean of fairway, with the green like an island some way off, ahead and to the right. Two of the guys waiting over there were now sitting down, on the ground. "I don't know about this thing," Harry said. "Let me see those other clubs."

Kelp unshouldered the bag and put it on the ground, so Harry could make his selection. While Harry frowned over his holdings in clubs, Kelp said, "What is it keeps you from being one hundred percent enthusiastic?"

Harry nodded, still looking at the clubs in the bag. Then he looked at Kelp. "I'll tell you," he said. "This is *his* heist. I never been around him when it's his own thing. Ralph and me, we'd bring him in, point to a door, a gate, a safe, whatever, say, 'Open that, Kirby,' and he'd do it. Competent. Not an artist, but competent. How is he when it's his own piece of work? I can't give you a recommendation."

"Okay," Kelp said.

Harry pointed at one of the clubs in the bag, one of the big-headed ones. "That one, you think?"

Kelp, the judicious caddy, considered the possibilities, then pointed at a different one, with an even bigger head. "That one, I think."

It didn't help.

4

New York City made Kirby Querk nervous. Well, in fact, everything made him nervous, especially the need to never let it show, never let anybody guess, that he was scared.

He'd been away too long, is what it was, away from New York and also away from the entire world. That last six and a half years inside had broken him, had made him lose the habit of running his own life to his own plans. Jail was so seductive that way, so comfortable once you gave up and stopped fighting the system. Live by the clock, their clock, their rules, their rhythms, just go along and go along. Six and a half years, and then all at once they give you a smile and a pep talk and a handshake and an open door, and there you are, you're on your own.

On his own? His two previous periods of incarceration had both been shorter, and he'd been younger, and the rhythms and routines of stir hadn't engraved themselves so deeply into his brain. This time, when he was suddenly free, loose, on his own, he'd lost his own, didn't have any own to be anymore.

Which was the main reason, as soon as those prison doors had clanged shut behind him, that he'd headed for Darbyville and Cousin Claude, even though he and Cousin Claude had never been close and didn't really have that much use for one another, Claude having been a straight arrow his entire life while Querk had from the beginning been rather seriously bent.

But it was to Darbyville that Querk had gone, on a beeline, with a warning phone call ahead of time to ask Claude where he would recommend Querk find housing. The excuse was that Querk had learned the printing trade while inside (or so he'd thought), and he'd known the Sycamore Creek Printery was in the town of Sycamore, not far from Darbyville, one hundred miles north of New York City. Claude was a decent guy, married, with four kids, two out of the nest and two still in, so he'd invited Querk to move into the bedroom now vacated by the oldest, until he found a more permanent place for himself, and now, a year and a half later, Querk was still there.

He hadn't known it then, and he still didn't know it now, but the reason he'd gone to Cousin Claude in the first place was that he'd felt the need for a warden; someone to tell him when it's exercise time, when it's lights out. It hadn't worked that way exactly, since Claude and his wife Eugenia were both too gentle and amiable to play warden, and the printing trade skills that were supposed to have given him a grounding had turned out to be just one more bubble blown into the air, but that was all right. He had the job at the printery, riding the forklift truck, which put some structure into his life, and he'd found somebody else to play warden.

And it was time to phone her.

One of the many things that made Querk nervous about New York City these days was the pay phones. He was afraid to use a phone on the street, to be talking into a phone while all these hulking people went by, many of them behind him, all of them unknowable in their intentions. You had to *stop* to make a call from a pay phone, but Querk didn't want to stop on the street in New York City; he couldn't get over the feeling that, if he stopped, a whole bunch of them would jump on him, rob him, hurt him, do who knew what to him. So if he was out and about in New York City, he wanted to keep moving. But he still had to make that phone call.

Grand Central Station was not exactly a solution, but it was a compromise. It was indoors and, even though there were just as many people hurtling by as out on the street, maybe more, it was possible to talk on the phone in Grand Central with his back to a wall, all those strangers safely out in front.

So that's what he did. First he got a bunch of quarters and dimes, and then he chose a pay phone from a line of them not far from the Metro North ticket windows, where he could stand with his back mostly turned to the phone as he watched the streams of people hustle among all the entrances and all the exits, this way, that way, like protons in a cyclotron. He could watch the buttons over his shoulder when he made the call, then drop coins into the slot when the machine-voice told him how much it was.

One ring: "Seven Leagues."

"Is Frank there?"

"Wrong number," she said, and hung up, and he looked toward the big clock in the middle of the station. Five minutes to two in the afternoon, not a particularly hot time at

Grand Central but still pretty crowded. He now had five minutes to wait, while she walked down to the phone booth outside the Hess station, the number for which he had in his pocket.

He didn't like standing next to the phone when he wasn't making a call; he thought it made him conspicuous. He thought there might be people in among all these people who would notice him and think about him and maybe even make notes on his appearance and actions. So he walked purposefully across the terminal and out a door onto Lexington Avenue and around to an entrance on 42nd Street, then down to the lower level and back up to the upper level, where at last the clock said two, straight up.

Querk dialed the pay phone number up in Sycamore, and it was answered immediately: "Hello."

"It's me."

"I know. How's it going?"

"Well, I got a couple guys," Querk said. "I think they're gonna be okay."

"You tell them what we're doing?"

"Not yet. We all hadda check each other out. I'm seeing them today at four o'clock. If they say yes, if they think *I* check out, I'll tell them the story."

"Not the whole story, Kirby."

Querk laughed, feeling less nervous, because he was talking to the warden. "No, not the whole story," he said. "Just the part they'll like."

5

For this meet they would be in a car, which Kelp would promote. He picked up Querk first, at the corner of Eleventh Avenue and 57th Street, steering the very nice black Infiniti to a stop at the curb, where Querk was rubbernecking up 57th Street, eastward. Kelp thought he'd have to honk, but then Querk got in on the passenger side next to him and said, "I just saw Lesley Stahl get out of a cab up there."

"Ah," said Kelp, and drove back into traffic, uptown.

"I used to watch *60 Minutes* regular as clockwork," Querk said, "every Sunday. Even the summer reruns."

"Ah," said Kelp.

"When I was inside," Querk explained. "It was kind of a highlight."

"Ah," said Kelp.

"I don't watch it so much any more, I don't know why."

Kelp didn't say anything. Querk looked around the interior of the car and said, "I happened to notice, you got MD plates."

"I do," Kelp agreed.

"You aren't a doctor."

"I'm not even a car owner," Kelp told him.

Querk was surprised. "You boosted this?"

"From Roosevelt Hospital, just down the street. I give all my automotive trade to doctors. They're very good on the difference between pleasure and pain. Also, I believe they have a clear understanding of infinity."

"But you're driving around— You're still in the neighborhood, with a very hot car."

"The hours they make those doctors work?" Kelp shrugged. "The owner's not gonna miss this thing until Thursday. In the private lot there, I picked one without dust on it. There's John."

They were on West End Avenue now, stopped at the light at 72nd Street, and Dortmunder was visible catty-corner across the street, standing on the corner in the sunlight as though a mistake had been made here. Anybody who was that slumped and bedraggled should not be standing on a street corner in the summer in the sunlight. He had looked much more at home in the bar where he and Kelp had conferred. Out here, he looked mostly like he was waiting for the police sweep.

The green arrow lit up, and Kelp swept around to stop next to Dortmunder who, per original plan, slid into the backseat, saying, "Hello."

Querk said, "Andy boosted this car."

"He always does," Dortmunder said, and to Kelp's face in the rearview mirror as they turned northward on the West Side Highway, he said, "My compliments to the doctor."

Traffic on the highway was light; Kelp drove moderately in the right lane, and nobody said anything until Dortmunder leaned forward, rested his forearms on the seatback, and said to Querk, "Jump in any time."

"Oh." Querk looked out ahead of them and said, "I thought we were headed somewhere."

"We are," Kelp told him. "But you can *start.*"

"Okay, fine."

As Dortmunder leaned back, seated behind Kelp, Querk half-turned in his seat so he could see both of them, and said, "One of the things the printery prints, where I work, is money."

That surprised them both. Kelp said, "I thought the mint printed the money."

"*Our* money, yes," Querk said. "But the thing is, your smaller countries, they don't have the technology and the skills and all, they farm out the money. The printing. Most of the money in Europe and Africa is printed in London. Most of the money in South America is printed in Philadelphia."

"You're not in Philadelphia," Kelp pointed out.

"No, this outfit I'm with, Sycamore, about ten years ago they decided to get some of that action. They had a big Canadian investor, they put in the machinery, hired the people, started to undercut the price of the Philadelphia people."

"Free enterprise," Kelp commented.

"Sure." Querk shrugged. "Nobody says the money they do is as up to date as the Philadelphia money, with all the holograms and anti-counterfeiting things, but you get a small enough country, poor enough, nobody *wants* to counterfeit that money, so Sycamore's got four of the most dragglyassed countries in Central and South America, and Sycamore makes their money."

Dortmunder said, "You're talking about stealing money you say isn't worth anything."

"Well, it's worth *something*," Querk said. "And I'm not talking about stealing it."

"Counterfeiting," Dortmunder suggested, as though he didn't like that idea either.

But Querk shook his head. "I'm the guy," he said, "keeps track of the paper coming in, signs off with the truck drivers, forklifts it here and there, depending what kinda paper, what's it for. Each of these countries got their own special paper, with watermarks and hidden messages and all. Not high tech, you know, pretty sophomore, but not something you could imitate on your copier."

"You've got the paper," Dortmunder said. He still sounded skeptical.

"And I look around," Querk said. "You know, I thought I was gonna be a printer, not a forklift jockey, so I'm looking to improve myself. Get enough ahead so I can choose my own life for myself, not to have to answer every whistle. You know what I mean."

"Huh," Dortmunder said.

"That's back," Querk pointed out. "That throat thing." He looked forward as Kelp steered them off the highway at the 125th Street exit. "Isn't this Harlem?" He didn't sound as though he liked the idea.

"Not exactly," Kelp said.

Dortmunder said, "Go on with your story."

"I don't think I can yet," Querk said. He was frowning out the windshield as though rethinking some earlier decisions in his life.

"Be there in a couple minutes," Kelp assured him.

Nobody talked while Kelp stopped at the stop sign, made the left around the huge steel pillars holding up the West Side Highway, drove a block past scruffy warehouses, turned left at the light, stopped at a stop sign, then drove across, through the wide opening in a chain-link fence, and turned left into a narrow long parking lot just above the Hudson River.

Querk said, "What is this?"

"Fairway," Kelp told him, as he found a parking space on the left and drove into it, front bumper against fence. It was hot outside, so he kept the engine on and the windows shut.

Querk said, "I don't get it."

"What it is," Kelp told him, putting the Infiniti in park, "Harlem never had a big supermarket, save money on your groceries, they only had these little corner stores, not much selection on the shelves. So this Fairway comes in, that used to be a warehouse over there, see it?"

Querk nodded at the big warehouse with the supermarket entrance. "I see it."

Kelp said, "So they put in a huge supermarket, great selections, everything cheap, the locals love it. But also the commuters, it's easy on, easy off, see, there's your northbound ramp back up to the highway, so they can come here, drop in, buy everything for the weekend, then head off to their country retreat."

Querk said, "But why us? What are *we* doin' here?"

Dortmunder told him, "You look around, you'll see one, two people, even three, sitting in the cars around here. The wife—usually, it's the wife—goes in and shops, the husband and the houseguests, they stay out here, keep outa the way, sit in the car, tell each other stories."

Kelp said, "Tell us a story, Kirby."

Querk shook his head. "I been away too

long," he said. "I hate to have to admit it. I don't know how to maneuver anymore. That's why I need a cushion."

Dortmunder said, "Made out of South American money."

"Exactly," Querk said, "I'm pretty much on my own at the plant, and I've always been handy around machinery—starting with locks, you know, that was my specialty—and also including now the printing presses they don't use anymore, and so I finally figured out the numbers."

Kelp said, "Numbers?"

"Every bill in your pocket," Querk told him, "has a number on it, and no two bills in this country have the same number. That's the same for every country's money. Everything's identical on every bill except the number changes every time, and it never goes back. That's part of the special machinery they bought, when they went into this business."

Kelp said, "Kirby, am I all of a sudden ahead of you here? You figured out how to make the numbers go back."

Querk was pleased with himself. "I know," he said, "how to tell the machine, 'That last run was a test. *This* is the real run.' " Grinning at Dortmunder, he said, "I also am the guy puts the paper here and there inside the plant, and checks it in when it's delivered, and maybe makes it disappear off the books. So you see what I got."

Kelp said, "It's the real paper, on the real machine, doing the real numbers."

"There's no record of it anywhere," Querk said. "It isn't counterfeit, it's real, and it isn't stolen because it was never there."

As they drove back down the West Side Highway toward midtown, each of them drinking a St. Pauli Girl beer Kelp had actually paid for in Fairway, Dortmunder said, "You know, it seems to me, there's gotta be more than one chapter to this story."

"You mean," Querk said, "what do we do with it, once we got it."

"We can't take it to a bank a hundred dollars a time to change it back," Dortmunder said.

"No, I know that."

Kelp said, "I suppose we could go to the country and buy a hotel or something . . ."

Dortmunder said, "With cash?"

"There's that. And then sell it again for dollars." He shook his head. "Too complicated."

"I got a guy," Querk said. His shoulders twitched.

They gave him their full attention.

"He's from that country, it's called Guerrera," Querk said. "He's a kind of a hustler down there."

Dortmunder said, "What is he up here?"

"Well, he isn't up here," Querk said. "Basically, he's down there."

Dortmunder said, "And how do you know this guy?"

"I got a friend," Querk said, "a travel agent, she goes all over, she knows the guy."

Dortmunder and Kelp exchanged a glance in the rearview mirror at that pronoun, which Querk didn't appear to see. "We run off the money," he went on, "and it comes out in cardboard boxes, already packed by the machinery, with black metal straps around it. We get it out of the plant, and I got a way to do that, too, and we turn it over to this guy, and he gives us fifty cents on the dollar."

"Half," Kelp said. "What are we talking about here?"

"The most useful currency for Rodrigo—that's my guy—is the twenty million siapa note."

Kelp said, "Twenty *million*?"

Dortmunder said, "How much is that in money?"

"A hundred dollars." Querk shrugged. "They been havin' a little inflation problem down there. They think they got it under control now."

Kelp said, "So how much is this run?"

"What we'll print? A hundred billion."

Dortmunder said, "Not dollars."

"No, siapas. That's five thousand bills, all the twenty million siapa note."

Dortmunder, pretending patience, said, "And what's *that* in money?"

"Five hundred grand," Querk said.

Kelp said, "Now *I'm* getting confused. Five hundred. This is in dollars?"

"Five hundred thousand dollars," Querk said.

Dortmunder said, "And we get half. Two hundred fifty thousand. And Kelp and me?"

"Half of the half," Querk said promptly.

They were now back down in a realm where Dortmunder could do calculations in his head. "Sixty-two thousand, five hundred apiece," he said.

"And a little vacation in the mountains," Kelp said.

"Next week," Querk said.

They looked at him. Dortmunder said, "Next week?"

"Or maybe the week after that," Querk said. "Anyway, when the plant's shut down."

"We," Dortmunder decided, "are gonna have to talk more."

6

"May?" Dortmunder called, and stood in the doorway to listen. Nothing. "Not home yet," he said, and went on into the apartment, followed by Kelp and Querk.

"Nice place," Querk said.

"Thanks," Dortmunder said. "Living room's in here, on the left."

"I used to have a place in New York," Querk said. "Years ago. I don't think I'd like the pace now."

They trooped into the living room, here on East 19th Street, and Dortmunder looked around at the sagging sofa and his easy chair with the maroon hassock in front of it and May's easy chair with the cigarette burns on the arms (good thing she quit when she did) and the television set where the colors never would come right and the window with its view of a brick wall just a little too far away to touch and the coffee table with all the rings and scars on it, and he said, "I dunno, the pace don't seem to bother me that much. Take a seat. Anybody want a beer?"

Everybody wanted a beer, so Dortmunder went away to the kitchen to play host. When he was coming back down the hall toward the living room, spilling beer on his wrists because three was one more can than he could carry all at once, the apartment door at the other end of the hall opened and May came in, struggling with the key in the door and the big sack of groceries in her arm. A tall thin woman with slightly graying black hair, May worked as a cashier at Safeway until Dortmunder should score one of these times, and she felt the sack of groceries a day was a perk that went with the position, whether management thought so or not.

"*Damn*, May!" Dortmunder said, spilling more beer on his wrists. "I can't help you with that."

"That's okay, I got it," she said, letting the door close behind her as she counted his beer cans. "We've got company."

"Andy and a guy. Come in and say hello."

"Let me put this stuff away."

As May passed the living room doorway, Kelp could be heard to cry, "Hey, May!" She nodded at the doorway, she and Dortmunder slid by each other in the hall, and he went on into the living room, where the other two were both standing, like early guests at a party.

Distributing the beers, wiping his wrists on his shirt, Dortmunder said, "May'll come in in a minute, say hello."

Kelp lifted his beer. "To crime."

"Good," said Querk, and they all drank.

May came in, with a beer of her own. "Hi, Andy," she said.

Dortmunder said, "May, this is Kirby Querk." They both said hello, and he said, "Whyn't we all sit down? You two take the sofa."

Sounding surprised, Querk said, "You want me to tell this in front of, uh, the lady?"

"Aw, that's nice," May said, smiling at Querk as she settled into her chair.

Dortmunder said, "I'll just tell her anyway, after you go, so you can save me some time."

"Well, all right."

They all seated themselves, and Dortmunder said to May, "Querk has a job up-state at a printery, where one of the things they print is South American money, and he's got a way to run off a batch nobody knows about."

"Well, that's pretty good," May said.

"Only now, it turns out," Dortmunder said, "there's some kind of deadline here, so we come over to talk about it."

Kelp explained, "Up till now, we weren't sure we were all gonna team up, so we met in other places."

"Sure," May said.

"So now," Dortmunder said, "Querk's gonna explain the deadline."

They all looked at Querk, who put his beer can on the coffee table, making another mark, and said, "The plant's called Sycamore Creek, and there's this creek runs through town, with a dam where it goes under the road, and that's where the electricity comes from to run the plant. But every year in August there's two weeks when they gotta open the dam and just let the water go, because there's always a drought up there in the summer and it could get too low downstream for the fish. So the plant closes, two weeks, everybody gets a vacation, they do their annual maintenance and all, but there's no electricity to run the plant, so that's why they have to close."

Dortmunder said, "Your idea is, you do this when there's no electricity."

"We bring in our own," Querk said.

Dortmunder visualized himself walking with a double handful of electricity, lots of little blue sparks. *Zit-zit*; worse than beer cans. He said, "How do we do that?"

"With a generator," Querk told him. "See, up there, it's all volunteer fire departments and rescue squads, and my cousin, where I've been living temporarily until I find a place, he's the captain of the Combined Darby County Fire Department and Rescue Squad, and what they got, besides the ambulance and the fire engine, is a big truck with a generator on it, for emergencies."

Dortmunder said, "So first you boost this truck—"

"Which I could do with my eyes closed," Querk said. "The locks up there are a joke, believe me. And the keys to the emergency vehicles are kept right in them."

Kelp said, "Do we do it day or night?"

"Oh, night," Querk said. "I figure, we go pick up the generator truck around one in the morning, there's *nobody* awake up there at one in the morning, we take it over to the plant, hook up the stuff we need, the run'll take just about three hours for the whole thing, we take the boxes with the money, we put the generator truck back, we're done before daylight."

Dortmunder said, "You're gonna have to have some light in there. And some noise."

"Not a problem," Querk said.

Dortmunder said, "Why, is this plant out in the woods all by itself or something?"

"Not really," Querk said. "But nobody can see it."

Kelp said, "How come?"

"High walls, low buildings." Querk spread his hands. "The way I understand it, in the old days the plant used to dump all its waste straight into the creek, the people downstream used to make bets, what color's the water gonna be tomorrow. Every time the state did an inspection, somehow the plant got tipped off ahead of time, and that day the water's clean and clear, good enough to drink. But finally, about thirty years ago, they got caught. People'd been complaining about noise and stink outa the plant, in addition to this water even an irreligious person could walk on, so they did a consent.

The plant upgraded its waste treatment, and did a sound-baffle wall all around, and planted trees so people wouldn't have to look at the wall, and now those trees are all big, you'd think it's a forest there, except the two drives in, with the gates, one for the workers and one for deliveries, and they're both around on the stream side, no houses across the way."

Dortmunder said, "We'd have to go up there, ahead of time, take a look at this place."

"Definitely," Kelp said.

"That's a good idea," Querk said, "you can help me refine the details. I could drive you up there tomorrow, I've got my cousin's van, I've been sleeping in it down in Greenwich Village."

"Nice neighborhood," May commented.

"Yeah, it is."

Dortmunder said, "We oughta have our own wheels, we'll drive up, meet you there."

Grinning, Querk said, "Another doctor gonna be on his feet?"

"Possibly," Kelp said. "You say this place is a hundred miles upstate? About two hours?"

"Yeah, no more. You go up the Taconic."

Dortmunder said, "If this is a plant, with

workers, there's probably a place to eat around it."

"Yeah, just up from the bridge, you know, where the dam is, there's a place called Sycamore House. It's mostly a bar, but you can get lunch."

Dortmunder nodded. "You got a problem, up there, being seen with us?"

"No, it's not *that* small a town. You're just people I happen to know, passing through."

"So before you leave here," Dortmunder said, "do a little map, how we find this town, we'll get some lunch there, come out at one o'clock, there you are."

"Fine," Querk said.

Kelp said, "What if there's an emergency around there, the night we go, and we've got the generator truck?"

"For three hours in the middle of the night in August?" Querk shrugged. "There isn't gonna be a blizzard. The three vehicles in the garage are in separate bays, so even if they come for the fire engine or the ambulance, which would almost never happen, middle of the summer, they still won't see the generator truck's gone."

"But what if," Kelp said.

"Then we're screwed," Querk said. "Me more than you guys, because there won't be any question who put the generator truck in the printery, and there goes my quiet life not being on the run."

Kelp said, "So you'll take the chance."

"The odds are so extreme," Querk said. "I mean, unless one of you guys is a Jonah, I don't see I've got anything to worry about. I'll risk it."

Nobody said anything.

7

First Querk split, and then Kelp, and then Dortmunder filled May in on the rest of the setup; Rodrigo, and the half of a half of a half, and the barely mentioned female travel agent.

"Well, she's the one behind it all," May said.

"Yeah, I got that part," Dortmunder said. "So what was your reading on the guy?"

"Rabbity."

"Yeah."

"Something's bothering you," May said.

Dortmunder shook his head. "I don't even know what it is. The thing is, this job *seems* to be doing everything you shouldn't do, and yet somehow it doesn't. You should never rip off the place where you work or you used to work, because you're who they look at, but that's what Querk's doing, but this time it's supposed to be okay, because, like Querk says, nobody's supposed to know any rip-off happened. If they know there's a hundred billion siapas gone missing, then the job's no good."

"I can't imagine money like that," May said. "But how do you get *your* money, that's the question. The dollars."

"We gotta work on that," Dortmunder said. "So far, Querk hasn't made any suggestions. And the other thing, I keep thinking about what Harry Matlock said, how he knew Querk was all right, not a star, when he was just a sideman in somebody else's scheme, but he couldn't say how Querk would be when the scheme was his own. And this is a weird scheme."

"In parts," May agreed.

"In all the parts. You got a factory closed because they open the dam to help out the fish downstream, you like that part?"

"Well, if that's what they do," May said.

"I guess." Dortmunder frowned, massively. "It's the country, see, I don't know what makes sense in the country. So that's what's got me geechy. Querk talks about how he isn't comfortable in the city anymore, but you know, I *never* been comfortable in the country. Why can't they print these siapas in the city? In Brooklyn somewhere."

"Well," May said, "there isn't any fish downstream in the city."

"Oh, yes, there is," Dortmunder said. "I just hope I'm not one of them."

8

As Querk walked toward Cousin Claude's van, he thought what a pity it was he couldn't phone now, give this progress report. But it was after five, so Seven Leagues was closed, and he couldn't call her at home, even if she'd got home so soon. Well, he'd see her in the morning, when he drove up to Sycamore, so he'd tell her then.

And what he'd tell her was that it was all coming together. Yes, it was. The two guys he'd wound up with were sharp enough to do the job without lousing anything up, but not so sharp as to be trouble later. He had a good feeling about them.

Walking along, he kept his hands in his pockets, even though it was a very hot August afternoon, because otherwise they'd shake like buckskin fringe at the ends of his arms. Well, when this was over, when at last they'd be safe—and rich—he wouldn't tremble at *all*. Hold a glass of wine, not a single wave in it.

Traveling from Dortmunder's place on East 19th Street to where he'd parked the van in the West Village seemed to just naturally lead Querk along West 14th Street, the closest thing Manhattan has to a casbah. Open-fronted stores with huge signs, selling stuff you never knew you wanted, but cheap. Gnomish customers draped with gnomish children and lugging shopping bags half their size roamed the broad littered sidewalk and oozed in and out of the storefronts, adding more and more *things* to their bags.

What got to Querk in this spectacle, though, was the guard on duty in front of every one of those stores. Not in a uniform or anything, usually in just jeans and a T-shirt, bulky stern-looking guys positioned halfway between the storefront and curb, some of them sitting on top of a low ladder, some of them just standing there in the middle of the sidewalk, but all of them doing nothing but glaring into their store. Usually, they had their arms folded, to emphasize their muscles, and a beetle-browed angry look on their faces to emphasize their willingness to dismember shoplifters.

Walking this gauntlet, Querk was sorry his hands were in his pockets, because those guys could see that as a provocation, particularly in this August heat, but he figured, if they saw him trembling all over instead that would not be an improvement in his image.

Finally, he got off 14th Street and plodded on down to 12th, which was much more comforting to walk along, being mostly old nineteenth-century townhouses well-maintained, intermixed with more recent bigger apartment buildings that weren't as offensive as they might be. The pedestrians here were less frightening, too, being mostly people either from the townhouses or who had things to do with the New School for Social Research, and therefore less likely to be homicidal maniacs than the people on 14th Street or up in Midtown.

When Greenwich Village becomes the West Village, the numbered grid of streets common to Manhattan acts all at once as though it's been smoking dope, at the very least. Names start mingling with the numbers—Jane, Perry, Horatio, who *are* these people?—and the numbers themselves turn a little weird. You don't, for instance, expect West 4th Street to *cross* West 10th Street, but it does . . . on its way to cross West 11th Street.

Cousin Claude's van was parked a little beyond that example of street-design as fun-house mirror, on something called Greenwich Street, lined with low dark apartment buildings and low dark warehouses, some of those being converted into low dark apartment buildings. The van was still there—it always surprised him, in New York City, when something was still there after he'd left it—and Querk unlocked his way in.

This was a dirty white Ford Econoline van that Claude used mostly for fishing trips or other excursions, so behind the bucket front seats he had installed a bunk bed and a small metal cabinet with drawers that was bolted to the side wall. Querk could plug his electric razor into the cigarette lighter, and could wash and brush teeth and do other things in restaurant bathrooms.

It was too early for dinner now, not yet six, so he settled himself behind the wheel, looked at the books and magazines lying on the passenger seat, and tried to decide what he wanted to read next. But then, all at once, he thought: Why wait? I'm done here. I don't have to wait here all night and drive up there in the morning. It's still daylight, I'm home before eight o'clock.

Home.

Janet.

Key in ignition. Seatbelt on. Querk drove north to West 11th Street, seeming none the worse for wear after its encounter with West 4th Street, turned left, turned right on the West Side Highway, and joined rush hour north. Didn't even mind that it was rush hour; just to be going home.

After a while he passed the big Fairway billboard on top of the Fairway supermarket. Those two guys sure know the city, don't they?

Well, Querk knew Sycamore.

9

In the end, Kelp decided to leave the medical profession alone this morning and rent a car for the trip upstate, which would mean fewer nervous looks in the rear-view mirror for a hundred miles up and a hundred miles back. Less eyestrain, even though this decision meant he would have to go promote a credit card, which in turn meant a visit to Arnie Albright, a fence, which was the least of the things wrong with him.

Kelp truly didn't want to have to visit with Arnie Albright, but when he dropped by at John's apartment at eight-thirty in the morning, just in time to wish May bon voyage on her journey to Safeway, to suggest that *John* might be the one to go promote the credit card, John turned mulish. "I've done my time with Arnie Albright," he said. "Step right up to the plate."

Kelp sighed. He knew, when John turned mulish, there was no arguing with him. Still, "You could wait out front," he suggested.

"He could look out the window and see me."

"His apartment's at the back."

"He could *sense* me. You gonna use O'Malley's?"

"Sure," Kelp said. O'Malley's was a single-location car rental agency that operated out of a parking garage way down on the Bowery near the Manhattan Bridge. Most of the clientele were Asians, so O'Malley mostly had compact cars, but more important,

O'Malley did *not* have a world-wide interconnected web of computers that could pick up every little nitpick in a customer's credit card and driver's license, so whenever Kelp decided to go elsewhere than doctors for his wheels it was O'Malley got the business.

"I'll meet you at O'Malley's," John demanded, "at nine-thirty."

So that was that. Kelp walked a bit and took a subway a bit and walked a bit and pretty soon there he was on 89th Street between Broadway and West End Avenue, entering the tiny vestibule of Arnie's building. He pushed the button next to *Albright*, waited a pretty long time, and suddenly the intercom snarled, "Who the hell is that?"

"Well, Andy Kelp," Kelp said, wishing it weren't so.

"What the hell do *you* want?"

He wants me to tell him *here*? Leaning confidentially closer to the intercom—he'd been leaning fastidiously away from it before this—Kelp said, "Well, I wanna come upstairs and tell you *there*, Arnie."

Rather than argue any more, Arnie made the awful squawk happen that let Kelp push the door open and go inside to a narrow hall that smelled of cooking from some ethnicity that made you look around for shrunken heads. Seeing none, Kelp went up the long flight of stairs to where the unlovely Arnie stood at his open door, glaring out. A grizzled gnarly guy with a tree-root nose, he had chosen to welcome summer in a pair of stained British Army shorts, very wide, a much-too-big bilious green polo shirt, and black sandals that permitted views of toes like rotting tree stumps; not a wise decision.

"It's buy or sell," this gargoyle snarled as Kelp neared the top of the stairs, "buy or sell, that's the only reason anybody comes to see Arnie Albright. It's not my lovable *personality* is gonna bring anybody here."

"Well, people know you're busy," Kelp said, and went past Arnie into the apartment.

"Busy?" Arnie snarled, and slammed the door. "Do I look *busy*? I look like somebody where the undertaker said, 'Don't do the open coffin, it would be a mistake,' and the family went ahead anyway, and now they're sorry. That's what *I* look like."

"Not that bad, Arnie," Kelp assured him, looking around at the apartment as a relief from looking at Arnie, who, in truth, would look much better with the lid down.

The apartment was strange in its own way. Small underfurnished rooms with big dirty viewless windows, it was decorated mostly with samples from Arnie's calendar collection, Januarys down the ages, girls with their skirts blowing, Boy Scouts saluting, antique cars, your ever-popular kittens in baskets with balls of wool. Among the Januarys starting on every possible day of the week, there were what Arnie called his "incompletes," calendars hailing June or September.

Following Kelp into the living room, Arnie snarled, "I see John Dortmunder isn't with you. Even *he* can't stand to be around me anymore. Wha'd you do, toss a coin, the loser comes to see Arnie?"

"He wouldn't toss," Kelp said. "Arnie, the last time I saw you, you were taking some medicine to make you pleasant."

"Yeah, I was still obnoxious, but I wasn't angry about it anymore."

"You're not taking it?"

"You noticed," Arnie said. "No, it made me give money away."

Kelp said, "What?"

"I couldn't believe it myself, I thought I had holes in my pockets, the super was coming in to lift cash—not that he could *find* the upstairs in this place, the useless putz—but it turned out, my new pleasant personality, learning to live with my inner scumbag, every time I'd smile at somebody, like out in the street, and they'd smile back, I'd give them money."

"That's terrible," Kelp said.

"You know it is," Arnie said. "I'd rather be frowning and obnoxious and *have* money than smiling and obnoxious and throwing it away. I suppose you're sorry you didn't get some of it."

"That's okay, Arnie," Kelp said, "I already got a way to make a living. Which by the way—"

"Get it over with, I know," Arnie said. "You want outa here, and so do I. You think I *enjoy* being in here with me? Okay, I know, tell me, we'll get it over with, I won't say a word."

"I need a credit card," Kelp said.

Arnie nodded. As an aid to thought, he sucked at his teeth. Kelp looked at Januarys.

Arnie said, "How long must this card live?"

"Two days."

"That's easy," Arnie said. "That won't even

cost you much. Lemme try to match you with a signature. Siddown."

Kelp sat at a table with incompletes shellacked on the top—aircraft carrier with airplanes flying, two bears and a honeypot—while Arnie went away to rummage and shuffle in some other room, soon returning with three credit cards, a ballpoint pen, and an empty tissue box.

"Hold on," he said, and ripped the tissue box open so Kelp could write on its inside. "I'll incinerate it later."

Kelp looked at his choice of cards. "Howard Joostine looks pretty good."

"Give it a whack."

Kelp wrote *Howard Joostine* four times on the tissue box, then compared them with the one on the credit card. "Good enough for O'Malley," he said.

10

Dortmunder's only objection to the car was the legroom, but that was objection enough. "This is a *sub*-compact," he complained.

"Well, no," Kelp told him. "With the subcompact, you gotta straddle the engine block."

They were not the only people fleeing the city northbound on this bright hot morning in August, but it is true that most of the other people around them, even the Asians, were in cars with more legroom. (O'Malley's bent toward Oriental customers was because his operation was on the fringe of Chinatown. However, he was also on the fringe of Little Italy, but did he offer bulletproof limos? No.)

In almost every state in the Union, the state capital is not in the largest city, and the reason for that is, the states were all founded by farmers, not businessmen or academics, and farmers don't trust cities. In Maryland, for instance, the city is Baltimore and the capital is Annapolis. In California, the city is Los Angeles and the capital is Sacramento. And in New York, the capital is Albany, a hundred fifty miles up the Hudson.

When the twentieth century introduced the automobile, and then the paved road, and then the highway, the first highway in every state was built for the state legislators; it connected the capital with the largest city, and let the rest of the state go fend for itself. In New York State, that road is called the Taconic Parkway, and it's *still* underutilized, nearly a century later. That's planning.

But it also made for a pleasant drive. Let others swelter in bumper-to-bumper traffic on purpose-built roads, the Taconic was a joy, almost as empty as a road in a car commercial. The farther north of the city you drove, the fewer cars you drove among (and no trucks!), while the more beautiful became the mountain scenery through which this empty road swooped and soared. It was almost enough to make you believe there was an upside to the internal combustion engine.

After a while, the congeniality of the road and the landscape soothed Dortmunder's put-upon feelings about legroom. He figured out a way to disport his legs that did not lead immediately to cramps, his upper body settled comfortably into the curve of the seat, and he spent his time, more fruitfully than fretting about legroom, thinking about what could go wrong.

An emergency in town while they were in possession of the generator truck, that could go wrong. The woman travel agent who was running Querk, and whose bona fides and motives were unknown, she could go wrong. (Harry Matlock's instincts had been right, when he'd said he could recommend Querk as a follower but not as a leader. He was still a follower. The question was, who vouched for the leader?)

Other things that could go wrong. Rodrigo, for one. No, Rodrigo for four or five. Described as mostly a hustler down on his home turf, he could run foul of the law himself at just the wrong moment, and have neither the cash nor the leisure to take delivery on the print job. Or, as unknown as the travel agent, he could be planning a double-cross from the get-go. Or, he could be reasonably trustworthy himself, but unaware of untrustworthy friends waiting just out of sight. Or, he could get one of those South American illnesses that people get when they leave the five boroughs, and die.

All in all, it was a pleasant drive.

Querk's instructions had said to exit the Taconic at Darby Corners and turn east and then north, following the signs past Darbyville, where Querk lived temporarily with his cousin, and on to Sycamore, where the Sycamore Creek Printery stood in woodland disguise beside Sycamore Creek.

They approached Sycamore from the south, while the creek approached the town from the north, so for the last few miles they were aware of the stream in the woods and fields off to their right, spritzing in the sun as it rushed and tumbled the other way.

There were farmhouses all along the route here, some of them still connected to farms, and there were fields of ripe corn and orchards of almost-ripe apples. The collapse of the local dairy farming industry due to the tender loving care of the state politicians meant several of the farms they passed were growing things that would have left the original settlers scratching their heads: llamas, goats, anemones, ostriches, Christmas trees, Icelandic horses, long-horn cattle.

The town was commercial right from the city line: lumberyard on the left, tractor dealership on the right. Far ahead was the only traffic light. As they drove toward it, private housing was mixed with shops on the left, but after the tractor man it was all forested on the right almost all the way to the intersection, where an Italian restaurant on that side signaled the return of civilization.

"That'll be it in there," Kelp said, taking a hand off the steering wheel to point at the dubious woodland.

"Right."

"And all evergreens, so people don't have to look at it in winter, either."

"Very tasteful," Dortmunder agreed.

It wasn't quite eleven-thirty. The traffic light was with them, so Kelp drove through the intersection, and just a little farther, on the right, they passed Sycamore House, where they would eat lunch. It was a very old building, two stories high, the upper story extending out over and sagging down toward an open front porch. The windows were decorated with neon beer logos.

A little beyond Sycamore House a storefront window proclaimed SEVEN LEAGUES TRAVEL. This time, Kelp only pointed his nose: "And there *she* is."

"Got it."

Kelp drove to the northern end of town—cemetery on left, church on right, "Go and Sin No More" the suggestion on the announcement board out front—where he made a U-turn through the church's empty parking lot and headed south again. "We'll see what we see from the bridge," he said.

Here came the traffic light, this time red. Moderate traffic poked along, locals and summer folk. Kelp turned left when he could, and now the pocket forest was on their right, and the creek up ahead. Just before the creek, where the bosk ended, a two-lane road ran off to the right, between the evergreens and creek, marked at the entrance by a large black-on-white sign:

PRIVATE
SYCAMORE CREEK PRINTERY
NO TRESPASSING

Right after that, there was what seemed to be a lake on their left, and a steep drop to a stream on their right, so the road must be the dam. Dortmunder craned around, banging his legs into car parts, trying to see something other than pine trees along the streamside back there, and just caught a glimpse of something or other where the private road turned in. "Pretty hid," he said.

There were no intersections on the far side of the creek, and in fact no more town over here. All the development was behind them, along the west side of the creek. On this side the land climbed steeply through a more diversified woods, the road twisting back and forth, and when they finally did come to a turnoff, seven miles later, it was beyond the crest, and the turnoff was to a parking area where you could enjoy the view of the Berkshire Mountains in Massachusetts, farther east.

They didn't spend a lot of time contemplating the Berkshires, but drove back to Sycamore, ignoring the traffic that piled up behind them because they insisted on going so slowly down the twisty road, trying to see signs of the printing plant inside the wall of trees. Here and there a hint, nothing more.

"So if he's careful," Kelp said, "with the light and the noise, it should be okay."

"I'd like to get in there," Dortmunder said, "just give it the double-o."

"We'll discuss it with him," Kelp said.

11

It was still too early for lunch. Kelp parked the little car in the parking lot next to Sycamore House, in among several cars owned by people who didn't know it was too early for lunch, and they got out to stretch, Dortmunder doing overly elaborate knee-bends and massaging of his thighs that Kelp chose not to notice, saying, "I think I'll take a look at the League."

"I'll walk around a little," Dortmunder said, sounding pained. "Work the kinks out."

They separated, and Kelp walked up the block to Seven Leagues Travel, the middle shop in a brief row of storefronts, a white clapboard one-story building, with an entrance and a plate glass display window for each of the three shops. The one on the right was video rental and the one on the left was a frame shop.

Kelp pushed open the door for Seven Leagues, and a bell sounded. He entered and shut the door, and it sounded again, and a female voice called, "Just a minute! I got a bite!"

A bite? Kelp looked around an empty room, not much deeper than it was wide. Filing cabinets were along the left wall and two desks, one behind the other, faced forward on the right. Every otherwise empty vertical space was covered with travel posters, including the side of the nearest filing cabinet and the front of both desks. The forward desk was as messy as a Texas trailer camp after a tornado, but the desk behind it was so neat and empty as to be obviously unused. At the rear, a door with a travel poster on it was partly open, showing just a bit of the lake formed by the dam and the steep wooded slope beyond.

Kelp, wondering if assistance was needed here—if a person was being bitten, that was possible—walked down the length of the room past the desks, pulled the rear door open the rest of the way, and leaned out to see a narrow roofless porch and a woman on it fighting with a fishing pole. She was middle-aged, which meant impossible to tell exactly, and not too overweight, dressed in full tan slacks, a man's blue dress shirt open at the collar and with the sleeves cut off above the elbow, huge dark sunglasses, and a narrow-brimmed cloth cap with a lot of fishing lures and things stuck in it.

"Oh!" he said. "A *bite*!"

"Don't break my concentration!"

So he stood there and watched. A person, man or woman, fighting a fish can look a little odd, if the light is just so and the fishing line can't be seen. There she was with the bent rod, and nothing else visible, so that she looked as though she were doing one of those really esoteric Oriental exercise routines, bobbing and weaving, hunching her shoulders, kicking left and right, spinning the reel first one way, then the other, and muttering and grumbling and swearing beneath her breath the entire time, until all at once a *fish* jumped out of the water and flew over the white wood porch railing to start its own energetic exercise program on the porch floor. The fish was about a foot long, and was a number of colors Kelp didn't know the names of.

She was gasping, the woman (so was the fish), but she was grinning as well (the fish wasn't). "Isn't he a beauty?" she demanded, as she leaned the pole against the rear wall.

"Sure," Kelp said. "What is it? I mean, I know it's a fish, but what's his name?"

"Trout," she said. "I can tell already, I give you one more word, it's gonna get too technical."

"Trout is good enough," he agreed. "They're good to eat, aren't they?"

"They're wonderful to eat," she said. "But not this one." Going to one knee beside the flopping fish, she said, "We do catch and release around here."

Kelp watched her stick a finger into the fish's mouth to start working the hook out of its lower lip. He imagined a hook in his own lower lip, then was sorry he'd imagined it, and said, "Catch and *release*? You let it go again?"

"Sure," she said. Standing, she scooped the fish up with both hands and, before it could shimmy away from her, tossed it well out into the lake. "See you again, fella!" she called, then said to Kelp, "Just let me wash my hands, I'll be right with you."

They both went back into the office and she headed for the bathroom, a separate wedge in the rear corner of the room. Opening its door, she looked back at him and waved her free hand toward her desk. "Take a seat, I'll be right with you."

He nodded, and she went inside, shutting the door. He walked over to the diorama of tornado damage and noticed, half-hidden under a cataract of various forms and brochures, one of those three-sided brass plaques with a name on it, this one JANET TWILLEY.

He wandered around the room, looking at the various travel posters, noting there was none to tout Guerrera, and that in fact the only South American poster showed some amazing naked bodies in Rio, and then the toilet flushed and a minute later Janet Twilley came out, shut the bathroom door, frowned at Kelp, and said, "I told you, take a seat."

"I was admiring the posters."

"Okay." Coming briskly forward, she gestured at the chair beside the front desk. "So *now* you can take a seat."

Bossy woman. They both sat, and she said, "So where did you want to go?"

"That's why I was looking at the posters," he said. He noticed she kept her sunglasses on. Then he noticed a little discoloration visible around her left eye.

She peered at him through the dark glasses. "You don't know where you want to *go?*"

"Well, not exactly," he said.

She disapproved. "That's not the usual way," she said.

"See," he told her, "I have this problem with time zones."

"Problem?"

"I change time zones, it throws me off," he explained, "louses up my sleep, I don't enjoy the trip."

"Jet lag," she said.

"Oh, good, you know about that."

"Everybody knows about jet lag," she said.

"They do? Well, then, you know what I mean. Me and the wife, we'd like to go somewhere that we don't change a lot of time zones."

"Canada," she said.

"We been to Canada. Very nice. We were thinking of somewhere else, some other direction."

She shook her head. "You mean Florida?"

"No, a different country, you know, different language, different people, different cuisine."

"There's Rio," she said, nodding at the poster he'd been admiring.

"But that's so far away," he said. "I mean, really far away. Maybe somewhere not quite that far."

"Mexico has many—"

"Oh, Mexico," he said. "Isn't that full of Americans? We'd like maybe somewhere a little off the beaten path."

Over the next ten minutes, she suggested Argentina, Belize, Peru, Ecuador, all of the Caribbean, even Colombia, but not once did she mention the name Guerrera. Finally, he said, "Well, I better discuss this with the missus. Thank you for the suggestions."

"It would be better," she told him, a little severely, "if you made your mind up *before* you saw a travel agent."

"Yeah, but I'm closing with it now," he assured her. "You got a card?"

"Certainly," she said, and dumped half the crap from her desk onto the floor before she found it.

12

The less said about lunch, the better. After it, Dortmunder and Kelp came out to find Querk perched on the porch rail out front. Dortmunder burped and said, "Well, look who's here."

"Fancy meeting you two," Querk said.

Kelp said, "We should all shake hands now, surprised to see each other."

So they did a round of handshakes, and then Dortmunder said, "I feel like I gotta see the plant."

"I could show you a little," Querk said. "Not inside the buildings, though, around the machines, the management gets all geechy about insurance."

"Just for the idea," Dortmunder said.

So they walked to the corner, crossed with

the light, and turned left, first past the Italian restaurant (not open for lunch, unfortunately), and then the abrupt stand of pines. Looking into those dense branches, Dortmunder could occasionally make out a blank grayness back in there that would be the sound-baffle wall.

At the no-trespassing sign, they turned right and trespassed, walking down the two-lane blacktop entrance drive with the creek down to their left, natural woods on the hillside across the way, and the "forest" on their right.

A big truck came slowly toward them from the plant entrance, wheezing and moving as though it had rheumatism. The black guy driving—moustache, cigar stub, dark blue Yankees cap—waved at Querk, who waved back, then said, "He delivers paper. That's what I'll be doing this afternoon, move that stuff around." With a look at his watch, he said, "I should of started three minutes ago."

"Stay late," Dortmunder suggested.

At the entrance, the shallowness of the tree-screen became apparent. The trees were barely more than two deep, in complicated diagonal patterns, not quite random, and behind them loomed the neutral gray wall, probably ten feet high.

Passing through the entrance, Dortmunder saw tall gray metal gates opened to both sides, and said, "They close those when the plant is shut?"

"And lock them," Querk said. "Which is my specialty, remember. I could deal with them before we get the truck, leave them shut but unlocked."

And the closed gates, Dortmunder realized, would also help keep light in here from being seen anywhere outside.

They walked through the entrance, and inside was a series of low cream-colored corrugated metal buildings, or maybe all one building, in sections that stretched to left and right and were surrounded by blacktop right up to the sound-baffle wall, which on the inside looked mostly like an infinitude of egg cartons. The only tall item was a gray metal water tower in the middle of the complex, built on a roof. The roofs were low A shapes, so snow wouldn't pile too thick in the winter.

Directly in front of them was a wide loading bay, the overhead doors all open showing a deep, dark, high-ceilinged interior.

One truck, smaller than the paper deliverer, was backed up to the loading bay and cartons were being unloaded by three workmen while the driver leaned against his truck and watched. Beyond, huge rolls of paper, like paper towels in Brobdingnag, were strewn around the concrete floor.

"My work for this afternoon," Querk said, nodding at the paper rolls.

"That driver's doing okay," Dortmunder said.

Querk grinned. "What did Jesus Christ say to the Teamsters? 'Do nothing till I get back.'"

Dortmunder said, "Where's the presses?"

"All over," Querk said, gesturing generally at the complex of buildings. "The one we'll use is down to the right. We'll be able to park down there, snake the wires in through the window."

Kelp said, "Alarm systems?"

"I've got keys to everything," Querk said. "I studied this place, I could parade elephants through here, nobody the wiser." Here on his own turf he seemed more sure of himself, less, as May had said, rabbity.

Kelp said, "Well, to me it looks doable."

Querk raised an eyebrow at Dortmunder. "And to you?"

"Could be," Dortmunder said.

"I like your enthusiasm," Querk said. "Shall we figure to do it one night next week?"

"I got a question," Dortmunder said, "about payout."

Querk looked alert, ready to help. "Yeah?"

"When do we get it?"

"I don't follow," Querk said.

Dortmunder pointed at the building in front of them. "When we leave there," he said, "what we got is siapas. *Money* we get from Rodrigo."

"Sure," Querk said.

"How? When?"

"Well, first the siapas gotta go to Guerrera," Querk said, "and then Rodrigo has stuff he's gonna do, and then the dollars come up here."

"What if they don't?" Dortmunder said.

"Listen," Querk said, "I trust Rodrigo, he'll come through."

"I dunno about this," Dortmunder said.

Querk looked at his watch again. He was antsy to get to work. "Lemme get a message to him," he said, "work out a guarantee. What if I come back to the city this Saturday? We'll meet. Maybe your place again?"

"Three in the afternoon," Dortmunder

said, because he didn't want to have to give everybody lunch.

"We'll work it out then," Querk said. "Listen, I better get on my forklift, I wouldn't want to get fired before vacation time."

He nodded a farewell and walked toward the loading bay, while Dortmunder and Kelp turned around and headed out. As they walked toward the public street, Kelp said, "Maybe the dollars should come up *before* the siapas go down."

"I was thinking that," Dortmunder said. "Or maybe one of us rides shotgun."

"You mean, *go* to this place?" Kelp was astonished. "Would you wanna do that?"

"No," Dortmunder said. "I said, 'one of us.' "

"We'll see how it plays," Kelp said. They turned toward the intersection, and he said, "I talked to Seven Leagues."

"Yeah?"

"Her name is Janet Twilley. She's bossy, and she's got a black eye."

"Oh, yeah?" Dortmunder was surprised. "Querk doesn't seem the type."

"No, he doesn't. I think we oughta see is there a Mr. Twilley."

13

Roger Twilley's shift as a repairman for Darby Telephone & Electronics (slogan: "The 5th Largest Phone Co. in New York State!") ended every day at four, an hour before Janet would close her travel agency, which was good. It gave him an hour by himself to listen to the day's tapes.

Twilley, a leathery, bony, loose-jointed fellow who wore his hair too long because he didn't like barbers, was known to his coworkers as an okay guy who didn't have much to say for himself. If he ever *were* to put his thoughts into words (which he wouldn't), their opinion would change, because in fact Twilley despised and mistrusted them all. He despised and mistrusted everybody he knew, and believed he would despise and mistrust everybody else in the world if he got to know them. Thus the tapes.

Being a phone company repairman, often alone on the job with his own cherry picker, and having a knack with phone gadgets he'd developed over the years on the job, Twilley had found it easy to bug the phones of everybody he knew that he cared the slightest bit about eavesdropping on.

His mother, certainly, and Janet, naturally, and half a dozen other relatives and friends scattered around the general Sycamore area. The bugs were voice-activated, and the tapes were in his "den" in the basement, a room Janet knew damn well to keep out of, or she knew what she'd get.

Every afternoon, once he'd shucked out of his dark blue Darby Telephone jumpsuit and opened himself a can of beer, Twilley would go down to the den to listen to what these people had to say for themselves. He knew at least a few of them were scheming against him—Mom, for instance, and Janet—but he hadn't caught any of them yet. It was, he knew, only a matter of time. Sooner or later, they'd condemn themselves out of their own mouths.

There are a lot of factors that might help explain how Twilley had turned out this way. There was his father's abrupt abandonment of the family when Twilley was six, for instance, a betrayal he'd never gotten over. There was his mother's catting around for a good ten years or more after that first trauma, well into Twilley's sexually agonized teens. There was the so-called girlfriend, Renee, who had publicly humiliated him in seventh grade. But the fact is, what it came down to, Twilley was a jerk.

The jerk now sat for thirty-five minutes at the table in his den, earphones on as he listened to the day the town had lived through, starting with Janet. Her phone calls today were all strictly business, talking to airlines, hotels, clients. There was nothing like the other day's "wrong number," somebody supposedly asking for somebody named Frank, that Twilley had immediately leaped on as code. A signal, some kind of signal. He'd played that fragment of tape over and over— "Is Frank there?" "Is Frank there?" "Is Frank there?"—and he would recognize that voice if it ever called again, no matter what it had to say.

On to the rest of the tapes. His mother and her friend Helen yakked the whole goddam day away, as usual—they told each other recipes, bird sightings, funny newspaper items, plots of television shows—and as usual Twilley fast-forwarded through it all, just dropping in for spot checks here and there— ". . . and she said Emmaline looked pregnant to *her* . . ."—or he'd be down here in the den half the night, listening to two women who had raised boringness to a kind of holy art form. Stained glass for the ear.

The rest of the tapes contained nothing useful. Twilley reset them for tomorrow and went upstairs. He sat on the sofa in the living room, opened the drawer in the end table beside him, and his tarot deck had been moved. He frowned at it. He always kept it lined up in a neat row between the coasters and the notepad, and now all three were out of alignment, the tarot deck most noticeably.

He looked around the room. *Janet* wouldn't move it. She wouldn't open this drawer. Had somebody been in the house?

He walked through the place, a small two-bedroom Cape Cod, and saw nothing else disturbed. Nothing was missing. He must have jostled the table one time, walking by.

He did a run of the cards on the living room coffee table, a little more hastily than usual, to be done before Janet got home. He wasn't embarrassed by the cards and his daily consultation of them, he could certainly do anything he damn well pleased in his own home, but it just felt a little awkward somehow to shuffle the deck and deal out the cards if he knew Janet could see him.

Nothing much in the cards today. A few strangers hovered here and there, but they always did. Life, according to the tarot deck, was normal.

He put the deck away, neatly aligned in the drawer, and when Janet came home a quarter hour later he was sprawled on the sofa, watching the early news. She took the sunglasses off right away, as soon as she walked in the door, to spite him. He squinted at her, and that shouldn't look that bruised, not four, five days later. She must be poking her thumb in her eye to make it look worse, so he'd feel bad.

You want somebody to poke a thumb in your eye, is that it? Is that what you want? "How was your day?" he said.

"I caught a fish." She'd been speaking to him in a monotone for so long he thought it was normal. "I'll see about dinner," she said, and went on through toward the kitchen.

Watching antacid commercials on television, Twilley told himself he *knew* she was up to something, and the reason he knew, she didn't fight back anymore. She didn't get mad at him anymore, and she almost never tried to boss him around anymore.

Back at the beginning of the marriage, years ago, she had been an improver and he had been her most important project. Not her only project, she bossed everybody around, but the most important one. She'd married him, and they both knew it, because she'd believed he needed improving, and further believed he'd be somebody she'd be happy to live with once the improvement was complete.

No. Nobody pushes Roger Twilley. Roger Twilley pushes back.

But she wasn't pushing any more, hardly at all, only in an automatic unguarded way every once in a while. Like a few days ago. So that's how he knew she was up to something. Up to something.

"Is Frank there?"

14

Since he didn't plan to stay overnight in the city this time, Querk didn't borrow Claude's van but drove his own old clunker of a Honda with the resale value of a brick. But it would take him to New York and back, and last as long as he'd need it, which wouldn't be very long at all.

Three o'clock. He walked from his

parked heap to the entrance to Dortmunder's building and would have rung the bell but Kelp was just ahead of him, standing in front of the door as he pulled his wallet out. "Whadaya say, Kirby?" he said, and withdrew a credit card from the wallet.

A credit card? To enter an apartment building? Querk said, "What are you doing?" but then he saw what he was doing, as Kelp slid the credit card down the gap between door and frame, like slicing off a wedge of soft cheese, and the door sagged open with a little forlorn *creak.*

"Come on in," Kelp said, and led the way.

Following, Querk said, "Why don't you ring the doorbell?"

"Why disturb them? This is just as easy. And practice."

Querk was not pleased, but not surprised either, when Kelp treated the apartment door upstairs the same way, going through it like a movie ghost, then pausing to call down the hallway, "Hello! Anybody there?" He turned his head to explain over his shoulder, "May doesn't like me to just barge in."

"No," agreed Querk, while down the hall Dortmunder appeared from the living room, racing form in one hand, red pencil in the other and scowl on face.

"God damn it, Andy," he said. "The building spent a lot of money on those doorbells."

"People spend money on anything," Kelp said, as he and Querk entered the apartment, Querk closing the door, yet wondering why he bothered.

Dortmunder shook his head, giving up the fight, and led the way into the living room as Kelp said, "May here?"

"She's doing a matinee." Dortmunder explained to Querk, "She likes movies, so if I got something to do she goes to them."

"You don't? Like movies?"

Dortmunder shrugged. "They're okay. Siddown."

Querk took the sofa, Dortmunder and Kelp the chairs. Kelp said, "So here we all are, Kirby, and now you're going to ease our minds."

"Well, I'll try." This was going to be tricky now, as Querk well knew. He said, "Maybe I should first tell you about the other person in this."

"Rodrigo, you mean," Kelp said.

"No, the travel agent."

"*That's* right," Kelp said, "you said there

was a travel agent, he's the one gonna ship the siapas south."

"She," Querk corrected him. "Janet Twilley, her name is. She's got a travel agency, up there in Sycamore."

"Oh, ho," said Kelp. He looked roguish. "A little something happening there, Kirby?"

"No no," Querk said, because he certainly didn't want them to think *that.* "It's strictly business. She and I are gonna split our share, the same as you two."

"Half of a half," Kelp said.

"Right."

Dortmunder said, "You trust this person."

"Oh, absolutely," Querk said.

Dortmunder said, "Without anything special between you, just a business thing, you trust her."

Treading with extreme caution, Querk said, "To tell you the truth, I think she's got an unhappy marriage. I think she wants money so she can get away from there."

"But not with you," Kelp said.

"No, not with an ex-con." Querk figured if he put himself down it would sound more believable. "She just wants to use me," he explained, "to make it so she can get out of that marriage."

Dortmunder shrugged. "Okay. So she's the one takes the siapas to Rodrigo. *You* trust her to come back with the dollars. But we still got the same question, why do *we* trust her?"

"We talked about that," Querk said, "Janet and me, and the only thing we could come up with is, one of you has to travel with her."

Kelp nodded at Dortmunder. "Told you so."

"See," Querk said, hurrying through the story now that they'd reached it, "she's putting together this travel package, I dunno, fifteen or twenty people on this South American bus tour. Plane down, then bus. And she'll have the boxes in with the whole container load of everybody's luggage. So what she can do, she can slip in one more person, and she'll get the ticket for free, but you'll have to tell me which one so she'll know what name to put on the ticket."

Dortmunder and Kelp looked at each other. Kelp sighed. "I knew this was gonna happen," he said.

Querk said, "It won't be bad. A few days' vacation, and you come back."

Kelp said, "Can she promote two tickets?"

"You mean, both of you go down?"

"No," Kelp said. "I mean my lady friend. I could see myself doing this, I mean it would be easier, if she could come along."

"Sure," Querk said, because why not, and also because this was turning out to be easier than he'd feared. "Just give me her name. Write it down on something."

Dortmunder, rising, said, "I got a pad in the kitchen. Anybody want a beer?"

Everybody wanted a beer. Dortmunder went away, and Kelp said to Querk, "Her name is Anne Marie Carpinaw. Your friend—Janet?—they'll like each other."

"I'm sure they will," Querk said. Then, because he was nervous, he repeated himself, saying, "It won't be bad. A few days' vacation, that's all. You'll have a good time."

"Sure," Kelp said.

Dortmunder came back with a notepad and three unopened beer cans. "Here, everybody can open their own," he said.

Kelp took the pad and wrote his lady friend's name on it, while the other two opened their beer cans, Dortmunder slopping beer onto his pants leg. "Damn!"

"Here it is," Kelp said, and handed the slip of paper to Querk.

"Thanks." Querk pocketed the paper and lifted his beer. "What was that toast of yours? To crime."

Kelp offered the world's blandest smile. "To crime, with good friends," he said.

"Hear, hear," Dortmunder and Querk said.

15

Wednesday. The last thing Janet did before shutting Seven Leagues for the day was cut the two tickets, in the names of Anne Marie Carpinaw and Andrew Octavian Kelp, JFK to San Cristobal, Guerrera, change in Miami, intermediate stop in Tegucigalpa, Honduras, departure 10 P.M. tomorrow night, arrival 6:47 A.M., first leg Delta, second leg the charter carrier InterAir. She tucked these two tickets into her shoulder bag, put on her sunglasses, locked up the shop, took a last long look at it through the front plate glass window, and drove home to the rat.

At almost the exact same instant Janet was opening the door of her hated home, Kelp was opening the driver's door of another O'Malley special (small but spunky) rented with another short-life-expectancy credit card. Dortmunder tossed his bag in the back and slid in beside Kelp.

Kirby Querk, being on vacation along with the entire workforce of Sycamore Creek Printery, spent the afternoon fishing with a couple of friends from the plant, well downstream from town. (It was while fishing this part of this stream, almost a year ago, that he'd first met Janet, beautiful in her fishing hat and waders.) The unusually high water made for a rather interesting day, with a few spills, nothing serious. The influx of water from the opened dam starting last Saturday had roiled the streambed for a while, making turbid water in which the fishing would have been bad to useless, but by Wednesday Sycamore Creek was its normal sparkling self and Querk spent a happy day playing catch and release with the fish. There were times he almost forgot his nervousness about tonight.

Roger Twilley watched television news every chance he got, a sneer on his face. He despised and mistrusted them all, and watched mainly so he could catch the lies. A lot of the lies got past him, he knew that, but some of them he caught, the blatant obvious untruths the powers that be tell to keep the shmos in line. Well, Roger Twilley was no shmo; he was on to them, there in their 6:30 network news.

Meanwhile Janet, allegedly in the kitchen working on dinner, was actually in the bedroom, packing a small bag. Toiletries, cosmetics, a week's worth of clothing. She left much more than she took, but still the bag was crammed full when she was finished, and surprisingly heavy. She lugged it from the bedroom through the kitchen, out the back door, and around to the side of the house where a band of blacktop had been added, for her to keep her car. (*His* car got the attached garage, of course, which was all right in the summer, less so in the winter.) She heaved the bag into the trunk, which already contained her fishing gear, and went back into the house to actually make dinner, asking herself yet again, as she did every evening at this time, why she didn't just go ahead and poison the rat. But she answered the question, too, as she always did, with the knowledge that she'd simply never get away with it. A battered wife and a poisoned husband; even a Darby County cop could draw that connector.

Using the same credit card that had promoted the rental car, outside which now

Dortmunder was stretching and groaning and wailing, "Why me?" Kelp took two adjoining rooms in the Taconic Lakes Motel, just about twenty miles north of Sycamore. It was not quite 7:30; even leaving the city in the middle of rush hour, they'd made good time.

Querk ate a bland dinner (meat loaf, mashed potatoes, green beans, water) with Cousin Claude and Eugenia and the two kids, then went into "his" room and packed his own bag. His years of being in and out of various jails had left him a man of very few possessions, all of which either fit into the bag or he wouldn't mind leaving behind. He put the bag on the floor next to the bed, on the side away from the door, and went out to watch television with the family.

Dortmunder and Kelp, after resting a little while in the motel, drove down to Sycamore and had dinner in the Italian restaurant by the traffic light there, the printery's forest crowding in on it from two sides. Dinner wasn't bad, and the same credit card still had some life in it. After dinner, they strolled around town a while, seeing how absolutely dense and black that forest was. There was some traffic, not much, and by evening the other joint in town, Sycamore House, where they'd had that lunch they were trying to forget, turned out to be where the rowdies hung out, the kind of place where the usual greeting is, "Wanna fight?" Their bark was presumably worse than their bite, though, because there was absolutely no police presence in town, neither around Sycamore House nor anywhere else, nor did it appear to be needed. Maybe on weekends.

When Janet washed her hair, which she usually did about three evenings a week, she was in the bathroom absolutely *forever.* This was a one-bathroom house, so Roger complained bitterly about the time she hogged in the bathroom, forcing him to go outside to piss on the lawn, but secretly this was the time he would take to search her possessions. Sooner or later, she would slip, leave something incriminating where he could find it.

And tonight, by God, was it! His hand shook, holding the airline tickets, and something gnawed at his heart, as though in reality he'd never wanted to find the proof of her perfidy after all, which was of course nonsense. Because here it was. *She* was Anne

Marie Carpinaw, of course, a stupid alias to try to hide behind. But who was Andrew Octavian Kelp?

Cousin Claude and his family were early to bed, early to rise, and usually so was Querk; jail does not encourage the habit of rising late. This evening, as usual, the entire household was tucked in and dark before eleven o'clock, but this evening Querk couldn't sleep, not even if he wanted to, which he didn't. He lay in the dark in "his" room, the packed bag a dark bulk on the floor beside the bed, and he gazed at the ceiling, thinking about the plan he and Janet had worked out, seeing how good it was, how really good. They'd gone over it together he didn't know how many times, looking for flaws, finding some, correcting them. By now, the plan was honed as smooth as a river rock.

Janet almost always went to bed before Roger, and by the time he got there she would be asleep or at least pretending. Tonight, without a word, she went off to the bedroom and their separate beds just as he started watching the eleven o'clock news. He listened, and when he heard the bedroom door close he quietly got up, went to the kitchen, then through the connecting door to the garage. There was an automatic electric garage door opener, but it was very loud, and it caused a bright light to switch on for three minutes, so tonight Roger opened his car door to cause the interior light to go on, and by that light he found the red-and-white cord he could pull to separate the door from the opener, designed for emergencies like the power being off. Then he lifted the door by hand, leaned into the car to put it in neutral, and pushed it backward out of the garage. There was a slight downhill slope from garage to street, so the car did get away from him just a little bit, but there was no traffic on this residential side street this late at night, so he just followed it, and it stopped of its own accord when the rear wheels reached the street. He turned the wheel through the open window, and wrestled the car backward in a long arc until it was parked on the opposite side of the street one door down. A dark street, trees in leaf, a car like any other. Janet would have no reason to notice it. He went back to the house, into the garage, and pulled the door down. He could reattach the cord in the morning.

11:45 said Querk's bedside clock, red

numbers glowing in the dark. He got up, dressed quickly and silently, picked up his bag, and tiptoed from the house. Tonight, he had parked the Honda down the block a ways. He walked to it, put the bag on the passenger seat, and drove away from there.

In their separate beds in the dark room, Janet and Roger were each convinced the other was asleep. Both were fully clothed except for their shoes under the light summer covers, and both worked very hard to breathe like a sleeping person. They had each other fooled completely.

Every time Janet, lying on her left side, cautiously opened her right eye to see the table between the beds, plus the dark mound of Roger over there, the illuminated alarm clock on the table failed to say midnight. She had no fear of accidentally falling asleep, not tonight of all nights, but why did time have to *creep* so? But then at last she opened that eye one more time and now the clock read *11:58,* and darn it, that was good enough. Being very careful, making absolutely no noise—well, a faint rustle or two—she rolled over and rose from the bed. She stooped to pick up her shoes, then carried them tiptoe from the room.

The instant he heard Janet move, Roger tensed like a bowstring. He forced himself to keep his eyes shut, believing eyes reflect whatever light might be around and she might see them and know he was awake. It wasn't until the rustle of her movements receded toward the bedroom door that he dared to look. Yes, there she goes, through the doorway, open now because it was only shut if she was in bed while he was watching television.

Janet turned left, toward the kitchen, to go out the back door and around to the car. It was too bad she'd have to start its engine so close to the house, but the bedroom was way on the other side, with the bulk of the house and the garage in between, so it should be all right. In any case, she was going.

The instant Janet disappeared from the doorway, Roger was up, stepping into his loafers, streaking silently through the house to the front door, out, and running full tilt across the street to crouch down on the far side of his car. Hunkered down there, he heard her car motor start, saw the headlights switch on, and then saw the car come out and swing away toward town, which is what he'd been hoping. It meant his car was faced the right way. He let her travel a block, then jumped into the car, started it, didn't turn the lights on, and drove off in pursuit.

12:20 by the dashboard clock, and Querk parked in the lot next to Sycamore House. There was no all-night street parking permitted in Central Sycamore, but there were always a few cars left at Sycamore House, by people whose friends had decided maybe they shouldn't drive home after all, so the Honda wouldn't attract attention. He got out and walked down the absolutely deserted silent street to the traffic light doggedly giving its signals to nothing, then crossed and walked to the entrance to Sycamore Creek and on in.

There was no problem unlocking the main gate, nor temporarily locking it again behind him. He crossed to the building, unlocked the one loading bay door with a faulty alarm he happened to know about, and made his way through the silent, dark, stuffy plant to the managers' offices, where it was a simple matter to disarm the alarm systems, running now on the backup batteries. Then he retraced his steps, out to the street.

Janet had expected to be the only person driving around this area this late at night, but partway to town another car's headlights appeared in her rearview mirror. Another night owl, she thought, and hoped he wasn't a drunken speed demon who would try to pass her. These roads were narrow and twisty. But, no; thankfully, he kept well back. She drove on into town, turned into the Sycamore House parking lot, recognized the Honda right away, and parked next to it.

Roger had kept well back, sorry he had to use his headlights at all but not wanting to run into a deer out here, the deer population having exploded in this part of the world once all of the predator animals had been removed, unless you count hunters, and don't. He followed the car ahead all the way into town, and when he saw the brake lights go on he thought at first she was braking for the traffic light up ahead, but then she suddenly made the left turn into the Sycamore House parking lot. Damn! He hadn't expected that. Should he go past? Should he stop? If he tried to park along here, you just knew some damn cop would pop out of nowhere to give him both a hard time and a ticket, while Janet got away to who knows where. Guerrera, that's where. San Cristobal, Guerrera.

He drove on by, peering in at the Sycamore House parking lot, but she'd switched her lights off and there was nothing to see. He got to the corner, and the light was against him, so he stopped, while no traffic went by in all directions. Diagonally across the street was Luigi's, the Italian restaurant, and at the far end of it, he knew, was a small parking lot, hemmed in by the fake forest. He could leave the car there and hoof it back to Sycamore House, just as soon as this damn light changed. When would it—? Ah! At last.

He drove across the empty intersection, turned left at the small and empty parking lot, and stopped, car's nose against pine branches. He switched off lights and engine, so now it was only by the vague streetlight glow well behind him that he saw, in his rearview mirror, the apparition rise from the floor behind the front seat, *exactly* like all those horror stories! He stared, convulsed with terror, and the apparition showed him a wide horrible smile, a big horrible pistol and a pair of shiny horrible handcuffs. "Didn't that tarot deck," it asked him, "tell you not to go out tonight?"

16

When Querk walked back into the Sycamore House parking lot, Janet's Chrysler Cirrus was parked next to his little Honda; a bigger, more comfortable car, though not very new. She must have seen him in the rearview mirror because she popped out of her car, the brief illumination of the interior light showing the hugeness of her smile but still the dark around her left eye. Then the door closed, the light went out, and she was in his arms.

They embraced a long time, he feeling her body tremble with the release of weeks of tension. Months. But now it was over. He was off parole, a free man. She was out of that house, a free woman. Start here.

At last he released her and whispered, "Everything's going fine. Three, four hours, it'll be all over."

"I know you'll do it," she whispered, then shook a finger at him. "Don't let them get any ideas."

"I won't."

He took his bag from the Honda and put it in the Chrysler, then kissed her one last time, got into the Honda, and drove out to the street. He turned left, ignored the red light, drove through the intersection, and stopped next to the Hess station across the street from Luigi's. Promptly, Dortmunder stepped out of the dimness inside the phone booth there, crossed the sidewalk, and slid in next to him.

Querk looked around. "Where's Kelp?"

"A couple things came up," Dortmunder told him, "nothing to do with us. He'll take care of them, then catch up with us later."

Querk didn't like this, didn't like the idea that one of his partners was going to be out of sight while the job was going down. "We're gonna need Kelp in the plant there," he said.

"He'll be there," Dortmunder promised. "He'll be right there when we get back with the truck."

There was nothing Querk could do about this development short of to call the whole thing off, which he didn't want to do, so he nodded reluctantly and said, "I hope nothing's gonna get screwed up."

"How could it? Come on, let's go."

The Combined Darby County Fire Department and Rescue Squad existed in an extremely fireproof brick building in the middle of nowhere. Seven local volunteer fire departments and two local volunteer ambulance services, each with its own firehouse or garage, had been combined into this organization, made necessary by the worsening shortage of volunteers, and political infighting had made it impossible to use any of the existing facilities. A local nob had donated land here in the middle of the responsibility area, and the building was erected, empty and alone unless a fundraiser dinner were being held or the volunteers' beepers sounded off.

Querk parked the Honda behind the building, out of sight, and used a copy of Cousin Claude's key to unlock the right garage door. He lifted it, stepped inside, and drove out the truck, which was red like a fire engine, with high metal sides full of cubicles containing emergency equipment, a metal roof, but open at the back to show the big generator bolted to the truck body in there.

Querk waited while Dortmunder lowered

the garage door and climbed up onto the seat next to him. "Pretty good machine," he said.

"It does the job," Querk said.

It was with relief that Querk saw Kelp actually standing there next to the NO TRESPASSING sign. Kelp waved, and Dortmunder waved back, while Querk drove down to the closed entrance gates. "They're unlocked," he assured Dortmunder, who climbed out to open the gates, then close them again after the truck and Kelp had both entered.

Driving slowly alongside the building toward the window he wanted, Querk saw in all his rearview mirrors, illuminated by a smallish moon, Dortmunder and Kelp walking along in his wake, talking together. Kelp must be telling Dortmunder what he'd done about whatever problem he'd gone off to fix.

Querk wondered; should he ask Kelp what the problem was? No, he shouldn't. Dortmunder had said it was nothing to do with tonight's job, so that meant it was none of his business. The fact that Kelp was here was all that mattered. A tight-lipped man knows when other people expect him to be tight-lipped.

17

Dortmunder was bored. There was nothing to do about it but admit it; he was bored.

Usually, in a heist, what you do is, you case the joint, then you plan and plan, and then there's a certain amount of tension when you break into whatever the place is, and then you *grab* what you came for and you get *out* of there.

Not this time. This time, the doors are open, the alarms are off, and nobody's around. So you just waltz in. But then you don't *grab* anything, and you certainly don't get *out* of there.

What you do instead, you shlep heavy cable off a wheel out of the generator truck, shove it through a window Querk has opened, and then shlep it across a concrete floor in the dark, around and sometimes into a lot of huge machines that are not the machine Querk wants, until at last you can hook the cables to both a machine and a control panel. This control panel also controls some lights, so finally you can see what you're doing.

Meanwhile, Querk has been collecting his supplies. He needs three different inks, and two big rolls of special paper, that he brings over with his forklift. He needs one particular size of paper cutter, a wickedly sharp big rectangle criss-crossed with extremely dangerous lines of metal, that has to be slid into an opening in the side of the machine without sacrificing any fingers to it, and which will, at the appropriate moments, descend inside the machine to slice sheets of paper into many individual siapas.

The boxes for the siapas already exist, but laid out flat, and have to be inserted into a wide slot in the back of the machine. The nasty wire bands to close the boxes—hard, springy, with extremely sharp edges—have to be inserted onto rolls and fed into the machine like feeding movie film into a projector. Having three guys for this part is a help, because it would take one guy working alone a whole lot longer just to set things up, even if he could wrestle the big paper roll into position by himself, which he probably couldn't.

But after everything was in position, then you *really* needed three guys. It was a three-guy machine. Guy number one (Querk) was at the control panel, keeping an eye on the gauges that told him how the ink flow was coming along, how the paper feed was doing, how the boxes were filling up. Guy number two (Kelp) was physically all around the machine, which was a little delicate and touchy, following Querk's orders on how to adjust the various feeds and watch the paper, which would have liked to jam up if anybody looked away for a minute.

And guy number three, Dortmunder, was the utility man. It was his job to replenish the ink supply when needed, which was rarely. It was also his job to wrestle the full boxes off the end of the chute at the back of the machine, but since in three hours there were only going to be five boxes, that didn't take up a lot of his time. It was also his job occasionally to go out to see how the generator truck was coming along, which was fine. In addition, it was his job to keep checking on the laid-out boxes inside the machine with the money stacking up on them, and the alignment of the big papercutter, to make sure nothing was getting off kilter and to warn Querk to shut down temporarily if something did, which only happened twice. And generally it was his job to stand chicky; but if anybody were to come into the plant that they wouldn't like to come in, it would already be too late to do anything about it.

So here he was, the gofer in a slow-motion heist, and he was bored. It was like having an actual job.

They'd started at ten after one, and it was just a few ticks after four when the last of the paper rolled into the machine and Querk started shutting its parts down, one section at a time until the fifth and final box came gliding out of the chute and Dortmunder wrestled it over onto the concrete floor with the others. Five boxes, very heavy, each containing a thousand bills compressed into the space, a thousand twenty million siapa notes per box, for a value of a hundred thousand dollars per box. In Guerrera.

Dortmunder stepped back from the final box. "Done," he said. "At last."

"Not exactly done," Querk said. "Remember, this run never happened. We gotta clean up everything in here, put it all back the way it was."

Yes; exactly like having a job.

18

Querk's nervousness, once they'd driven the generator truck actually onto the plant property, had turned into a kind of paralysis, a cauterizing in which he couldn't feel his feelings. He was just doing it, everything he'd been going over and over in his mind all this time, acting out the fantasy, reassuring Janet and himself that everything would work out just fine, playing it out in his head again and again so that, when the time came to finally *do* it, actually in the real world do it, it was as though he'd already done it and this was just remembering.

And the job went, if anything, even better than the fantasy, smooth and quick and easy. Not a single problem with the two guys he'd found to help, and that had always been one of the scarier parts of the whole thing. He couldn't do it alone, but he couldn't use locals, none of these birds around here had the faintest idea how to keep their mouths shut. Amateurs. He had to use pros, but he didn't know anybody anymore.

Nevertheless, if he was going to do it, he would have to reach out, find *somebody* with the right résumé that he could talk into the job, and boy, did he come up lucky. Dortmunder and Kelp were definitely pros, but at the same time they were surprisingly gullible. He could count on them to do the job and to keep their mouths shut, and he could also count on them to never even notice what he was really up to.

The cleaning up after the print job took another half hour. The next to the last thing they did, before switching off the lights, was forklift the five boxes of siapas out to the generator truck, where they fit nicely at the back. Then it was disconnect the cables, reel them back into the truck, and drive out of there, pausing to lock the big gates on the way by.

Still dark on the streets of Sycamore. Still no vehicles for the dutiful traffic light to oversee. Dortmunder and Kelp rode on the wide bench seat of the truck beside Querk, who drove down the street to stop in front of Seven Leagues. "I'll just unlock the door," he said, as he climbed down to the street.

The story he'd told them was that the travel group going down there to Guerrera contained a bunch of evangelicals, looking for converts, so Janet would ship the boxes out of the United States as missals and hymnals. Tonight, they'd leave the boxes at

Seven Leagues, and in the morning she'd cover them with all the necessary tags and stickers, and the van carrying all the tour group's luggage would come by to pick them up and take them down to JFK.

Once the boxes had been lugged into Seven Leagues and the door relocked, Querk said, "You fellas need a lift to your car?"

"No, that's okay," Kelp said, pointing vaguely north, out of town. "We're parked just up there."

Dortmunder said, "You want to get the truck back."

"I sure do."

Should he shake hands with them? He felt he should; it would be the more comradely thing to do. Sticking his hand out in Kelp's direction, he said, "It's been good working with you."

Kelp had a sunny smile, even in the middle of the night. Pumping Querk's hand, he said, "I wouldn't miss it for the world."

Shaking Dortmunder's hand, bonier than Kelp's but less powerful, Querk said, "We'll be in touch."

"You know it," Dortmunder said.

"You know where to find me."

"Sure do," Dortmunder said.

Well. That was comradely enough. "I better get this truck back before sunup," he said.

"Sure," they said, and waved at him, and he got into the truck.

He had to make a K turn to go back the other way, cumbersome with this big vehicle. He headed toward the traffic light as Dortmunder and Kelp walked off northward, disappearing almost immediately into the darkness, there being streetlights only here in the center of town.

As he drove toward the traffic light, he passed Sycamore House on his left, and resisted the impulse to tap the horn. But Janet would see him, and a horn sounding here in the middle of the night might attract attention. Attention from Dortmunder and Kelp, in any case.

So he drove on, the traffic light graciously turning green as he reached the intersection. Behind him, Janet in the Cirrus would now have seen the truck go by twice, and would know the job had gone well. He could hardly wait to get back to her.

Querk grinned all the way to the garage, where he put the truck away, backing it in the way it had been before. Then he got into the Honda for the last time in his life and drove it back to Sycamore, not only grinning now but also humming a little and at times even whistling between his teeth. To his right, the sky was just beginning to pale; dawn was on the way.

Sycamore. Once again the traffic light gave him a green. He drove through the intersection, turned into the Sycamore House parking lot, and put the Honda next to the Cirrus. He switched off the lights and the engine and stepped out to the blacktop, leaving the keys in the car. Turning to the Cirrus, he expected Janet to either start the engine or step out to speak to him. When she did neither, he bent to look into the car, and it was empty.

What? Why? They'd agreed to meet here when the job was done, so what happened? Where was she?

Maybe she'd needed to go to the bathroom. Or maybe she started to get uncomfortable in the car, after almost four hours, and decided to go wait in the office instead. The whole purpose of her being here the whole time was so he'd have his own backup means of escape in case anything were to go wrong with the job. Once she'd seen the truck, she had to know the job had gone well.

So she must be up at Seven Leagues. Querk left the parking lot and walked up the street, taking the Seven Leagues key out of his pocket. When he reached the place, there were no lights on inside. That was strange.

He unlocked the door, entered, closed the door, felt around on the wall for the light switch, found it, and stared, unbelieving.

"Surprise," Dortmunder said.

19

Between dinner and the job, in fact, Dortmunder and Kelp had found a number of things to keep them interested, if not completely surprised. Primarily, they'd wanted to know what part Janet Twilley planned to take in tonight's exercises, if any, and so had driven out to the Twilley house a little before eleven, seeing lights still on in there. They'd visited that house last week, learning more about Roger Twilley than anybody else on Earth, and had found none of it pleasant. If Janet Twilley wanted to begin life anew with Kirby Querk, they couldn't argue the case, not with what they knew of Roger, just so she didn't plan to do it with their siapas.

They were parked down the block from the Twilley residence, discussing how to play this—should Kelp drive Dortmunder back to town, to keep an eye on the plant, while Kelp kept the car and maintained an observation post chez Twilley—when Roger decided their moves for them. The first thing they saw was the garage door open over there.

"The light didn't come on," Dortmunder said.

"I knew there was something," Kelp said.

Next, a car backed out of the garage, also with no lights on, and moving very slowly. Not only that, Roger himself came trotting out of the garage right after the car, so who was driving?

Turned out, nobody. Fascinated, they watched Roger push his car around in a great loop to park it on their side of the street, about two houses away.

"He, too, knows something's up," Kelp said.

Dortmunder said, "But he doesn't know what."

"He's gonna follow her."

"So we," Dortmunder said, "follow him."

"I got a better idea," Kelp said. "Have we got that bag in the back?"

"In the trunk? Yeah."

On an outing like this, they always traveled with that bag. Small, it was packed with extra materials that, who knew, might come in handy. Tools of various kinds, ID of various kinds, weapons of various kinds, and handcuffs of just one kind.

"What do you need from it?" Dortmunder asked.

"The cuffs. I'll ride in the back of the peeping tom's car, take him out if there's a problem, borrow it myself if she doesn't come out to be followed. You stash this car in town, tell Kirby I'll meet up with you guys at the plant."

So that's what they did, Dortmunder learning some more along the way, beginning with the fact that the driver's seat had even less legroom than the passenger seat. He stashed the compact in the Sycamore House parking lot, but stayed with it, and was there when Querk arrived, parked his Honda, and went off to set things up over at the printery.

A little later, he was also about to leave when Janet Twilley drove in, shut down, but didn't get out of her car. That was interesting. Not wanting to call attention to himself, he removed the bulb from the compact's interior light so that everything remained dark when he eased out of the car and out of the parking lot to go over to the Hess station and wait for Querk.

One thing about the phone booth outside the Hess station; it had legroom. Dortmunder leaned his back against the phone, folded his arms, and watched the traffic light change. After a while he saw Querk cross the street and walk north, and then here he came in the Honda south.

After the job at the plant and the departure of Querk to return the generator truck, there'd been nothing left to do but gather up Janet Twilley, still at her post in her Chrysler Cirrus, and use her keys to gain entrance to Seven Leagues. As for her husband, he could stay where he was, trussed up on the floor of his own car down by Luigi's. Good place for him.

And now it was simply a matter of waiting for Querk. And here he is.

20

Querk stared, pole-axed with shock. Janet was gagged and tied to her office chair, wide-eyed and trembling. Even her bruise was pale. Kelp, still with that sunny smile, sat near her in the client's chair. And Dortmunder stood near Querk; not too near, but close enough so that, if Querk decided to spin around and pull the door open and run, it wouldn't happen.

Stammering, the tremble in his hands back and worse than ever, Querk said, "What? What happened?"

"We came to settle up," Dortmunder said, while Kelp got to his feet, walked back to the unused desk, took the client's chair from it, and brought it back to stand facing himself and Janet. "Take a load off," he offered.

Dortmunder said, "Andy, turn the desk light on, will you? It's too bright in here."

Kelp did, and Dortmunder switched off the overheads that Querk had switched on. It became much dimmer in the long room, the light softer, though not what Querk thought of as cozy. Watching all this, he tried desperately to think, without much success. What was going on? What were they going to do? He said, "What's wrong? Fellas? I thought everything was okay."

"Not exactly okay," Dortmunder said, as he perched on the corner of Janet's desk.

Kelp said, "Come on, Kirby, take a chair. We'll tell you all about it."

So Querk sat in the chair Kelp had brought for him, and folded his shaking hands in his lap. He could feel Janet's eyes on him, but he couldn't bring himself to look directly at her. He was supposed to make things *better* for her. Tied up in a chair by two heisters from New York wasn't *better.*

Kelp said, "You know, Kirby, the thing was, at first we believed there really was a Rodrigo." He still seemed cheerful, not angry or upset, but Querk didn't believe any of it.

"You got us there, for a while," Dortmunder agreed. He sounded sullen, and that Querk could believe.

"What we figured," Kelp said, "why would you go through this whole scheme unless you had a payout coming? So that's why we believed in Rodrigo. Until, of course, we heard about Janet. Just as a by the by."

"Just dropped in the conversation," Dortmunder said.

"And Harry Matlock said you were a better follower than a leader," Kelp said, "so we began to wonder, who exactly were you following? So when we came up here last week, I stopped in to see Janet."

What? Querk now did stare directly at Janet, and she was frantically nodding, eyebrows raised almost to her hairline. "She—" Querk had to clear his throat. "She didn't tell me."

"She didn't know," Kelp said. "See, I was a customer, I was interested in going somewhere in South America, I wasn't sure where, and we talked about, oh . . ." He looked at Janet, amiable, inquiring. "About fifteen minutes, right?" Looking at Querk again, he said, "And the funny thing, never once did she mention that tour going to Guerrera. In fact, she never even mentioned Guerrera, the whole country."

"Probably," Querk said, even though he knew it was hopeless, "the tour was full by then."

"Which gets to how easy the extra two tickets were," Kelp said. "First she can wangle one ticket, but then two tickets is easy, no sweat, you don't even have to check back with her. But I'm getting ahead of my story."

"I thought you were buying it," Querk said.

Kelp's grin got even wider. "Yeah, I know. Anyway, when I was here that time, I noticed the shiner on Janet, and you didn't seem the type—"

"We both thought that," Dortmunder said.

"Thank you," Querk said.

"So we checked out her house," Kelp said, "and that's some winner she decided to marry."

"I guess he didn't seem that bad at first," Querk said.

"Maybe," Kelp said. "Anyway, here's this bossy woman—"

Janet gave him a glare, which Kelp ignored.

"—with a shiner and a bad husband. And here's you, likes to be bossed around. So we decided, what it was, you didn't have any Rodrigo, because how is this Janet here in upstate New York gonna make that kinda connection. Also, this is not a really successful travel agency here, which you can see by the fact that the other desk isn't used, so if she ever had an assistant or a partner the business couldn't support that person. So *maybe,* just maybe, the idea is, you'll run these half million dollars' worth of siapas, and you and Janet will *drive* to Guerrera, down through Mexico and all that, maxing out your credit cards along the way. And when you get there, you find a nice place to stay, you start living on the siapas. You put 'em in a few banks down there, you can even come back up to the States sometimes and spend them like money. Of course, there wouldn't be any for *us.*"

"I'm sorry," Querk said.

Dortmunder nodded. "You certainly are."

"You needed two guys," Kelp said. "You couldn't go with local amateurs, so you had to reach out for pros, and what you got was us."

"I underestimated you," Querk said.

"Don't feel bad," Kelp advised him. "That's what *we* specialize in. So here you are, you've kissed us off, and Anne Marie and me are gonna feel really stupid tomorrow night at JFK with those imitation tickets—"

"I'm sorry," Querk said again.

"We know," Dortmunder said. He didn't sound sympathetic.

"But, you know," Kelp said, "this is better for you, because *Roger* knew something was up. You know, the paranoid is sometimes right, and Roger was right. So he was following Janet tonight, and if it hadn't been for us, Roger would be making a whole lot of trouble for you people right now."

Querk was rather afraid of Roger Twilley. "Roger?" he said. "Where is he?"

"Tied up in his car, down at Luigi's."

Dortmunder said, "You owe us for that one."

"Well," Kelp said, "he owes us for the whole score."

"That's true," Dortmunder said.

Rising, Kelp said, "I'll go get our wheels, you explain it."

Kelp was the pleasant one. Why couldn't Dortmunder go get their car? But, no; Kelp nodded at Querk and left the shop, and it was Dortmunder who said, "This is what we're gonna do. We're gonna leave you one box of the siapas, that's a hundred grand you can take down to Guerrera, get you started. In six months, you come up to New York, you buy at least one more box from us, half price. Fifty grand for a hundred grand of siapas. You can buy them all then, or you can buy a box every six months."

Querk said, "Where am I gonna get that money?"

"You're gonna steal it," Dortmunder told him. "That's what you do, remember? You gave up on reform."

Querk hung his head. The thought of a Guerreran jail moved irresistably through his mind.

Meanwhile, Dortmunder said, "If you *don't* show up in six months, the four boxes go to the cops with an anonymous letter with your names and a description of the scheme and where you're hiding out, and the probable numbers on your siapas. And then you've got nothing."

"Jeez," Querk said.

"Look at it this way," Dortmunder suggested. "You lied to us, you abused our trust, but we aren't getting even, we aren't hurting you. Because all we want is what's ours. So, one way or another, you keep your side of the bargain, and we keep ours." Looking past Querk at the window, he said, "Here's the goddam compact. I hope we can fit these boxes in there. Come on, Querk, help me carry the loot."

"All right." Rising, Querk said, "What do we do about Roger?"

"Nothing," Dortmunder said. "Luigi's cook'll find him in the morning, let *him* decide what to do. Come on, grab a box."

So Querk did, the two of them shlepping the boxes one at a time, Kelp busily moving crap around inside the car. They managed to cram three of the boxes into the trunk and one on its side on the alleged back seat, with their luggage on top.

At the end, feeling humble, Querk said to them both, on the sidewalk, "I wanna thank you guys. You could of made things a lot tougher for me."

"Well," Dortmunder said, "I wouldn't say you were getting off scot free." He nodded at Seven Leagues. "Sooner or later, you're gonna have to take off that gag."

WALTER MOSLEY

Walter Mosley has forged a successful mystery career in the tradition of authors like Chester Himes and Carroll John Daly, but he added the complex issue of race relations and an in-depth look at the lethal heart of a major city that few authors can even come close to. He is the author of twenty books and has been translated into twenty-one languages. His popular mysteries featuring Easy Rawlins and his friend Raymond "Mouse" Alexander began with *Devil in a Blue Dress,* which was made into the film of the same name starring Denzel Washington and Jennifer Beals. Others in the series were *A Red Death, White Butterfly, Black Betty, A Little Yellow Dog,* and *Bad Boy Brawley Brown*; a prequel to the Rawlins mysteries, *Gone Fishin'*, and a series of short stories collected in *Six Easy Pieces.* His other character, ex-con Socrates Fortlow, lives in Los Angeles, infusing his episodic tales with ethical and political considerations. Excerpts from his collection *Always Outnumbered, Always Outgunned: The Socrates Fortlow Stories* have been published in *Esquire, GQ, USA Weekend, Buzz,* and *Mary Higgins Clark Mystery Magazine.* One of these new stories was an O. Henry Award winner for 1996 and is featured in *Prize Stories 1996: The O. Henry Awards,* edited by William Abraham. In 1996 he was named the first Artist-in-Residence at the Africana Studies Institute, New York University. Since that residency, he has continued to work with the department, creating an innovative lecture series entitled "Black Genius" which brings diverse speakers from art, politics, and academe to discuss practical solutions to contemporary issues. Designed as a "public classroom" these lectures have included speakers ranging from Spike Lee to Angela Davis. In February 1999, a collection of these lectures was published with the title *Black Genius,* with a Mosley introduction and essay. His most recent novels include *The Wave* and *Fortunate Son.*

WALKING THE LINE

Walter Mosley

1

I saw the first ad on a Tuesday in the *Wall Street Journal.*

> REQUIRED: SCRIBE
> A. LAWLESS IN THE TESSLA BUILDING

The next notice appeared on Thursday in the classified section of the daily *New York Times.*

Originally published in the hardcover edition of *Transgressions* under the title "Archibald Lawless, Anarchist at Large: Walking the Line."

AAL LTD. SEEKS SCRIBE
APPLY AT OFFICES IN TESSLA BUILDING

Then, the next week, on the back page of the *Village Voice* and in the classified section of the *Amsterdam News.*

SCRIBE SOUGHT KL-5-8713

The last ads gave no address but I knew that it had to be put there by A. Lawless at AAL Ltd. in the Tessla Building. I called and got an answering machine.

"If you are applying for the position leave your name and number," a throaty woman's voice said. "And please let us know where you heard about the position."

Then came the tone.

"Felix Orlean," I said. I gave my phone number and added, "I saw your ad in the *Times*, the *Journal*, the *Amsterdan News*, and the *Village Voice.*"

Much later that night, hours after I'd gone to sleep, the phone rang giving me a sudden fright. I was sure that my mother or father had gotten sick down home. I grabbed the phone and whined, "What? What's wrong?"

"Mr. Orlean?" He said *or-leen* not *or-le-ahn* as I pronounce my name.

"Yes? What's wrong?"

"Nothing's wrong, son," he sad in a deep gravelly voice that reminded me of Wallace Beery from the old films. "Why would you think something's wrong?"

"What time is it?"

"I just went through the tape," he said. "You were the only one who saw all four ads. Do you read all those New York papers?"

"Yeah," I said. "The *Washington Post* too. And the *International Herald Tribune* when I can get it."

I turned on the light next to my bed to see the clock but was blinded by the glare.

"Are you a student?" he asked.

"Yeah," I said. "At Columbia." If I had been more awake I wouldn't have been so open.

"Come to the office this morning," he said. "I'll be in by five but you don't have to get there till ten to six."

"Huh?"

He hung up and my eyesight cleared enough to see that it was three forty-five.

I wondered what kind of man did his work at that time. And what would possess him to call a potential employee hours before the sun came up? Was he crazy? Must be, I thought. Of course I had no intention of going to his office at six A.M. or at any other time. I turned out the light and pulled the covers up to my chin but sleep did not return.

I had been intrigued for days about the job description of *scribe.* I had thought it was just a fancy way to say secretary who takes dictation. But after the call I wasn't so sure. Who was A. Lawless? Was it that cool woman's voice on the answering machine? No. It had to be the raspy late-night caller.

What kind of job could it be?

"It's too bad yo' daddy and them named you Felix," Aunt Alberta, the Ninth Ward fence, said to me once. And when I asked her why she said, " 'Cause that's a cartoon cat and we all know what curiosity do for a cat."

I loved my Aunt Alberta. She's the one who encouraged me when I wanted to come up to New York to study journalism. My parents had always planned on me becoming a lawyer like my father, and his father. Even my great-grandfather had studied law, although he wasn't able to get a license to practice in Louisiana. In those days colored lawyers, even extremely light ones, were rare down south.

My father had harangued me for a week to stop my foolishness and make a decision about which law school to attend. I finally told him that Alberta thought it was a good idea for me to try journalism.

"And how would you know what Alberta thinks?" he asked. My father is a big man but I'm just small, taking after the men on my mother's side.

"I asked her," I said shaking a little under the shadow of JP Orlean.

"You what?"

"I went down to the county jail and saw her, poppa." I closed my eyes involuntarily, expecting to be knocked on my can.

I had been hit by my father before. He was a violent man. *Stern but fair,* my mother used to say. But I never saw what was fair about whipping a child with a strap until red welts rose up all over his body.

"I thought I told you that Alberta Hadity is no longer to be considered family," my father said in a voice as quiet as the breeze.

And that was my chance. After twenty-one years of obeying my father, or lying to him, the gate was open. All I had to do was stay quiet. All I had to do was keep my mouth shut and he would see it as insubordination.

I looked down at his brown shoes.

Blutcher's we called them down south. They're known as wing tips in New York. Chub Wilkie, I knew, had shined those shoes that morning. He shined my father's shoes every week day morning. JP used to say that Chub Wilkie was the finest man in the law building where he practiced. But he never invited Mr. Wilkie to dinner as he did the law partners at Hermann, Bledsoe, and Orlean.

Mr. Wilkie was too dark-skinned and too poor to be seen on our social level.

My father and mother were no more than café au lait in their coloring. My sister and I were lighter even than that.

"Well?" my father said. I could feel the weight of his stare on my neck.

It was a great concession for him to ask anything of me. I was supposed to say that I was sorry, that I would never speak to my felon auntie again. The words formed in my mouth but I kept my teeth clamped down on them.

"I expect you out of the house before your mother returns home," he said.

But still he hesitated.

I knew that he expected me to fold, to gasp out an apology and beg for his indulgence. I had always lived at home, never worked a day in my life. But as dependent as I was on my father I was just as stubborn too.

After another minute the shoes carried him from the family den. I looked up and out of the glass doors that led to the garden at the back of the house. I knew then that it would be the last time I ever saw my mother's orchid and lily garden.

I almost yelled for joy.

After reliving my exile from the Orlean family sleep was impossible. At five I got out of bed and went to the tiny kitchen that separated my room from my soccer-star roommate, Lonnie McKay. I heated water in a saucepan instead of the kettle so as not to wake him.

Lonnie had a full scholarship in the engineering school for captaining the fledgling Columbia Ciceros (pronounced by those in the know as Kickeros). I had to borrow the thirty thousand dollars a year and then get part-time jobs to pay the outrageous rent and for anything else I might need—like instant coffee.

I poured the hot water and mixed in the

freeze-dried flakes. The coffee was bitter and yet tasteless but that was all right by me. The bitter taste was my life, that's what I was thinking.

And then I looked up.

The long red velvet curtain that covered Lonnie's doorway fluttered and a young woman walked through. There was only the small forty-watt bulb lighting the kitchen but I could see that she was naked except for the tan bikini panties. An inch shorter than I with smallish but shapely breasts. Her hair was long curly brown and her eyes were large. She was slender and pale skinned but somehow I knew that she was a colored woman, girl really—not more than nineteen. When she saw me she smiled, crossed her hands over her breasts, and sat down on the chair across from where I was standing.

"Hi," she said, smiling with false modesty.

"Hi." I looked away to hide my embarrassment.

"You must be Felix."

Forcing my head back I looked her in the eye. Eyes. They were light brown and laughing, full of life and encouraging me to stay where I was, not to run back to my room which is what I wanted to do more than anything.

"Yes," I said. I stepped forward and held out my hand like I always did when someone called me by name.

She looked at my hand, hesitated, then shifted, managing to keep her modesty and take my hand at the same time.

"Arrett," she said. "I'm a friend of Lonnie's."

"Pleased to meet you," I said.

We stared at each other for a moment, and then a moment more. Arrett seemed to be suppressing a laugh. I would have loved to see that laugh.

"Why are you up so early?" she asked.

"Going to apply for a job," I said. And there it was. My future was sealed. A near naked woman stumbling across my path in the early hours of the morning and I was thrown out of my orbit. My whole life had changed because of a girl I'd probably never see again.

Mr. Lawless would have said that it was my fate, that the moment he heard my light New Orleans drawl he knew that we were meant to come together.

"What kind of job?" she asked.

"I don't know."

She grinned and I felt my heart swell up in my chest.

A sound issued from Lonnie's room. It might have been her name.

"He wants me," she said. It was almost a question.

I almost said, *don't go.*

"Ari," Lonnie called from behind the red curtain.

She got up, forgetting her modesty, and said, "We'll see each other at school," and then ran through the red fabric into my roommate's den.

I sat down and considered going back to bed. But then Lonnie's first sigh of pleasure pierced the air. I hurried to my room, dressed and left the apartment before they could fill the house with their love.

2

The Tessla building is on West 38th Street. It's not the biggest building in midtown Manhattan but it's up there. Sixty-nine stories. The glass doors are modern but the lobby is thirties art deco to the max. Black, white, and red tiles of marble cover the floor in vaguely Egyptian designs. The marble on the walls is gray and light blue. A huge painting behind the guard's stone counter is of a bare-breasted, golden skinned Joan of Arc leading her French army out of a sun that you just know represents God.

"Yes?" the guard asked me. "Can I help you?"

"AAL Limited," I said.

The man behind the counter was African, I believed. His features were purely Negroid. The round head and almost almond shaped eyes, the dark skin had no blemishes and his lips seemed chiseled they were so perfect. My sister went out with a man like this for two weeks once and our parents decided to send her to Paris for two years. She was still there for all that I knew.

The man's eyes rose as a smile curved his sensual mouth.

"Mr. Lawless wants to see you?"

"I guess," I said. "He said to get here by ten to six."

"That's Mr. Lawless. No visitors after five fifty-five. He told me that himself," the guard said, sounding a little like he'd learned to speak English from an Englishman. "What do you do?"

"I'm a student," I said. "I study journalism."

This answer seemed to disappoint the

young guard. He shrugged his shoulders as if to say, too bad.

"Fifty-two eleven," he said. "Take the last elevator on the right. It's the only one we have working this early."

It was a utility elevator. Thick matting like gray bedspreads were hung over the walls to protect them from harm when heavy objects were moved. I pushed the button and the door closed but there was no sense of motion. A couple of times I looked up at the small screen that should have shown the floors as they passed by but the number was stuck at twelve.

Finally, after a long interval the doors opened and I got out wondering if I was on the right floor. The walls were painted the palest possible green and the floor was tiled with white stone veined in violet and dark jade. Two arrows on the wall opposite the elevator door pointed in either direction. Right was 5220 to 5244 and left was 5200 to 5219.

I turned left. After I passed the first few offices I realized that the door at the dead end of the hall was my destination.

That door was different than the rest. From the distance it seemed to be boarded up as if it were under construction or condemned. Five or six weathered boards were nailed into place, lengthwise but not neatly at all. Two shorter boards were nailed across these, more or less vertically. There was something that I couldn't discern hanging midway down the left side of the door.

I passed Tweed's Beads and then Thunderstruck, Personal Dating Service. I was wondering what other kind of date there was, other than personal that is, when I realized that the object hanging from the door at the end of the hall was a handmade doll with a black face and a striped yellow and red dress. The dress was painted on the cylindrical body made from a toilet paper roll or something like that.

The voodoo doll stopped me for moment. I'd seen many such fetishes in Louisiana. They're all over the French Quarter, for tourists mainly. But hanging there, from that boarded-up door, the manikin took on a sinister air.

What the hell was a voodoo doll doing there on the fifty-second floor of a skyscraper in New York City?

I gritted my teeth and took a deep breath through my nostrils. Then I walked forward.

There wasn't any doorknob or door that I could see. Just the grayed planking nailed to either side of the doorway covering something black and wooden behind. The doll had a slack grin painted on her round head. She seemed to be leering at me.

"Go on," I said to the doll.

I rapped on the boards.

No answer.

After a reasonable pause I knocked again.

No answer.

My fear of the doll was quickly being replaced by fury. What kind of trick was being played on me? Was the guard downstairs in on it? Did Lonnie put Arrett out there to run me out of the house?

My fingernails were pressing hard against my palms when a voice said, "Who's out there?"

There was no mistaking that raspy tone.

"Mr. Lawless?"

"Orleen?"

"Yes. I mean yes sir." The latter was added because I was raised on good manners down home.

The door opened into the room, which surprised me. The planks were arranged to give the illusion of a boarded-up portal but really they were cut to allow the door, boards and all, to open inward.

The man standing there before me had no double in the present day world or in history. He stood a solid six three or four with skin that was deep amber. His hair, which was mostly dark brown and gray, had some reddish highlights twined into a forest of thick dreadlocks that went straight out nine inches from his head, sagging only slightly. The hair resembled a royal head-dress, maybe even a crown of thorns but Mr. A. Lawless was no victim. His chest and shoulders were unusually broad even for a man his size. His eyes were small and deep set. The forehead was round and his high cheekbones cut strong slanting lines down to his chin which gave his face a definite heart shape. There was no facial hair and no wrinkles except at the corners of his eyes.

His stomach protruded from his open fatigue jacket but it didn't sag or seem soft against the buttoned-up rose colored shirt. His pants were tan and shapeless. His big feet were bare.

A. Lawless was forty-five or maybe sixty. But even a rowdy with a baseball bat would have thought twice before taking a swing at him.

"Orleen?" he asked me again.

"Yes sir."

"Come in, come." He gestured with hands that were small compared to the rest of the him. But that only reminded me of stories I'd read about the Brown Bomber, Joe Louis. He had small hands too.

Mr. Lawless went around me to close the boarded door. He threw three bolts down the side and then flipped down a bronze piece of metal at the base that served a buttress against anyone forcing their way in.

"Just so we don't have any unwanted guests," he said. Then he led the way back to the interior.

I followed my host through a moderate sized room that had a dark wood floor and wooden furniture that wasn't of this century or the last. Just a couple of tables with a chair and a cushionless couch. The thick pieces had seen a lot of use in the past hundred years or so but they were well varnished and sturdy.

There were two doors at the back of the room. Straight ahead was a frosted glass door that had no writing on it. Immediately to the left was an oak door upon which the word STORAGE was stenciled in highlighted gold lettering.

We went through the untitled glass door into a smallish room that I figured to be his office. At the back of the room was a window that had an unobstructed view of the Hudson River and New Jersey beyond. It was about six and the sun was just falling upon our misty neighbor state. There was a dark wood swivel chair next to the window, behind a small desk which was only large enough for the laptop computer that sat on it.

The room was filled with a musky odor that, while neither sweet nor sour, carried a pleasant notion. This odor I later came to associate with Archibald Lawless's life. He pervaded any situation with his presence and half-civilized genius.

The wall to my left had a series of shelves that held various oddities. There was a crusty old toy chest and a child's baby doll with a red sash around its throat. There was a rattlesnake suspended in fluid in a large jar, a parchment scroll tied with string, a replica of a human skull, a small stuffed animal (I didn't know what species at the time), and a necklace: a piece of costume jewelry in a plastic case held up by a W-shaped metal frame. This necklace was made up of gaudy pieces of glass representing emeralds and rubies mainly, with a ribbon of fake diamonds snaking through. There were other pieces on the shelves but that's all I was able to make out on first sight.

The wall opposite the shelves was dominated by a giant blown-up photograph rendered in sepia tones. It was the face of some German or Russian from a bygone age. The man, whoever he was, had a big mustache and a wild look in his eye. I would have said it was a picture of Nietzsche but I knew it wasn't him because I had just finished reading *Thus Spake Zarathustra* for a class called the History of the West and there was a photograph of the German philosopher on the cover of the book.

"Bakunin," A. Lawless said. "It's Bakunin."

"The anarchist?"

"He's why I'm here today talking to you. And he's why you're here today talking to me."

"Oh," I said trying to think of a way into the conversation.

"Sit down," the big man said.

I noticed that there were two tree trunks diagonally across from the swivel chair. Real tree trunks, plucked right out of the ground. Each one was about two and a half feet high with curves carved into them for a comfortable seat.

I sat.

"Archibald Lawless, Anarchist at Large," my host said formally. He sat in the swivel chair and leaned back.

"What does that mean exactly?"

"What do you think it means?"

"That you plan to overthrow the government in hopes of causing a perpetual state of chaos throughout the world?"

"They aren't much on reality at Xavier or Columbia, are they?"

I didn't remember telling him that I did my undergrad work at Xavier but I didn't remember much before Arrett.

"What do you do?" I asked.

"I walk the line."

"What line?"

"Not," he said raising an instructive finger, "what line but the line between what forces?"

"Okay," I said. "The line between what forces?"

"I walk the line between chaos and the man."

3

Archibald Lawless brought two fingers to his lower lip speculating, it seemed, about me and how I would fill the job opening.

But by then I had decided against taking the position. I found his presence disturbing. If he offered me a cup of tea I'd take it out of civility, but I wouldn't swallow a drop.

Still, I was intrigued. The line between chaos and the man seemed a perfect personal realization of the philosophy he followed. It brought to mind a wild creature out at the edges of some great, decaying civilization. Interesting for a college paper but not as a profession.

I had just begun considering how to refuse if he offered me the job when a knock came on the front door of the office. Three fast raps and then two slower ones.

"Get that will you, Felix?" Lawless said.

I didn't want to sound off so I went back through the Americana room and said, "Yes," through the door.

"Carlos for A L," a slightly Spanish, slightly street accented voice answered.

I didn't know what to do so I threw the locks, kicked up the buttress, and opened the door.

The man was my height, slight and obviously with a preoccupation for the color green. He wore a forest green three-button suit over a pale green shirt with a skinny dark green tie.

His shoes were reptile definitely and also green. His skin was olive. He was past forty, maybe past fifty.

"Hey, bro," Carlos said and I really didn't know what to make of him.

"Wait here please," I said.

He nodded and I went back to Archibald Lawless's office. The anarchist was sitting back in his chair, waiting for my report.

"It's a guy named Carlos. He's all in green. I didn't ask what he wanted."

"Come on in, Carlos!" Archibald shouted.

The green man came in pushing open the office door.

"Hey, Mr. Big," Carlos greeted.

"What you got for me?"

"Not too much. They say he was drinking, she wasn't but she was just some girl he'd picked up at the bar."

"Couldn't you get any more?" Lawless wasn't upset but there was a certain insistence to his query.

"Maria tried, man, but they don't have it on the computer and the written files were sent to Arizona three hours after they were done. The only reason she got that much was that she knows a guy who works in filing. He sneaked a look for her."

Lawless turned away from Carlos and me and looked out over New Jersey.

"How's your mother?" Lawless asked Hoboken.

"She's fine," Carlos responded. "And Petey's doin' real good in that school you got him into."

"Tell him hello for me when you see him," Lawless said. He swiveled around and leveled his murky eyes at the green man. "See you later, Carlos."

"You got it, Mr. Big. Any time."

Carlos turned to go. I noticed that he seemed nervous. Not necessarily scared but definitely happy to be going. I followed him to the front door and threw all the locks into place after him.

When I returned Lawless was pulling on heavy work boots. He nodded toward a tree stump and I sat.

"Do you know what a scribe does?" he asked.

"I don't know if I'm really interested—"

"Do you know what a scribe does?" he asked again, cutting me off.

"They were monks or something," I said. "They wrote out copies of the bible before there was printing or moveable type."

"That's correct," he said sounding like one of my professors. "They also wrote for illiterate lords. Contracts, peace treaties, even love letters." Lawless smiled. "How much do you know about Bakunin?"

"Just his name."

"He was a great man. He knew about all the gross injustices of Stalin before Stalin was born. He was probably the greatest political thinker of the twentieth century and he didn't even live in that century. But do you know what was wrong with him?"

"No sir."

"He was a man of action and so he didn't spend enough time writing cohesive documents of his ideas. Don't get me wrong, he wrote a lot. But he never created a comprehensive document detailing a clear idea of anarchist political organization. After he died the writing he left behind made many small-minded men see him as a crackpot and a fool. I don't intend for my legacy to be treated like that."

"And that's why you need a scribe?"

"Mainly." He turned to watch Jersey again. "But also I need a simple transcriber.

Someone to take my notes and scribbles and to make sense out of them. To document what I'm trying to do."

"That's all?"

"Mostly. There'll be some errands. Maybe even a little research, you know—investigative work. But any good journalism student should love doing some field work."

"I didn't tell you I was a journalism student."

"No, you didn't. But I know a lot about you, Felix Orlean," he said, pronouncing my name correctly this time. "That's why I put that old doll of mine on the door, I wanted to see if you were superstitious. I know about your father too, Justin Proudfoot Orlean, a big time lawyer down in Louisiana. And your mother, Katherine Hadity, was a medical student before she married your father and decided to commit her life to you and your sister Rachel who now goes by the name Angela in the part of London called Brixton."

He might as well have hit me over the head with a twelve-pound ham. I didn't know that my mother had been a medical student but it made sense since she had always wanted Rachel to be a doctor. I didn't know that Rachel had moved to England.

"Where'd you get all that?"

"And that's another thing." Lawless cut his eyes at the laptop on the tiny desk. Then he held up that educational finger. "No work that you do for me goes on the computer. I want to wait until we get it right to let the world in on our work."

"I'm not w-working for you, Mr. Lawless," I said, hating myself for the stutter skip.

"Why not?"

"I don't know what you do for one thing," I said. "And I don't like people calling me at any hour of the night. You have your doors boarded up and you call yourself an anarchist. Some guy who looks like a street thug comes in to make some kind of report."

"I told you what I do. I'm an anarchist who wants to keep everything straight. From the crazed politico who decides that he can interfere with the rights of others because he's got some inside track on the truth to the fascist mayor trying to shut down the little guy so he can fill his coffers with gold while reinventing the police state.

"I'm the last honest man, an eastern cowboy. And you, Mr. Orlean, you are a young man trying to make something of himself. Your father's a rich man but you pay your own way. He wanted you to become a lawyer,

I bet, and you turned your back on him in order to be your own man. That's half the way to me, Felix. Why not see what more there is?"

"I can take care of my own life, Mr. Lawless," I said. "The only thing I need from a job is money."

"How much money?"

"Well, my rent which is five-fifty a month and then my other expenses. . . ."

"So you need forty-two thousand, before taxes, that is if you pay taxes." I had come up with the same number after an afternoon of budgeting.

"Of course I pay my taxes," I said.

"Of course you do," Lawless said, smiling broadly. "I'll pay you what you need for this position. All you have to do is agree to try it out for a few weeks."

I glanced at the blow-up of Bakunin and thought about the chance this might be. I needed the money. My parents wouldn't even answer one of my letters much less finance my education.

"I'm not sure," I said.

"About what?"

"The line you're talking about," I said. "It sounds like some kind of legal bound-ary. One side is law abiding and the other isn't."

"You're just an employee, Felix. Like anyone working for Enron or Hasbro. No one there is held responsible for what their employers may or may not have done."

"I won't do anything illegal."

"Of course you won't," Lawless said.

"I have to put my school work first."

"We can make your hours flexible."

"If I don't like what's happening I'll quit immediately," I said. "No prior notice."

"You sound more like a law student than a news hound," Lawless said. "But believe me I need you, Felix. I don't have the time to read every paper. If I know you're going through five or six of the big ones that'll take a lot of pressure off of me. And you'll learn a lot here. I've been around. From the guest of royalty in Asia to the prisons of Turkey and Mexico."

"No law breaking for me," I said again.

"I heard you." Lawless took a piece of paper from the ledge on the window behind him and handed it to me. "Over the next couple of days I'd like you to check up on these people."

"What do you mean?"

"Nothing questionable, simply check to see that they're around. Try to talk to them yourself but if you can't just make sure that they're there, and that they're okay."

"You think these people might be in trouble?"

"I don't worry about dolls hanging from doorknobs," he said. "They don't mean a thing to me. I'm just looking into a little problem that I picked up on the other day."

"Maybe you should call the police."

"The police and I have a deal. I don't talk to them and they don't listen to me. It works out just fine."

4

I wanted to talk more but Lawless said that he had his day cut out for him.

"I've got to go out but you can stay," he said. "The room next door will be your workplace. Here let me show you."

My new employer stood up. As I said, he's a big man. There seemed to be something important in even this simple movement. It was as if some stone monolith were suddenly sentient and moving with singular purpose in the world.

The room labeled STORAGE was narrow, crowded with boxes and untidy. There was a long table covered with papers, both printed and handwritten, and various publications. The boxes were cardboard, some white and some brown. The white ones had handwritten single letters on their fitted lids, scrawled in red. The brown ones on the whole were open at the top with all sorts of files and papers stacked inside.

"The white ones are my filing cabinet," Lawless said. "The brown ones are waiting for you to put them in order. There's a flat stack of unconstructed file boxes in the corner under the window. When you need a new one just put it together." He waved at a pile of rags set upon something in the corner.

"What's that?" I asked, pointing at a pink metal box that sat directly under the window.

"It's the only real file cabinet but we don't keep files in there." He didn't say anything else about it and I was too busy trying to keep up to care.

Through the window an ocean liner was making its way up river. It was larger than three city blocks.

"The papers are all different," Lawless said. "The legal sheets are my journal entries, reports, and notes. These you are to transcribe. The mimeoed sheets are various documents that have come to me. I need you to file them according to the way the rest of the files work. If you have any questions just ask me."

The liner let out a blast from its horn that I heard faintly through the closed window.

"And these newsletters," he said and then paused.

"What about them?"

"These newsletters I get from different places. They're very, very specialized." He was holding up a thick stack of printed materials. "Some of them come from friends around the world. Anarchist and syndicalist communes in America and elsewhere, in the country and the cities too. One of them's an Internet commune. That one will be interesting to keep tabs on; see if they got something there."

The big man stopped speaking for a moment and considered something. Maybe it was the Internet anarchist commune or maybe it was a thought that passed through his mind while talking. In the weeks to come I was to learn how deeply intuitive this man was. He was like some pre-Columbian shaman looking for signs in everything;

talking to gods that even his own people had no knowledge of.

"Then there are the more political newsletters. The friendlies include various liberation movements and ecological groups. And of course there's Red Tuesday. She gathers up reports of problems brewing around the world. Dictators rising, infrastructures failing, and the movements of various players in the international killkill games."

"The what?"

"How do you kill a snake?" he asked grabbing me by the arm with a frighteningly quick motion.

I froze and wondered if it was too late to tell him that I didn't want the job.

"Cut off his head," Lawless informed me. "Cut off his head." He let me go and held out his hands in wonder. "To the corporations and former NATO allies this whole world is a nest of vipers. They have units, killkill boys Red Tuesday calls them. These units remove the heads of particularly dangerous vipers. Some of them are well known. You see them on TV and in courtroom cases. Others move like shadows. Red tries to keep tabs on them. She has a special box for the killkill boys and girls just so they know that somebody out there has a machete for their fangs too."

He said this last word like a breathy blast on a toy whistle. It made me laugh.

"Not funny," he told me. "Deadly serious. If you read Red's letters you will know more than any daily papers would ever dare tell you."

I wondered, not for the last time, about my employer's sanity.

"She's crazy of course," Lawless said as though he had read my mind.

"Excuse me?"

"Red. She's crazy. She also has a soap box about the pope. She's had him involved in every conspiracy from that eyeball on the dollar bill to frozen aliens in some Vatican subbasement."

"So how can you trust anything she says?"

"That's just it, son," Lawless said boring those pinpoint eyes into mine. "You can't trust anyone, not completely. But you can't afford not to listen. You have to listen, examine, and then make up your own mind."

The weight of his words settled in on me. It was a way of thinking that produced a paranoia beyond paranoia.

"That sounds like going into the crazy

house and asking for commentary on the nightly news," I said, trying to make light of his assertions.

"If the world is insane then you'd be a fool to try and look for sanity to answer the call." Archibald Lawless looked at me with that great heart-shaped face. His bright skin and crown of thorns caused a quickening in my heart.

"The rest of these newsletters and whatnot are from the bad guys. White supremacist groups, pedophile target lists, special memos from certain key international banks. Mostly it's nothing but sometimes it allows you to make a phone call, or something." Again he drifted off into space.

I heard the threat in his voice with that *or something* but by then I knew I had to spend at least a couple of hours with those notes. My aunt Alberta was right about my curiosity. I was always sticking my nose where it didn't belong.

"So you can spend as much time as you want making yourself at home around here. The phone line can be used calling anywhere on the planet but don't use the computer until I show you what's what there." He seemed happy, friendly. He imparted that élan to me. "When you leave just shut the door. It will engage all the locks by itself, electrically."

As he opened the door to leave my storage office, I asked, "Mr. Lawless?"

"Yeah, son?"

"I don't get it."

"Get what?"

"With all this Red Tuesday, pedophiliac, white supremacist stuff how can you know that you should trust me? I mean all you've done is read some computer files. All that could be forged, couldn't it?"

He smiled and instead of answering my question he said, "You're just like a blank sheet of paper, Orleen. Maybe a name and a date up top but that's all and it's in pencil. You could be my worst nightmare, Felix. But first we've got to get some words down on paper." He smiled again and went out of his office. I followed.

He threw the bolts open and kicked up the buttress. Then he pulled open the door. He made to go out and then thought of something, turned and pointed that teacher's finger at me again.

"Don't open this door for anybody. Not for anyone but me. Don't answer it. Don't say anything through it. You can use this," he tapped a small video monitor that was mounted on the wall to the right of the door, "to see, but that's it."

"W-why?" I stammered.

"The landlord and I have a little dispute going."

"What kind of dispute?"

"I haven't paid rent in seven years and he thinks that it's about time that I did."

"And you don't?"

"The only truth in the bible is where it says that stuff about money and evil," he said and then he hurried out. The door closed behind him, five seconds later the locks all flipped down and the buttress lowered. I noticed then that there was a network of wires that led from the door to a small black box sitting underneath the cushionless couch.

The box was connected to an automobile battery. Even in a blackout Archibald Lawless would have secure doors.

5

I spent that morning inside the mind of a madman or a genius or maybe outside of what Lawless refers to as *the hive mind, the spirit that guides millions of heedless citizens through the aimless acts of everyday life.*

The mess on my office table was a treasure trove of oddities and information. Xeroxed copies of *wanted* posters, guest lists to conservative political fund raisers, blueprints of corporate offices and police stations. Red Tuesday's newsletter had detailed information about the movements of certain *killkills* using their animal code names (like Bear, Ringed Hornet, and Mink). She was less forthcoming about certain saboteurs fighting for anything from ecology to the liberation of so-called political prisoners. For these groups she merely lauded their actions and gave veiled warnings about how close they were to discovery in various cities.

Lawless was right about her and the Catholic Church. She also had a box in each issue surrounded by a border of red and blue crosses in which she made tirades against Catholic crack houses paying for political campaigns and other such absurdities. Even the language was different. This article was the only one that had misspellings and bad grammar.

At the back of every Red Tuesday newsletter, on page four, was an article signed only in the initials AAL. Everything else was written by Red Tuesday. This regular column had a title, REVOLUTIONARY NOTES. After flipping through about fifteen issues I found one column on Archie and the rent.

> Never give an inch to the letter of the law if it means submitting to a lie. Your word is your freedom not your bond. If you make a promise, or a promise is made to you, it is imperative that you make sure the word, regardless of what the law says, is upheld. Lies are the basis for all the many crimes that we commit every day. From petty theft to genocide it is a lie that makes it and the truth that settles the account.
>
> Think of it! If only we made every candidate for office responsible for every campaign promise she made. Then you'd see a democracy that hasn't been around for a while. My own landlord promised me whitewashed walls and a red carpet when I agreed to pay his lousy rent. He thought the lie would go down easy, that he could evict me because I never signed a contract. But he had lied. When I took his rooms for month to month he needed the rent and told me that a contract wasn't nec-

essary. He told me that he'd paint and lay carpet, but all that was lies.

It's been years and I'm still here. He hasn't painted or made a cent. I brought him to court and I won. And then, because a man who lies cannot recognize the truth, he sent men to run me out . . .

Never lie and never lie down for a lie. Live according to your word and the world will find its own balance.

I was amazed by the almost innocent and idealistic prattle of such an obviously intelligent man.

The thought of a landlord sending up toughs to run me out of the rooms stopped my lazy reading and sent me out on the job I had been given.

The first person on my list was Valerie Lox. She was a commercial real estate broker on Madison Avenue, just above an exclusive jewelry store. I got there at about eleven forty-five. The offices were small but well appointed. The building was only two floors and the roof had a skylight making it possible for all of the lush green plants to flourish between the three real estate agents' desks.

"Can I help you?" a young Asian man at the desk closest to the door asked.

I suppressed the urge to correct him. *May I*, my mother inside me wanted to say. But I turned my head instead looking out of the window onto posh Madison. Across the street was a furrier, a fancy toy store, and a German pen shop.

"Yes," I said. "I want to see Ms. Lox."

The young man looked me up and down. He didn't like my blue jeans and ratty, secondhand Tibetan sweater—this college wear wasn't designed for Madison Avenue consumption.

"My father is thinking of opening a second office in Manhattan and he wanted me to see what was available," I further explained.

"And your father is?" Another bad sentence.

"JP Orlean of Herman, Bledsoe, and Orlean in New Orleans."

"Wait here." The young man uttered these words, rose from his chair, and walked away.

The two young women agents, one white and the other honey brown, looked from me to the young man as he made his way past them and through a door at the back of the garden room.

I was missing my seminar on the History of the West but that didn't bother me much. I could always get the notes from my friend Claude. And working for Lawless promised to hone my investigative potentials.

"Making sense out of a seemingly incomprehensible jumble of facts." That's what Professor Ortega said at the first lecture I attended at Columbia. His class was called the Art in Article.

I wasn't sure what Lawless was looking for but that didn't worry me. I knew enough from my father's practice to feel safe from involvement in any crime. The test was that even if I went to the police there was nothing concrete I could tell them that they didn't already know.

I was beginning to wonder where the agent had gone when he and a small woman in a dark blue dress came out of the door in back. He veered off and the woman walked straight toward me.

"Mr. Orlean?" she asked with no smile.

"Ms. Lox?" I did smile.

"May I see some form of identification?"

This shocked. When did a real estate agent ask for anything but a deposit? But I took out my wallet and showed her my student ID and Louisiana driver's license. She looked them over carefully and then invited me to follow her into the back.

The head woman's office was no larger than an alcove, there was no skylight or window. Her workstation was a one-piece, salmon pink high school desk next to which sat a short black filing cabinet. She sat and put on a telephone headset, just an earphone and a tiny microphone in front of her mouth.

I stayed standing even though there was a visitor's chair, because I had my manners to maintain.

"Sit," she said, not unkindly.

I did so.

Valerie Lox was a mild blend of contradictions. Her pale skin seemed hard, almost ceramic. Her tightly wound blond hair was in the final phase of turning to white. The hint of yellow was illusive. The face was small and sharp, and her features could have been lightly sculpted and then painted on. Her birdlike body was slender and probably as hard as the rest of her but the blue dress was rich in color and fabric. It was like a royal cloak wrapped around the shoulders of a white twig.

"Why did you need to see my ID?"

"This is an exclusive service, Mr. Orlean," she said with no chink of humanity in her face. "And we like to know exactly who it is we're dealing with."

"Oh," I said. "So it wasn't because of my clothes or my race?"

"The lower races come in all colors, Mr. Orlean. And none of them get back here."

Her certainty sent a shiver down my spine. I smiled to hide the discomfort.

She asked of what assistance she could be to my father. I told her some lies but I forget exactly what. Lying comes easily to me. My aunt Alberta had once told me that lying was a character trait of men on my father's side of the family. That was why they all became lawyers.

"Lawyer even sounds like liar," she used to say. "That's a good thing and it's a bad thing. You got to go with the good, honey chile, no matter what you do."

I spent forty-five minutes looking over photographs and blueprints of offices all over the Madison Avenue area. Nothing cost less than three hundred and fifty thousand a year and Ms. Lox got a whole year's rent as commission. I was thinking maybe I could marry a real estate agent while I worked the paper trade.

Ms. Lox didn't press me. She showed me one office after another asking strategic questions now and then.

"What sort of law would he be practicing?" she asked at one point. "I mean would he need a large waiting room?"

"If he did," I answered, "I wouldn't be here talking to you. Any lawyer with a waiting room is just two steps away from ambulance chasing."

That was the only time I saw her smile.

"Is your father licensed to practice in New York?" she asked at another time.

"You should know," I said.

"Come again?"

"I gave your assistant my father's name and he came back here for five minutes or more. If I were you I would have looked up JP Orlean in the ABA Internet service. There I would have seen that he is not licensed in this state. But you must be aware that he has many clients who have investments and business in the city. A lawyer is mostly mind and a license is easy to rent." These last words were my father's. He used them all the time to out-of-state clients who didn't understand the game.

It struck me as odd that Ms. Lox was so suspicious of me. I was just looking at pictures of commercial spaces. There was nothing top secret that I could steal.

The young Asian man, Brian, brought me an espresso with a coconut cookie while I considered. And when I was through he led me to the front door and said good-bye using my name. I told him, as I had told Valerie Lox, that I would be in touch in a few days after my father and I had a chance to talk.

As I was leaving I saw Valerie Lox standing at the door in back looking after me with something like concern on her porcelain face.

The next stop was a construction site on 23rd Street. Kenneth Cornell, the man I came to see, was some kind of supervisor there. The crew was excavating a deep hole getting ready for the roots of a skyscraper. There were three large cranes moving dirt and stone from the lower depths to awaiting trucks on a higher plane. There was a lot of clanging and whining motors, men, and a few women, shouting, and the impact of hammers, manual and automatic, beating upon the poor New York soil, trying once again to make her submit to their architectural dreams.

I walked in, stated my business, was fitted with a hard hat, and shown into the pit.

They led me to a tin shack half the way down the dirt slope. The man inside the shack was yelling something out of the paneless window at workers looking up from down below. I knew that he was yelling to be heard over the noise but it still gave me the impression that he was a man in a rage. And, being so small, I always stood back when there was rage going on.

Cornell was tall but a bit lanky for construction I thought. His pink chin was partly gray from afternoon shadow and his gray eyes were unsettling because they seemed to look a bit too deeply into my intentions.

"Yeah?"

"Mr. Cornell?"

"Yeah?"

"I'm Orlean," I said pronouncing it *or-leen* as Lawless had done.

"That supposed to mean something to me?"

"I called your office last week—about getting a job," I said.

His eyes tightened, it felt as though they were squeezing my lungs.

"Who are you?" he asked me.

It suddenly occurred to me that I was way out of my depth.

Cornell's hands folded up into fists as if to underscore the epiphany.

"Get the hell out of here," he said.

I didn't exactly run out of that hole but if I had been competing in a walking race I wouldn't have come in last.

6

Lana Drexel, fashion model, was the last name on my list. She was the one I most wanted to see but I didn't make it that day.

Henry Lansman was my second to last stop. He was an easy one, a barber at Crenshaw's, a popular place down in Greenwich Village. There was almost always a line at Crenshaw's. They were an old time barbershop that catered to the conservative thirty-something crowd. They gave classic haircuts in twelve minutes and so could afford to undercut, so to speak, the competition.

The shop, I knew from friends, had nine barber chairs that were all busy all of the time. But because this was a Tuesday at two-thirty there were only about ten or twelve customers waiting in line at the top of the stairwell of the shop. You had to go down a half flight of stairs to get into the establishment. I can't say what the inside of the place looked like because I never made it there.

"Hey," someone said in a tone that was opening to fear. "Hey, mister."

"Excuse me," a man in a red parka said before he shouldered me aside hard enough to have thrown me down the stairwell if there hadn't been a portly gentleman there to block my fall.

"Hey, man! What the fuck!" the big man I fell against hollered. He was wearing some kind of blue uniform.

I wanted to see who it was that pushed me. I did catch a glimpse of the top of the back of his head. It had partly gray close-cut hair. He was crouching down and the parka disguised his size, and, anyway, the big guy I slammed into needed an apology.

"I'm sorry . . ." I said and then the shouting started.

"Hey, mister. Mister! Hey I think this guy's havin' a heart attack!"

The big man had put his hand on my shoulder but the terror in the crackling tone distracted him long enough for me to rush to the side of the young man who was screaming. I wish I could say that it was out of concern for life that moved me so quickly but I really just wanted to save myself from being hit.

The screamer was a white man, tall and well built. He was tan and wore an unbuttoned black leather jacket and a coal colored loose-knit shirt that was open at the neck revealing a thick gold chain that hung around his throat. He had a frightened child's eyes. His fear was enough to convince me to clear out before the danger he saw could spread. I would have run away if it wasn't for the dying man at my feet.

I crouched down on one knee to get a closer look at the heart attack victim. There was a fleck of foam at the corner of his mouth. The lips were dark, the panic in his wide eyes was fading into death. He wore a short-sleeved nylon shirt which was odd because this was late October and on the chilly side. His gray slacks rode a little high. He was almost completely bald.

The struggle in his eyes was gone by the

time I had noticed these things. I cradled the back of his head with my hand. A spasm went through his neck. His back arched and I thought he was trying to rise. But then he slumped back down. Blood seeped out of his left nostril.

"He's dead," the someone whispered.

Men and women all around were voicing their concern but I only made out one sentence, "Mr. Bartoli, it's Henry, Henry Lansman!" a man's voice shouted.

I was watching the color drain from the dead man's face thinking that I should clear out or tell somebody what I knew. But all I could do was kneel there holding the heavy head, watching the drop of blood making its way down his jowl.

"Out of the way! Let him go!" a man ordered.

A round man, hard from muscle, pushed me aside. He was wearing a white smock. At first I thought it was a doctor. But then I realized it must be someone from the barbershop.

I moved aside and kept on going. The screamer with the gold chain was leaning against the window of the shoe store next door. His tan had faded. I remember thinking that some poor woman would have to have sex with him all night long before the color came back.

Henry Lansman was dead. People were shouting for someone to call an ambulance. I stayed watching until I heard the first far-off whine of the siren then I walked away from the scene feeling guilty though not knowing why.

I went over to Saint Mark's Place, a street filled with head shops, twelve-step programs, and wild youths with punk hair and multiple piercings. There was a comic book store that I frequented and a quasi-Asian restaurant that was priced for the college student pocketbook.

I ordered soba noodles with sesame sauce and a triple espresso. I finished the coffee but only managed about half of the entrée. I sat there thinking about the ceramic woman, the angry man, and the dead barber. That morning I was just a college student looking for a job. By afternoon I had witnessed a man dying.

I considered my options. The first one was calling my father. He knew lawyers in

New York. Good ones. If I told him what was wrong he'd be on the next plane. JP would be there. He'd body block anyone trying to hurt me. He'd do anything to save me from danger. But then he'd take me back down to Louisiana and tell me how stupid I was and which law school I was to attend. He might even tell me that I had to live at home for a while.

And how could I say no if I begged him to save me?

And anyway it looked like a heart attack that killed Lansman. I decided that I was just being oversensitive to the paranoia of Lawless and Red Tuesday.

The man was just sick.

"Didn't you like it?" the slightly overweight, blue-haired, black waitress asked. Actually her hair was brown with three bright blue streaks running back from her forehead.

"I like you," I said, completely out of character.

She gave me a leery look and then walked away to the kitchen. She returned with my bill a few moments later. At the bottom was her telephone number and her name, Sharee.

I called Lawless's answering machine from a pay phone on the street.

"Lox and Cornell are fine," I said after the tone. "But Lansman died of a heart attack. He fell dead just when I got there. I didn't get to Drexel and I quit too. You don't have to pay me."

From there I went up to the special lab room that was set up for us at Columbia. There were three computers that were connected to AP, UPI, and Reuters news databases. There were also lines connected to police and hospital reports in Manhattan. Lansman's death wasn't even listed. That set my mind at ease some. If there was no note of his death it had to be some kind of medical problem and not foul play.

I followed breaking news in the Middle East and Africa until late that night. There had been a car bomb near the presidential residence in Caracas, Venezuela. I wondered, briefly, what Red Tuesday would have made of that.

It was midnight by the time I got to 121st Street. I made it to our apartment house, the Madison, and climbed six floors. I was walking down the hall when a tall man in a dark suit appeared before me.

"Mr. Orlean?"

"Yes?"

"We need to speak to you."

"It's late," I complained and then made to walk around him.

He moved to block my way.

Backing up I bumped into something large and soft so I turned. Another obstacle in the form of a man in a suit stood before me.

The first man was white, the second light brown.

"We need to talk to you at the station," the brown man informed me.

"You're the police?"

Instead of speaking he produced a badge.

"What do you want with me?" I asked, honestly confused. I had put my dealings with Archibald Lawless that far behind me.

"You're a witness to a possible crime," the man behind me said.

I turned and looked at him. He had a big nose with blue and red veins at the surface. His breath carried the kind of halitosis that you had to take pills for.

The brown man pulled my arms behind my back and clapped handcuffs on my wrists.

"You don't arrest witnesses," I said.

"You've been moving around a lot, son," the white cop said, exhaling a zephyr of noxious fumes. "And we need to know some answers before we decide if we're going to charge you with something or not."

"Where's your warrant?" I said in a loud voice intended to waken my roommate. But I was cut short by the quick slap from the man I came to know as August Morganthau.

7

They took me to the 126th Street station. There were police cars parked up and down the block. I was taken past a waiting room full of pensive looking citizens. They weren't manacled or guarded so I figured they were there to make complaints or to answer warrants. I *was* a felon in their eyes, cuffed and manhandled, shoved past them like a thief.

They took me to a Plexiglas booth where a uniformed officer filled out what I came to know later as an entry slip.

"Name?" the sentry asked.

I was looking at the floor to avoid the nausea caused by Morganthau's breath.

"Name?"

I realized that I was expected to answer the question. It seemed unfair. Why should I tell him my name? I didn't ask to be there.

"Felix Orlean," I said taking great pleasure in withholding my middle names.

"Middle name?"

I shook my head.

"Case number?"

"I don't know," I said, trying now to be helpful. I regretted the childish withholding of my name.

"Of course you don't, stupid," Morganthau said. He shoved me too.

"Case six-three-two-two-oh, homicide," the chubby brown man, Tito Perez, said.

"Charges?"

"Pending," Officer Morganthau grunted.

There was a Plexiglas wall next to the booth with a rude door cut into it. The edges were all uneven and it had only a makeshift wire hanger handle. I got the impression that one day the police realized that if someone got loose with a gun there would be a lot of casualties unless they put up a bulletproof barrier between them and the phantom shooter. So they bought some used Plexiglas and cut it into walls and doors and whatnot. After that they never thought about it again.

Perez pulled open the door. It wasn't locked, couldn't be as far as I could see. They pushed me along an aisle of cubicles. Men and women wearing headsets were sitting behind the low-cut walls talking to the air or each other. Some of them were in uniform, some not. Mostly it was women. Almost all of them white. The room was shabby. The carpet under my feet was worn all the way to the floor in places. The cubicles were piled high with folders, scraps of pink and white papers, coffee cups, and small heaps of sweaters, shirts, and caps. The tan cubicle walls weren't all straight. A few were missing, some were half rotted away or stained from what must have been water damage of some sort.

If this was the nerve center of police intelligence for that neighborhood, crime was a good business opportunity to consider.

I see how slipshod the police seemed now. But that night, while I merely recorded what I saw with my eyes, my mind was in a state of full-blown horror. As soon as I got to a phone I was going to call my father's twenty-four-hour service. Betty was the woman on the late night shift. She'd get to him no matter where he was.

We reached a large cubicle that was not only disheveled but it also smelled. The smell was sharp and unhealthy. Morganthau sat down on one of a pair of gray steel desks that faced each other. He indicated the chair that sat at the desk for me.

"Can you take these things off my hands?" I asked.

"Sorry," he said with an insincere gray smile. "Policy."

I lifted my arms to go behind the back of the chair and sat slightly hunched over.

"I'm Morganthau and this is Officer Perez," he said. "Tell us what you know about Hank Lansman."

The "Hank" threw me off for a second. I frowned trying to connect it.

"Come on, kid," Perez said. "You were seen at the barbershop. We know you were there."

My mind flooded with thoughts. How did they know I was there? Was Lansman murdered? Even if someone saw me how would they know my name? I didn't tell anyone. I don't have a record or even any friends in that part of town.

All of this was going on just barely in the

range of consciousness. Most of what I felt was fear and discomfort. Morganthau's breath was beginning to reach my nostrils again. That coupled with the sharp odor of the cubicle started to seriously mess with my stomach.

"I want to make a phone call."

"Later," Perez said. His voice was soft.

"I have a right . . ." I began but I stopped when Morganthau put his shod foot, sole down, on my lap.

"I asked you a question," he said.

"A man named Archibald Lawless hired me to see about four people. He didn't tell me why." I gave them the names of Lox, Lansman, Drexler, and Cornell. "He said that I should go see these people, make sure I saw them in the flesh."

"And then what?"

"That's all he said. He said see them. I suppose he wanted me to make a report but we didn't get that far."

"What were you supposed to say to these people when you saw them?" Perez asked.

"What was said didn't matter. Just make sure I saw them, that's all. Listen. I don't know anything about this. I answered an ad in the paper. It was for Lawless. He said that he wanted a scribe . . ."

"We know all about Lawless," Morganthau said. "We know about his *scribes* and we know about you too."

"There's nothing about me that has to do with him."

"One dead man," Perez suggested.

"I thought he had a heart attack?"

The officers looked at each other.

"We don't need any shit, kid," Morganthau said. "Who else is in the cell?"

It was at that moment I began to fear that even my father could not save me.

I had to swallow twice before saying, "What do you mean?"

Morganthau's foot was still in my lap. He increased the weight a little and said, "This is about to get ugly."

I felt cold all of a sudden. My head was light and my tongue started watering.

"Shit!" Morganthau shouted. He pulled his foot back from my thighs but not before I vomited soba noodles all over his pant leg. "Damn!"

He skipped away. Perez flung open a drawer in his desk and threw a towel to his partner who began wiping his pants as he went back down the corridor we came from.

"You're in trouble now, kid," Perez said.

If I had seen it on a TV show I would have sneered at the weak dialogue. But in that chair I was scared to death. I retched twice more and steeled my neck to keep from crying.

After he was sure that I was through being sick, Perez jerked me up by the arm and dragged me down another corridor until we came to a big room where there were other chained prisoners. All of them male.

The center of the room was empty of furniture except for a small table in the middle of the floor where a lone sentry sat. Along three walls ran metal benches that were bolted to the floor. Every four feet or so along each bench there was a thick eyebolt also planted in the concrete floor. There were three eyebolts along each bench. Six men were attached to these stations by manacles that also held their feet. All of these men were negroes.

"Finney," Perez said. "Grab me some bracelets for this one."

Finney was my age with pale strawberry hair. He was tall and long limbed. He had to stand up in order to kneel down and reach under the table for the restraints. Perez undid my handcuffs, made me sit at a station next to a big brown man who was rocking backward and forth and talking to himself. He was smiling through his words, which were mostly indistinct, and tapping his right foot on the concrete. Two places away, on the other side was a man so big that it didn't seem as if the chains he wore could possibly hold him. Across the way was a young, very mean looking man. All he wore was a pair of tattered jeans. His eyes bored into mine. It was as if I were his worst enemy and finally my throat was within his reach.

Perez didn't say anything to me or even look me in the face. He simply attached the new manacles to my ankles and wrists and secured the chains to the eyebolt in the floor. Then he went to fill out a form on Finney's table. After they exchanged words, which I couldn't make out, Perez left through the door we had entered.

8

I was relieved to be away from Morganthau's putrid breath. At least I had a few moments to think about what happened so far. If Lansman was murdered the man in the red parka had something to do with it. I wanted to tell the police about him but they seemed so sure of my guilt that I thought they might construe any information I gave them as confirmation of my culpability. I wasn't very experienced with police procedure but I knew a lot about the law from my father and grandfather, LJ Orlean.

I knew that I needed to speak to a lawyer before I could have any kind of meaningful dialogue with the law. But they didn't seem ready to allow me my Constitutional phone call. I was screwing up my courage to ask the midwestern looking Finney for my one call when the big guy two spaces to my left began speaking to me.

"You look like a cherry," he said. It was almost a question.

"Cherry, cherry, cherry . . ." the grinning rocker on the other side chanted.

"You might need a friend," the big man suggested.

"I'm all right," I said with nary a break in my voice.

". . . cherry, cherry, cherry . . ."

"You dissin' me, bitch?" the big man asked, this time it was hardly a question.

I didn't know what to say. An apology seemed inappropriate and getting down on my knees to beg was not what a man should do in such a situation.

The man across from me mouthed a sentence that was either announcing his intention of killing or kissing me, I didn't know which.

"Officer," I said. "Officer."

". . . cherry, cherry, cherry, cherry . . ."

"Officer."

"Shut up," Finney said.

"Officer, I haven't been given the right to a phone call yet. I want to make that call now."

The strawberry blond didn't respond. He was reading something. I honestly believe that he no longer heard me.

"I'ma bust you up, punk," the big man to my left proclaimed.

I started thinking about the possibility of weapons at my disposal.

A man is only as strong as his th'oat or his groin. My aunt Alberta's words came back to me with a flash of heat and then cold passing over my scalp. *Just remember, baby—don't hesitate, not for a minute.*

". . . cherry, cherry . . ."

I glanced at the big man. He had fists the width of a small tree's trunk. I decided that when I got the chance I'd go in low on him: hit him hard and ruin him for life. Jail had turned me into a felon and I hadn't been there an hour.

A phone rang, which in itself was not unusual but I couldn't see a phone anywhere in the room. It rang again.

". . . cherry, cherry, I want some," the rocking man sang.

The shirtless man across the way was still mouthing his violent flirtation.

The phone rang for the third time.

The guard turned the page of his magazine.

The big man on the left suddenly yanked on his chains with all his might. My heart leapt. I was sure that he'd break those flimsy shackles.

"Settle down, Trainer," the blond guard said. Then he got up and walked to the wall where there was a space between the benches.

The phone rang.

"You gonna suck my toes, niggah," the man called Trainer promised.

The kid across the way made me another promise.

The phone rang. The room started spinning. The guard located a hidden door in the wall and pulled it open. He reached in and came out with a yellow phone receiver connected to a black cord.

"Finney here," he said.

". . . cherry, cherry the best dessert," the rocking man said. "Cherry, cherry in the dirt."

Maybe he didn't say those words but that's what I remember. The room was spinning and my sweater smelled of vomit. Finney looked at me.

". . . cherry . . ."

". . . suck on my big black dick . . ."

". . . Orlean?" Finney said.

"What?"

"Are you Felix Orlean?" he asked.

"Yes sir."

"*Yes sir,*" Trainer said. He was trying to make fun of me but I think he realized that I might soon be beyond his reach.

"He's here," Finney said into the receiver.

He hung up the phone and went back to his chair and magazine.

"Hm," Trainer said. "Looks like they just wanted to make sure you was up here wit' me."

"Fuck you," I said. I didn't mean to, I really didn't. But I was sick and he was stupid . . .

"What did you say?"

"I said, fuck you, asshole."

Trainer's eyes widened. The veins on his neck were suddenly engorged with blood. His lips actually quivered. And then I did the worst thing I could have done to such a man—I laughed.

What did I have to lose? He was going to brutalize me if he could anyway. Maybe I could catch him by the nuts like my aunt Alberta had advised.

"You a dead man," Trainer promised.

"Mash his cherry, Jerry," the rocking man tapped his toe for each syllable.

I lowered my head and tried to remember the Lord's prayer.

I could not.

Then I heard the door to the strange room open. I looked up to see a white man walking through. He was tall and dressed in an expensive gray suit.

"Which one is Orlean?" the white man asked Blondie.

"Over there." Finney gestured with his chin.

"Unlock him."

"Rules are you need two guards to remove a recal," the guard replied.

"Get up off your ass, kid, or I will have you

mopping up vomit in the drunk tank for a month of Sundays." The gray suit had a deadly certain voice.

The guard got up and unlocked my fetters. I stood up and smiled at Trainer and the shirtless man across the way.

"This way, Felix," the man in the gray suit said.

"I'm gonna remember you, Felix Orlean," the prisoner Trainer said.

"Whatever you say, loser," I said smiling. "Maybe you'll learn something."

Again the prisoner named Trainer strained at his bonds. He jumped at me but there was no give to his chains. I was scared to death. The only way I kept from going crazy was taunting my helpless tormentor.

The man in the gray suit took me by the shoulder and guided me out of the room. The shirtless detainee spat on the floor as I left. Trainer screeched like a mad elephant.

We walked down a long corridor coming to a small elevator at last. The car went up seven floors and opened into a room that was almost livable. There were carpets and stuffed chairs and the smell of decent coffee.

"You can go in there and clean up," the suit said, pointing toward a closed door.

"What's your name?" I asked him.

"Captain Delgado."

The door led to a large restroom and shower area. I took off my college clothes and got under a spigot for at least fifteen minutes. After the shower I washed the vomit from my sweater. Between the lateness of the hour, the heat, dehydration, and fear I was so tired that it was hard to keep moving.

I staggered back to the room where Delgado waited. He was sitting in a big red chair, reading a newspaper.

"Feel better?"

"Uh-huh."

"Let's go then."

We retraced every step I'd taken through the station. Me sticking close to the slick policeman and him leading the way. Nobody stopped us, nobody questioned our passing.

We went to a '98 Le Sabre parked out in front of the station and Delgado drove us up further into Harlem.

"Where we going?" I asked.

"Up on One Fifty-sixth," he said.

"I'd like to go home."

"No you wouldn't. Take my word on that."

"What's going on, Captain?"

"I haven't the slightest idea, son."

We stopped in front of a large stone apartment building on 156th Street. Even though it was late there were young men and women hanging out around the front stoop.

"Eight twenty-one," Delgado said.

"What?"

"Apartment eight twenty-one. That's where you're going."

"I want to go home."

"Get out."

"Are you coming?"

"No."

I had never felt more vulnerable in my life.

I opened the door and all the faces from the stoop turned toward me.

"Who's up there?" I asked Delgado.

He pulled my door shut and drove off.

"You a cop, man?" a young man asked me.

He had climbed down from his seat on the top step of the stoop.

"No. No. He just gave me a ride."

My inquisitor was probably a year or two younger than I. His skin was very dark. Even though the air was chilly he wore only a T-shirt. His arms were slender but knotty with muscle.

"You fuckin' wit' me, man?"

"No. I'm supposed to go to an apartment upstairs."

Two other angry looking youths climbed down from the stoop. They flanked my interlocutor, searching me with their eyes.

"What for?" the youth asked.

"They told me that the man who had me released is up there."

I started walking. I had to go around my three new friends. Up the stoop I went and into the dark corridor of the first floor.

There was no light and I could almost feel the young men they followed me so closely. As we climbed the stairs they spoke to me.

"You with the cops you ain't gonna get outta here, mothahfuckah," one of them said.

"We should take him now, Durkey," another suggested.

"Let's see where he go," Durkey, the first one who had approached me, said. "Let's check it out."

I was breathing hard by the time I got to the eighth floor landing. Most of the journey was made through semi-darkness. Along the way there was some light from open apartment doors. Silent sentinels came to mark our passing: children, old people, women, and some men. But no one asked Durkey and his henchmen why they were following me.

I had been in places like this before, in the Ninth Ward, New Orleans. But I was always under the protection of my aunt Alberta and her boyfriends. Being from a light-skinned family of the upper crust of colored society I was always seen as an outsider.

I knocked on the door to apartment eight twenty-one and waited—and prayed.

"Nobody there," Durkey said.

He put a hand on my shoulder.

The door opened flooding the hallway with powerful light. I winced. Durkey's hand fled my shoulder.

Archibald Lawless appeared in the doorway.

"Mr. Madison," he said loudly. "I see that you've accompanied my guest upstairs."

"Hey, Lawless," Durkey said with deference. "I didn't know he was your boy."

"Uh-huh," the anarchist said. "You can go now."

My retinue of toughs backed away. My recent, and ex, boss smiled.

"Come on in, Felix. You've had a busy day."

9

It was an opulent room. The floors were covered in thick, rose-colored carpets. On the walls hung a dozen eighteenth-century paintings of countrysides and beautiful young men and women of all races. There was a fireplace with a gas blaze raging and a large dark-wood table set with cheeses, meats, fruits, and bottles of wine.

"Have a seat," Lawless said.

There was a big backless couch upholstered with the rough fur of bear or maybe beaver.

"What's going on?" I asked.

"Are you hungry?"

"I don't know. I threw up at the police station."

"Wine then," Archibald said. He took a dark green bottle and a slender water glass from the table. He filled the glass halfway with the dark red liquid and handed it to me.

It was the finest burgundy I'd ever tasted. Rich, fruity, almost smoky.

"Cheese?" Lawless asked.

"In a minute," I said. "Is this your apartment?"

"I own the building," he said blandly. "Bought it when the prices were still depressed."

"You're a landlord?"

"Building manager is the title I prefer. I collect a certain amount of rent from my tenants until they've paid for the cost of their unit. After that they pay whatever maintenance is necessary for taxes and upkeep."

I must have been gaping at him.

"It's the way Fidel does it in Cuba," he said.

"Castro's a dictator."

"And Bush is a democratically elected official," he replied.

"But . . ." I said.

Lawless held up his hand.

"We'll have enough time to discuss politics on slow days at the office," he said. "Right now we have some more pressing business."

I'd drunk the half glass and he replenished it.

"I left you a message," I said. "Did you get it?"

"Tell me about the murder," he replied.

"But I quit."

"No."

The wine felt good in my belly and in my blood. It warmed me and slowed the fear I'd felt since being taken by the police. I was safe, even hidden, with a man who seemed to be a force of nature all on his own. His refusal to accept my resignation made me tired. I took another swig, sat the glass down on an antique wooden crate used as a table, and let my head loll backward.

"I'm not working for you," I said. And then my eyes closed. I forced them open but couldn't keep focus. I closed my eyes again and I must have fallen asleep for a while.

The next thing I knew there was somebody whimpering somewhere . . .

"Ohhhhh the wolverines. The maggots and the ticks. Blood suckers and whores . . ."

The voice was high which somehow fit with the headache threaded behind my eyes. I sat up and regretted it. My stomach was still unsteady, my tongue dry as wood.

". . . whores and pimps and teachers sticking sticks in your ass . . ."

Lawless was rolling on the floor, whining

out these complaints. At first I thought he must have had too much wine. I went to him, touched his shoulder.

He rose under me like the ground in a terrible upheaval. Grabbing me by my hair and right shoulder he lifted me high above the floor.

"Don't you fuck with me, mother fucker!" he shouted.

His small eyes were almost large with the fear.

"It's me, Mr. Lawless," I said. "Felix. Your scribe."

He lowered me slowly, painfully because of his hold on my hair.

"I'm sick," he cried when he'd released me. "Sick."

He swayed left then right and then fell in a heap like a young child in despair. I looked around the room for something that might help him. I didn't see anything so I took a doorway that led me into a master bedroom painted dark blue with a giant bed in the center. There was a skylight in this room. Light came in from an outside source somewhere. There was a white bag on the bed made from the skin of what seemed to be an albino crocodile. You had to open the mouth and reach in past the sharp teeth to see what was inside. Therein I found a knife and pistol, an English bible and an old copy of the Koran in both English and Arabic. There was a clear plastic wallet filled with one-dollar bills and a small amber vial which contained a dozen or so tiny tablets.

There was no label on the glass tube.

Archibald Lawless had stripped off his clothes by the time I returned to the living room. He was squatting down and rocking not unlike the man in the police station.

I knelt down next him, held up the small bottle, and asked, "How many do you take, Mr. Lawless?"

His eyes opened wide again.

"Who are you?"

"Felix Orlean, your scribe. You hired me yesterday."

"Are you killkill?"

"I'm not on any of Red Tuesday's lists."

For some reason this made him laugh. He took the bottle from me and dumped all the pills in his mouth. He chewed them up and said, "I better get into the bed before I go unconscious—or dead."

I helped him into the bedroom. I think he was asleep before his head hit the mattress.

For the next few hours I hung around the big bed. Lawless was unconscious but fitful. He talked out loud in his sleep speaking in at least four different languages. I understood the Spanish and German but the other dialects escaped me. Most of his utterances were indistinct. But his tone was plaintive enough that I could feel the pain.

Now and then I went back into the living room. I had some cheddar and a sip of burgundy. After a while I started putting the food away in the kitchen, which was through a door opposite the bedroom entrance.

I stayed because I was afraid to leave. The police might still be after me for all I knew. Delgado seemed to owe a debt to Lawless but that didn't mean that Perez and Morganthau wouldn't grab me again. And somehow I'd been implicated in a murder. I had to know what was going on.

But there was more to it than that. The self-styled anarchist seemed so helpless when I'd come to. His mental state was definitely unstable and he did get me out of jail. I felt that I should wait, at least until he was aware and able to take care of himself.

There was a bookshelf in the bathroom. The books were composed of two dominant genres: politics and science fiction. I took out a book entitled *Soul of the Robot* by the author Barrington J. Bayley. It was written in the quick style of pulp fiction, which I liked because there was no pretension to philosophy. It was just a good story with incredible ideas.

I'd been reading on the bear or beaver couch for some while when there came a knock on the front door. Five quick raps and then silence. I didn't even take a breath.

I counted to three and the knock came again.

Still I didn't make a sound.

I might have stayed there silently, breathing only slightly. But then the doorknob jiggled.

I moved as quietly as I could toward the door.

"Who is it?" I called.

The doorknob stopped moving.

"Who is that?" a woman's voice asked.

"I'm Felix. I work for Mr. Lawless."

"Open the door, Felix." Her voice was even and in charge.

"Who are you?"

"My name is Maddie. I need to see Archie." A sweetness came into her voice.

I tried to open the door but there were three locks down the side that required specialized attention. One had a knob in a slot shaped like a simple maze. The next one had a series of three buttons that needed to be pressed.

"Are you going to let me in, Felix?" Maddie asked.

"Trying to get the locks."

The last lock was a bolt. The knob was on a spring that allowed it be pushed in. I squashed the knob inward but the bolt refused to slide. I tried pulling it out but that didn't work either.

"Felix?"

"I'm trying."

The hand on my shoulder made me jump into the door.

"What's wrong?" Maddie asked from her side.

"Nothing, M," Archibald Lawless said from behind me.

"Archie," the woman called.

"Meet me at Sunshine's at noon," Lawless said to the door, his hand still on my shoulder.

"Will you be there?" she asked.

"Absolutely. I can't let you in right now because I'm in the middle of something, something I have to finish."

"You promise to meet me," the disembodied woman said.

"You have my word."

He had on camouflage pants and a black T-shirt, black motorcycle boots and a giant green inlaid ring on the point finger of his left hand.

"Okay," Maddie said.

I inhaled deeply.

"You've got the job," he said.

10

Lawless drank a glass of wine, said, "Sleep on the couch," and stumbled back toward his bedroom.

I lay down not expecting to sleep a wink but the next thing I knew there was sunlight coming through a window and the smell of food in the air. There was a small table at the far end of the narrow kitchen. The chairs set there looked out of a window, down on the playground of an elementary school. He made griddle cakes with a sweet pecan sauce, spicy Andouille sausage, and broiled grapefruit halves with sugar glazed over the top, set off by a few drops of bourbon.

I tried to ask him questions while he was cooking but he put them all off asking me instead about parts of New Orleans that I knew well.

I loved talking about my city. The music and the food, the racial diversity and the fact that it was the only really French city in the United States.

"I used to go down there a lot," Lawless told me while flipping our cakes. "Not to the city so much as the swamplands. There's some people out around there who live like human beings."

When the breakfast was finally served he sat down across from me. There was a girl in the asphalt yard calling up to her mother in some apartment window. I couldn't discern what they were saying because I was studying the madman's eyes.

"I have a few disorders," he said after passing a hand over his food.

"You mean about last night?"

"Bipolar, mildly schizophrenic," he continued. "One doctor called it a recurring paranoid delusional state but I told him that if he had seen half the things that I have that he'd live in Catatonia and eat opium to wake up."

His laugh was only a flash of teeth and a nod. Everything Lawless did seemed pious and sacred—though I was sure he did not believe in God.

"Are you under a doctor's care?" I asked him.

"You might say that," he said. "I have a physician in New Delhi. A practitioner of ancient lore. He keeps me stocked with things like those pills you fed me. He keeps the old top spinning."

Lawless pointed at his head.

"Maybe you're addicted," I suggested.

"Tell me about the murder," he replied.

"I'm not working for you."

"Are you going to work for yourself?" he asked.

"What does that mean?"

"It means that it would be in your best interest to give me the information you have. That way I can make sure that the police and anybody else will leave you alone."

He was right of course. But I didn't want to admit it. I felt as if I had been tricked into my problems and I blamed A. Lawless for that.

"First I want *you* to answer some questions," I said.

Lawless smiled and held his palms up—as in prayer.

"Who was that guy in the green suit talking about in your office yesterday?" I asked.

"A diamond dealer named Benny Lamarr. He was from South Africa originally but he relocated to New York about five years ago."

"Why did you want to know about him?"

Lawless smiled. Then he nodded.

"I have a friend in the so-called intelligence center here in New York. She informs me when the government takes an interest in the arrests, detainments, deaths, or in the liberation of citizens, aliens, and government officials."

"This is someone in your employ?" I asked.

"In a manner of speaking. I maintain Nelly, but she only gives me information that is, or should be, public record. You know, Felix, the government and big business hide behind a mountain of data. They hide, in plain sight, the truth from us. I tease out that truth so that at least one man knows what's going on."

"What did this Nelly tell you?" I asked.

"The diamond dealer died in an automobile accident. There was no question of foul play on the local level but still the death was covered up. His files were sealed and sent to Arizona."

"Arizona?"

"There's a government facility outside of Phoenix where certain delicate information is handled."

"Did you know this Lamarr?" I asked.

"No."

"Then why are you so concerned with him?"

"When I looked into Lamarr's past I found that he had recently been seen in the company of a man named Tellman Drake. Drake had also moved to New York and changed his name to Kenneth Cornell. When I looked into both men together I found the other names on our list."

"So what?"

Archibald Lawless smiled.

"What are you grinning about?" I asked him.

"You're good at asking questions," he said. "That's a fine trait and something to know about you."

"You're only going to know me long enough to get me out of this trouble you started."

Lawless held up his palms again. "Lamarr was in diamonds. Valerie Lox leases expensive real estate around the world. Tellman Drake—"

"Kenneth Cornell," I said to make sure that I was following the story.

"Yes," the anarchist said. "Kenny Cornell is a world class demolitions expert. Henry Lansman was an assassin when he lived in Lebanon, and Lana Drexel . . . Well, Lana Drexel learned when she was quite young that men, and women too, would give up their most guarded secrets in the light of love."

"And the government was looking into all of these people?"

"I'm looking into them."

"Why?"

"Because Lamarr's murder was covered up."

"You said it was an accident."

"The facts were smothered, sent to Arizona," Lawless said. "That's enough for me."

"Enough for you to what?"

"Walk the line."

The words chilled me in spite of my conviction to treat Lawless as an equal.

"Are you working for someone?" I managed to ask.

"For everyone. For the greater good," Lawless said. "But now I've answered your questions. You tell me what happened when you saw Henry Lansman die."

"One more question." I said.

"Okay."

"Who is Captain Delgado to you?"

"An ambitious man. Not a man to trust but someone to be used. He wants to advance in the department and he knows that I have a reach far beyond his own. We get together every month or so. I point him where I might need some assistance and, in return, he answers when I call."

"It all sounds very shady."

"I need you, Felix," Archibald Lawless said then. "I need someone who can ask questions and think on his feet. Stick with me a day or two. I'll pay you and I'll make sure that all the problems that have come up for you will be gone."

"What is it that you're asking me to do?" I asked.

I thought I was responding to his offer of exoneration. But now, when I look back, I wonder if maybe it wasn't his unashamed admission of need that swayed me.

"Tell me about the death of Henry Lansman," he said for the third time.

I gave him every detail I remembered down to the waitress and the half-eaten meal.

"We need to talk to at least one of these players," Lawless said. "I want to know what's going on."

"Which one?"

"Lana Drexel I should think," he said. "Yes definitely Lana . . ."

He stood up from the table and strode back toward the living room. I followed. From under the fur divan he pulled a slender briefcase. When he opened it, I could see that it contained twenty amber colored bottles in cozy velvet insets.

"These are the medicines that Dr. Meta has prescribed for me. Here . . ." From the upper flap of the briefcase he pulled three sheets of paper that were stapled together. "These are the instructions about what chemical I need in various manifest states. This last bottle is an aerosol spray. You might need it to subdue me in case my mind goes past reason."

"You want me to tote this around behind you?"

"No," he said. "I just want you to see it. I have a variety of these bags. If I start slipping all I need is for you to help me out a little."

Hearing his plea I felt a twinge of emotion and then the suspicion that Archibald Lawless was messing with my mind.

11

"Lana Drexel," the anarchist was saying to me a while later. We were having a glass of fresh lemonade that he'd prepared in the kitchen. "She's the most dangerous of the whole bunch."

"What do you mean?"

"Valerie Lox or Kenny Cornell are like nine-year-old hall guards compared to her."

"She's the smallest," I said, "and the youngest."

"She swallows down whole men three times her age and weight," Lawless added. "But she's fair to look at and you're only young once no matter how long you live."

"Are you going to your meeting?" I asked him.

"What meeting?"

"The one with the woman you talked to through the door."

"Oh no," he said, shaking his head. "No. Never. Not me."

I was thinking about our conversation when I entered the Rudin apartment building on East 72nd.

Lawless had given me one of his authentic Afghan sweaters to make up for the sweater I vomited on. I looked a little better than I had before but not good enough to saunter past the doorman at Lana Drexel's building.

"Yes?" the sentry asked. He wore a dark blue coat festooned with dull brass buttons, a pair of pale blue pants with dark stripes down the side, and light blue gloves.

"Drexel," I said.

The doorman—who was also a white man and a middle-aged man—sneered.

"And your name is?" he asked as if he expected me to say, *Mud.*

"Lansman," I replied smugly. "Henry Lansman."

The doorman reached into his glass alcove-office and pulled out a phone receiver. He pressed a few digits on the stem, waited and then said, "A Mr. Lansman."

It was a pleasure to see his visage turn even

more sour, I think, when he looked to me that he was still half inclined to turn me away.

"Back elevator," he said. "Twenty-fifth floor."

"What's the apartment number?" I asked.

"It's the only door," he said getting at least some pleasure out of my naiveté.

The elevator was small but well-appointed, lined with rosewood, floored in plush maroon carpeting, and lit by a tasteful crystal chandelier. The doors slid open revealing a small red room, opposite a pink door. This door was held ajar by a small olive-skinned woman who had eyes twice the size they should have been. Her hair was thick, bronze and golden of color. Her cheekbones were high and her chin just a shade lower than where you might have expected it to be. She was beautiful the way the ocean is beautiful. Not a human charm that you could put your arms around but all the exquisiteness of a wild orchid or a distant explosion. It was a cold beauty that you knew was burning underneath. But there was no warmth or comfort in the pull of Lana Drexel's magnetism. There was only a jungle and, somewhere in the thickness of that hair, a tiger's claws.

She looked me up and down with and said, "You're not Lansman."

"Sorry," I said. "But he's dead."

I had practiced that line for two hours. Lawless had given me the job of getting in to see the fashion model and of convincing her to come to his office and share what she knew about the other names on his list. It was my idea to pretend that I was the dead man. I also decided that shock might loosen her tongue.

But if she was in any way alarmed I couldn't see it.

"He is?" she said.

"Yeah. The people around thought that it was a heart attack but then the police arrested me and said something about murder."

"So he was murdered?" she asked.

"I thought I'd come here and ask you."

"Why?"

"Because the police for some reason suspect me of being involved with you guys and your business. You see, I'm just a journalism student and I'd like them to leave me alone."

"Excuse me," she said, still holding the door against my entrée, still unperturbed by the seriousness of our talk, "but what is your real name?"

It was her turn to frighten me. I thought that if she was to know my name then she could send someone after me. I lamented, not for the last time, agreeing to work for the anarchist.

"I'm a representative of Archibald Lawless," I said, "anarchist at large."

Lana Drexel's confident expression dissolved then. She fell back allowing the door to come open. She wandered into the large room behind her.

I followed.

I began to think that you could understand the strange nature of denizens that peopled Archibald Lawless's world by their sense of architecture and design. The room I entered was as beautiful and intense as young Lana Drexel. The ceilings were no less than eighteen feet high and the room was at least that in width—and more in length. The outer wall was one large pane of glass. There was no furniture in the room except for the wide, cushioned bench that ran from the front door to the picture window. Nine feet up on either side were large platforms that made for rooms without walls. Underneath the platform on the right everything was painted dark gray. The room formed underneath the platform on the left was white.

Miss Drexel threw herself down in the middle of the banquette. She was wearing a maroon kimono that barely came down to the tops of her thighs. This garment exposed shapely legs and powerful hamstrings. Her toenails were painted bright orange.

I sat down a few feet from her, near the window that looked south upon midtown.

"What does he want?" Lana said covering her eyes with an upturned hand.

"I don't really know," I said. "But he seems to think that you and Lansman and a few others are in trouble."

"Who?" She sat up and leaned toward me. The intensity of her stare was captivating and cold.

"Valerie Lox, Henry Lansman, Kenneth Cornell, Benny Lamarr, and you," I said. "Lamarr is also dead."

"How did he die?"

"A car accident I think. He was with a woman."

"What was her name?"

"I don't know."

The beauty lowered her face to her hands, causing her hair to fall forward. I could see her breasts under the mane of hair but somehow that didn't matter much.

"What does he want from me?" she asked.

"He wants to see you," I said.

She looked up at me again. "Will you protect me from him?"

"Yes," I said without hesitation. My heart went out to her and I think I might have even challenged A. Lawless for her smile.

12

We reached the Tessla building at about two in the afternoon. There were various business types coming in and out. The guard sitting in front of the Joan of Arc mural was an elderly white man with a big mustache and a head full of salt and pepper hair.

"Hello, Mr. Orlean," he hailed. "Mr. Lawless is expecting you and the lady."

"He is?"

"Yes sir."

The guard's eyes strayed over to Lana. She wore a Japanese ensemble of work pants and jacket made from rough cotton. The color was a drab green but still it accented her beauty.

"What's your name?" I asked the guard.

"Andy."

"I thought Lawless was in trouble with the building, Andy."

"No sir, Mr. Orlean. Why would you say that?"

"It was something about the rent."

"Oh," he said. Andy's smile was larger even than his mustache. "You mean the owners don't like him. Well, that might be true but you know the *men* in this building, the union men, they love Mr. Lawless. He's a legend in unions all over the city and the world. The reason they can't trick him outta here is that no real union man would ever turn a key on him."

In the elevator Lana stood close to me. When the doors slid open she squeezed my left forearm. I touched her hand. She kissed me lightly on the lips and smiled.

In the six seconds between the door opening and our departure she raised my blood pressure to a lethal level.

Archibald was waiting for us. He opened the door before I could knock and ushered us into chairs in the outer room.

I was later to learn that Lawless never had anyone but his closest confidants in his office.

"Miss Drexel," he said, smiling broadly.

Timidly, and leaning toward me on the hardback sofa, she said, "I hope that you'll be kind."

"I'll do you one better, lady," he said. "I'll be honest and I'll be fair."

She shivered.

I put a hand on her shoulder.

Archibald Lawless laughed.

"Let's get something straight from the start, Lana," he said. "Felix is working for me. He won't jump, lady, so straighten up and talk to me."

Lana did sit up. The woman who met me at the pink door returned. She was self-possessed and distant, a European princess being held for ransom in a Bedouin camp.

"What do you want?" she asked.

"Why did you come?" he replied.

"Because your employee told me that Hank Lansman and Benny Lamarr had been murdered."

Lawless smiled. I think he liked Lana.

"Why would that bother you?"

"Don't you know?"

He shook his head then shrugged his shoulders. "Someone in the government has gone to great lengths to hide the accidental deaths of your two friends. You got precious gems, hide away real estate, explosives, security, and a siren all mixed up together and then the hammer drops . . ."

Lana's eyes cut toward me for a moment then she turned them on the madman.

"What are you in this for?" she asked.

Walking the line, I said in my mind.

"I've been hired by the insurance company to locate some property that has been—temporarily misplaced," he said.

I was lost. Every step along the way he had presented himself as a dedicated anarchist, a man of the people. Now all of a sudden he was working for the Man.

Lana sat back. She seemed to relax.

"How much will they pay?" she asked.

"Five percent with a conviction," he said. "Eight if I can keep things quiet."

"Four million is a lot of revolution," she said. "But the full fifty could topple a nation."

"Are you worried about surviving or retiring?" Archibald asked the beauty.

It was her turn to smile enigmatically.

"Because you know," Lawless continued, "whoever it was killed Lansman and Lamarr will certainly come to your door one day soon."

"I'll die one day anyway," she admitted with a half pouting lower lip. "But to stay alive you have to keep on moving."

How old was she? I wondered. Four years and a century older than I.

"I ask you again," Lawless said. "Why did you come here?"

"No one says no to Mr. Archibald Lawless," she opined. "Just ask Andy downstairs."

"What do you want?" Lawless asked Lana.

"Hardly anything. Two hundred and fifty thousand will pay for my ticket out of town. And, of course, I expect exemption from arrest."

"Of course."

Lana stretched, looked at his murky eyes, and then nodded.

"Who were you working for?" he asked after an appreciative pause.

"Lamarr."

"To do what?"

"To go with him to a party in the Hamptons," she said sounding bored. "To meet a man named Strangman. To make friends with his bedroom."

"And did you?"

Her stare was her response.

"And then what?" Archibald asked.

"I met with Lansman, told him where the hidey hole was and collected my fee."

"That's all?"

"I met with the other people on your list," she admitted.

"When?"

"The morning after I spent with Strangman," she said. "He was really a jerk."

"Where did you meet?" Lawless asked.

"A vacant house that Val was selling. They wanted to go over the layout with me."

"And this Strangman," Lawless asked. "He was in the same business that Lamarr was in, I suppose?"

"I suppose," she replied.

"And was the operation a success?"

"I was paid."

"By who?" Lawless asked.

I wanted to correct his grammar but held my tongue.

"Lamarr." Lana hesitated. Her vast eyes were seeing something that had been forgotten.

"There was a guy with Lamarr," she said. "Normal looking. White. Forties."

"Was his hair short?" I asked.

"I think so."

"With a little gray?"

She turned to me, bit her lower lip, and then shook her head.

"I don't remember," she said. "He didn't make much of an impression. I thought that maybe he worked for Lamarr. Actually I'm pretty sure of it."

"So we have Stangman and a fortyish white man that might have worked for Lamarr," Lawless said.

"And Valerie Lox and Kenneth Cornell," I added.

The existentialist detective shook his head.

"No," he said. "Cornell made a mistake with a blasting cap yesterday afternoon and took off the top of his skull. Valerie Lox has disappeared. Maybe she's just smart but I wouldn't put a dollar on seeing her breathing again."

"What about me?" Lana Drexel asked.

"You're still breathing," he said.

"What should I do?"

"Nothing you've ever done before. Don't go home. Don't use your credit cards. Don't call anyone who has been on your phone bill in the last three years."

The young woman had a slight smile on

her face as she listened to the anarchist's commandments.

"Do you have a suggestion of where I should go?" she asked.

"Sure. I'm full of advice. You just wait out here for a few minutes while I give my operative here his walking orders. Come on, Felix," he said to me. "Let's go in my office for a minute or two."

13

"She needs to be put somewhere very safe," Lawless told me, his profile set against the New Jersey landscape.

"Where?"

"There's a small chapel in Queens," he said. "Run by a defrocked priest I know."

"A friend of Red Tuesday's?"

He turned toward me and smiled. "That's why we're going to get along, kid," he said. "Because you know how to be funny."

"Do you want me to take her there?" I asked.

"No. If I let her spend more than an hour with you the next thing I know there you'd be face down with a knife in your back in some back alley in Cartagena."

His swampy eyes were laughing but I knew he believed what he said. *I* believed it. Inwardly I was relieved that I didn't have to accompany Lana Drexel to Queens.

"No," Lawless continued, "Lana can take care of herself and besides—I might have a little job for her."

"What kind of job?"

"The kind I wouldn't give you," he said.

"What should I do?"

"Follow the same plan I laid out for Miss Drexel. Don't do anything that you've done before."

"How can I not do anything I've done?" I asked. "I only have seven dollars on me. I don't know anything but my routine."

The anarchist smiled.

"Your first baby step outside the lies they have you living, young man."

"That doesn't help me."

"There's a hotel on East Thirty-fifth," he said. "Over by Park. It's called the Barony. Go there when you get tired. Tell Frederick that I told you to stay there tonight. Other than that you can do anything. Anything that you've never done before."

"Can I get an advance to eat with?"

"Frederick will feed you."

"What if want to go to a movie?"

Lawless shook his head. I could see his thoughts: *Here the child could do anything and all he can come up with is a movie.*

"Or maybe opera tickets," I added.

"I never carry more than ten dollars in cash myself," he said.

"But I don't have a credit card."

"Neither do I." He held his pious palms upward.

"How do you make it with only ten bucks in your pocket?"

"It's a challenge," he said. "And challenge is what makes life sing."

I must have looked miserable because he gave me his quick laugh and said, "In your office. The bottom half of the pink file. Eighteen, eighteen, nine."

With that he rose and went to the door.

"When do I see you again?" I asked.

"I'll call you," he said. "Be prepared."

With that he left the office. I heard him say a few words to Lana Drexel. She laughed and said something. And then they were gone.

I felt uncomfortable staying in his private office. It seemed so personal in there. There were private letters on his closed laptop and all those curiosities along the walls. I went to the storage room, what he called my office, and sat at the long table in a chair that seemed to be made from stoneware pottery clay. It was glazed a shiny dark red and slender in every aspect. I wouldn't have been surprised if it broke under the weight of a man Lawless's size.

I perused a couple of Red Tuesday's newsletters. The paranoia struck a note with me though and so I put them down.

I wondered about what Lawless had said; that we lived in a skein of lies. So many things he said seemed to be anchored in some greater truth. In many ways he was like my father, certain and powerful—with all of the answers, it seemed.

But Lawless was wild. He took chances and had received some hard knocks. He lived with severe mental illness and shrugged off threats that would turn brave men into jellyfish.

Don't do anything you've done before, he told me. I experienced the memory of his words like a gift.

I picked up the phone and entered a number from a slip of paper in my pocket.

"Hello?" she answered. "Who is this?"

There was a lot of noise in the background, people talking and the clatter of activity.

"Felix."

"Who?"

"The guy you gave your number yesterday at lunch . . . I had the soba noodles."

"Oh. Hi."

"I was wondering if you wanted to get together tonight. After work I mean."

"Oh. I don't know. I was going to go with some of the guys here to . . . But I don't have to. What did you want to do?"

"I'm pretty open," I said. "Anything you been really wanting to do?"

"Well," she hesitated.

"What?"

"There's a chamber music concert up at the Cloisters tonight. It's supposed to be wonderful up there."

"That sounds great," I said, really meaning it.

"But the tickets are seventy-five dollars . . . each."

"Hold on," I said.

I stretched the phone cord over to the tiny pink file cabinet. The drawers were facing the wall so I turned it around—it was much heavier than I expected.

I could see that the bottom drawer was actually a safe with a combination lock.

"Are you still there?" Sharee said.

"Oh yeah. Listen, Sharee . . ."

"What?"

"Can I call you right back?"

"Okay."

It took me a moment to recall the numbers eighteen, eighteen, nine. The combination worked the first time.

There was more cash in that small compartment than I had ever seen. Stacks of hundred-dollar bills and fifties and twenties. English pounds and piles of euros. There were pesos and other bills in white envelopes that were from other, more exotic parts of the world.

"Wow."

I took two hundred and fifty dollars leaving an IOU in its place. Then I hit the redial button.

"Felix?" she answered.

"What time do you get off work?"

Sharee was a music student at Juilliard. She studied oboe and flute. There was an oboe in the quartet and a violin that made my heart thrill. After the concert we walked along the dark roads of the Cloisters' park. I kissed her against a moss covered stone wall and she ran her hands up under my sweater scratching her long fingernails across my shoulder blades.

We took a taxi down to the Barony. At first the desk clerk didn't want to get Frederick but when I mentioned Mr. Lawless he jumped to the task.

Frederick was a tall man, white from his hair to his shoes. He guided us to a small elevator and brought us to a room that was small and lovely. It was red and purple and mostly bed.

I must have kissed Sharee's neck for over an hour before trying to remove her muslin blouse. She pulled the waistband of her skirt up over her belly and said, "Don't look at me. I'm fat."

That's when I started kissing around her belly button. It was an inny and very deep. Every time I pressed my tongue down there she gasped and dug her nails into my shoulders.

"What are you doing to me?" she said.

"Didn't anybody ever kiss you here before?" I asked her. "It's just so sexy." And then I jammed my tongue down deep.

We spent the night finding new places on each other. It was almost a game and we were almost children. We didn't even go to the bathroom alone.

At five I ordered room service. Salami sandwiches and coffee.

"Who are you, Felix Orlean?" she asked me as we stared at each other over the low coffee table that held our early morning meal.

"Just a journalism student," I said. "In over my head every way that I look."

She was wearing my sweater and nothing else. I wanted to kiss her belly but she looked too comfortable to unfold out of that chair.

"I have a kinda boyfriend," she said.

"Huh?"

"Are you mad?"

"How could I be mad?" I said. "What you gave me last night was exactly what I needed. And you're so beautiful."

"But I'm not very nice," she said, experimenting with the thought of being beautiful while at the same time feeling guilty about her deceit.

"I think you are."

"But here I am smelling like you in your

sweater and he's in the East Village sleeping in his bed."

"And here you are and here I am," I said. "Everybody's got to be someplace."

She came over and began kissing my navel then.

The phone rang. It was the last thing in the world that I wanted but I knew that I had to answer.

Sharee moaned in distress.

"Just a minute, honey," I said. "It might be business. Hello?"

"Between Sixth and Seventh on the north side of Forty-seventh Street," Archibald Lawless said. "Deluxe Jewelers. Nine thirty. I'll meet you out front."

The moment I hung up the phone Sharee whispered in my ear, "Give me three days and I'm yours."

I grunted and pulled her blue-streaked hair so that her lips met mine. And for a long time I didn't think about big-eyed models or anarchy or where the day might end.

14

I was standing across the street from the jewelry store at nine fifteen, sipping coffee from a paper cup and rubbing the sand from my eyes. When I say jewelry store I should be more specific. That block is all jewelers. Almost every doorway and almost every floor. There were Arabs and India Indians and Orthodox Jews, white men and Asian men and every other race counted on that block. Big black security guards joked with small wizened dealers. I heard French and Spanish, Hebrew and Yiddish, Chinese and even a Scandinavian tongue casually spoken by passersby.

I had put Sharee in a taxi an hour before. She said that she was going to get some sleep and that I should call her later that day. I told her that I'd call that day if I could and she asked if I was in trouble.

"Why you say that?"

"My daddy was always in trouble and you remind me of him."

"I like it when you call me daddy," I said before kissing her and closing the yellow cab door.

Deluxe Jewelers was just a glass door with unobtrusive gold letters telling of its name.

There was an older brown man, with an almond shaped head accented by a receding hairline, sitting on a fold-up metal chair inside the door. There were many more impressive stores on that block. Stores with display cases lined with precious stones set in platinum and gold.

I figured that the people who worked at Deluxe were Lawless's low-rent toehold in this world of unending wealth.

"Hey, kid," Archibald Lawless said.

He was standing there next to me as if he had appeared out of thin air.

"Mr. Lawless."

"Being on time is a virtue in this world," he said. I wasn't sure if that was a compliment or an indictment. "Shall we?"

We crossed the street and went through the modest entrance.

"Mr. Lawless," the seated guard hailed. "You here for Sammy?"

"I think I need Applebaum today, Larry."

The sentry nodded and said, "Go on then."

The room he sat in was no more than a vestibule. There was a black tiled floor, his chair, and an elevator door. Lawless pressed the one button on the panel and the door opened immediately. On the panel inside there were twelve buttons, in no particular order, marked only by colors. The anarchist chose orange and the car began to descend.

When the door opened we entered into another small and nondescript room. It was larger than Larry's vestibule but with no furniture and a concrete floor.

There was a closed door before us.

This opened and a small Asian woman came out. Her face was as hard as a Brazil nut until she saw Lawless. She smiled and released a stream of some Asian dialect. Archibald answered in the same language, somewhat slower but fluent still and all.

We followed the woman down a hall of open doorways, each one leading to rooms with men and women working on some aspect of gemstones. In one room there was an elderly Jewish man looking down on a black velvet-lined board. On the dark material lay at least a dozen diamonds, every one large enough to choke a small bird.

At the end of the hall was a doorless doorway through which I could see a dowdy office and an unlikely man.

He stood up to meet us but wasn't much taller than I am. He was brown with blond hair and striking emerald green eyes. He was both hideous and beautiful, qualities that don't come together well in men.

"Archie," he said in an accent I couldn't place. "It's been so long."

They shook hands.

"Vin, this is Felix. He's working for me," Lawless said.

"So happy to meet you." The jeweler took my hand and gazed into my eyes.

I suppressed a shudder and said, "Me too."

There were chairs and so we sat. Vin Applebaum went behind his battered oak desk. We were underground and so there were no windows. The office, which wasn't small, had been painted so long ago that it was a toss-up what color it had been originally. The lighting was fluorescent and the Persian carpet was threadbare where it had been regularly traversed.

Applebaum, who was somewhat over forty, wore an iridescent silver and green suit. It was well tailored with three buttons. His shirt was black and open at the throat.

The most surprising thing to me about his dress was that he wore no jewelry. No ring or chain or even a watch. He was like a gay male pimp who specialized in women or a vegan butcher.

"Strangman," Lawless said.

"Lionel," Vin replied.

"If you say so. What about him?"

"He was the luckiest man in the world there for a while. Through an investment syndicate he made a purchase that kings salivate over. Now he's in bad trouble. As bad as it can be."

"He was robbed?"

"That word doesn't begin to explain the loss of twenty-three nearly red diamonds."

"Red?" Lawless said. "I thought the most you could get in a diamond was pink or purple."

Applebaum nodded. "Yes. You might say that these stones, not one of which is less than six karats, are a deep or dark pink. But to the eye beholding they are red."

"Fifty million dollars red?"

"If you could sell the whole collection," Applebaum said, nodding. "Yes. Think of the necklace you could make with just nine of those gems."

"My scales run to starving, dying millions," Lawless said.

"You could feed a small country with Strangman's find."

"What about Lamarr?" Archibald Lawless asked then.

I wondered if he were really working for an insurance company. I realized that even if he had a client that their needs might dovetail like the interests of a gem dealer and a mad anarchist in a basement room in Manhattan.

"Benny?" Applebaum asked. "What about him?"

"Did he know Strangman?"

"Everyone knows Lionel. He's been on the periphery of our business for many years. Do you think that Benny had anything to do with the theft?"

"The diamonds were definitely stolen then?" Lawless asked.

"Definitely."

"Who has them?"

Applebaum shook his head.

"Who insured them then?" Lawless asked.

"Auchschlous, Anterbe, and Grenell. An Australian company." Again the odd jeweler shook his head.

"What's wrong with them?"

"Strangman is old-fashioned. He likes to carry stones around in his pocket," the ugly diamond dealer said. "A lot of the old-timers are like that. Somebody says that all they would need is fifty thousand dollars and life would even out and Strangman would pull two hundred thousand in diamonds out of his vest pocket just to show them how small they really are. Stupid."

"The insurance didn't cover personal delivery?" I asked just to feel that I wouldn't blend in with the colorless walls.

"That's right," Applebaum said with a generous smile. "Somebody made a deal with Strangman. A deal so sweet and so secure that he brought the stones home and made an appointment with the buyer."

Archibald Lawless's eyes were closed. His hands were held upward. He began nodding his head as if he were listening to a subtle tune coming from a bit too far off.

"Who is the investigating agent?" he asked behind still closed eyes.

"Jules Vialet," Applebaum said without hesitation.

The anarchist opened his eyes and asked, "How did you know that so quickly?"

"Because he's AAG's best man and even though they have a clause saying that he couldn't carry the jewels without proper protection he still might be able to make a case against them."

"And what about Strangman," Lawless asked. "Is he still around?"

"Up at Obermann's Sanitarium on Sixty-eighth."

"He's fakin' it?"

"I doubt it," Vin said. "He never had much money or much power. Those stones represented a whole new life for him on these streets. All he needed was that collection in his vault and he would have had the respect of the whole community. Now, of course, all of that is gone."

There was great deal of pleasure Applebaum felt about the professional demise of Lionel Strangman. I got the feeling that life in the jewelry district wasn't friendly or safe.

15

There was a silver-gray Cadillac waiting for us when we came out. A dark man with broad shoulders, and a neck an inch too short, climbed out of the driver's seat to greet us.

"Mr. Lawless," he said in a Caribbean-English accent. "Where do you wish to go, sir?"

"This is Felix Orlean," Lawless said. "Felix, meet Derek Chambers."

The chauffeur's hands were rough and

strong. He was shorter than Lawless, only about six feet.

"Pleased to meet you, Derek," I said.

"We're going to an address somewhere in Manhattan," Lawless said. "I'll need the phone books."

Derek opened the back door and Lawless slipped in, moving all the way to the other side in order to make room for me. I got in and the door shut behind me. The chauffeur went to the rear of the car, opened the trunk and closed it. After he'd climbed into the driver's seat he handed my temporary employer the white book and Yellow Pages for New York City.

Derek drove off and Lawless began thumbing through the Yellow Pages, the business to business volume.

"Corruption on this level is always pretty easy to crack," he was saying. "Big companies, rich men, and the government are all too arrogant to waste time hiding their crimes. They have official avenues to follow and reports to make, agents with health benefits and paramours who nurse aspirations of their own.

"Derek, take us to Second Avenue between Fifty-fourth and Fifty-fifth."

"Yes sir, Mister Lawless."

"Is that your real name?" I asked. "Lawless?"

The nihilist smiled at me and patted my knee.

"You would even question a man's name?" he asked, amazed.

"I mean what are the odds?" I said. "An anarchist named Lawless? That's just too perfect."

"What if my parents were revolutionists? What if I looked up my name and decided that that's what I'd become?"

"Your parents were revolutionaries that changed their names?" I asked.

"I am Archibald Lawless," he said. "I'm sitting here before you. You are looking into my eyes and questioning what you see and what you hear. On the streets you meet Asian men named Brian, Africans named Joe Cramm. But you don't question their obviously being named for foreign devils. You accept their humiliation. You accept their loss of history. You accept them being severed from long lines of heritage by their names. Why wouldn't you accept just as simply my liberating appellation?"

"I . . ." I said.

"Here we are," Derek announced.

The building must have been considered futuristic and quirky when it was newly built. It still had a personality, if somewhat cold. Gray steel and stone relieved by thick glass windows that were accented by just a touch of green tinting. Two guards sat at a violet kidney-shaped desk with computer screens embedded in the top.

"Yes?" the smaller one asked me.

"Lawless," I said. "Archibald and associate for Mr. Vialet."

There were lights on in the entranceway but darkness hovered at the corners of the room. That gloom ascended to the roof.

The guard flipped through a screen, found a number and then dialed it on an old-fashioned rotary phone.

"A man named Lawless and somebody else for Mr. Vialet," the guard said.

He listened for a beat or two and then said to us, "Please have a seat. Someone'll be down to get you."

There was a whole tree that had been split down the middle and then cut to the length of a twelve-foot bench for us to sit on. The tree-half had been heavily lacquered and fitted with dowels to keep it from rolling around when someone sat on it.

"They rule the world," Archibald Lawless hissed.

He was sitting next to me with his hands on his knees. He still wore black slacks and an army jacket buttoned half the way up his chest. Now that his jacket was open I noticed that he wore a necklace too. It was strung with chicken bones that were white from age and being exposed to the sun. The bones had a crazy clattery way about them. There wasn't much doubt why the security guard decided to ask me about our business.

"Who?" I asked.

"People in buildings like this one. They own farms in Turkey and solar generation plants in the Gobi desert. They decide on foreign legislation and cry over the deaths of their children. Even their love is hypocritical. Even with their deaths they cannot pay for their crimes . . ."

He would have said more but a young man in a lavender suit approached us.

"Mr. Lawless?" he asked me.

"No," I said.

The kid was pale and definitely an ectomorph. But he'd been doing his exercises. There was muscle under his lapels and on his toothpick shoulders. In his eyes however he was still a ninety-pound weakling. He stared at Lawless as if the big man were a plains lion hungry for a pale-boy snack.

"You're Lawless?"

"Mr. Archibald Lawless."

"Yes," the young man said. "I'm Grant Harley, Mr. Vialet's assistant. Please follow me."

He led us through a hallway that had as a path a raised ramp that went over a hall-long pond filled with oversized, multicolored carp. Bamboo sprouted from planters along the sides of the walls. We entered into a large room inhabited by five secretaries, each at her own pastel colored desk. There were windows in this room and classical flute playing instead of Muzak.

One of the secretaries, a forty-year-old black woman with a broad chest and small eyes, got up and approached us.

"You Lawless?" she asked me.

"I'm Mr. Lawless," Archibald said.

The woman didn't seem to like his sense of self-worth but I think she was more intimidated by his size and growl.

"This way," she said.

We went through a smallish doorway into a long dark hall. At the end of this hall was a white door. The secretary opened the door and brought us into a large room with a sunken office at its center. We had to walk down five stairs to get on an even plane with the desk behind which sat a man who was almost indescribable he was so plain.

He stood to his five foot nine height and looked at us with bland brown eyes. His hair was brown and his skin was off-white. His hands were as normal as you could be. The suit he wore was medium gray and the shirt might have had a few blue threads in the depths of all that white.

"Archibald," he said to the right man.

"Do I know you?" my would-be employer asked.

"No. But I sure know a lot about you. There was an emerald necklace that we lost in Sri Lanka six years ago that no one ever thought we'd recover. One day you just walked in and dropped it off. Gave the fee to some charity as I remember."

"Can we sit down, Mr. Vialet?"

"Certainly. Forgive me. What is your friend's name?"

"Felix," I said. "Orlean."

"Have a seat, Felix, Archibald. Right here on the sofa."

It was a fuzzy white sofa that sat across from his desk. There was a dark stained walnut coffee table before us. Vialet sat in a plain walnut chair.

"Anything to drink?" he offered.

"Lets talk about red diamonds," Lawless replied.

"I like a man who gets down to business," Jules Vialet said. "Business is what makes the world turn."

". . . like a stone over the bones of the innocent," Lawless added. "Who do you suspect in the theft?"

"I'm really not at liberty to discuss the disposition of any active case that we are pursuing, Mr. Lawless. But if—"

Archibald stood up.

"Come on, Felix," he said.

Before I could rise the insurance investigator was on his feet, holding up both hands.

"Don't be like that," he said. "You know there are rules that I have to follow."

"I don't have time for your rules, Mr. Insurance Man. People have been dying out there and your government is covering it up. There's something rotten in this business and I'm the one's going to sanitize and bleach it clean."

"What do you mean about the government?" Vialet asked.

"You answer me, Mr. Insurance Man, and then I'll share."

"That's hardly fair, you know," Vialet said. "What if I give you all my information and then you turn around and leave or tell me that you really don't know anything?"

"I'm not the liar here," Lawless said. "You are. This whole building is a lie. Your pale-faced boy and your snotty secretaries are lies. Maybe if you ate raw flesh at your desk and kept a pot of shit at each doorway then maybe you'd be halfway to the truth about something. No. I'm not a liar, Mr. Insurance Man. I'm the only true thing you've seen all year."

His voice sounded a little high, strained. I worried that maybe one of his psychological maladies was manifesting itself.

"Mr. Lawless," I said.

When he turned toward me I could see the madness in his eyes.

"What?"

"We don't have the briefcase with us so I won't be able to make complete notes."

For a moment he was bewildered but then his mind grabbed hold. He laughed and said, "It's okay, Felix. We'll just wing it until we have the case." He looked back at Vialet and said, "Tell me, who do you suspect in the theft?"

Vialet looked at us and sighed. He sat down and so did Lawless.

"A man named Lamarr," the insurance man said.

"Benny," Lawless agreed. "Him and Lana Drexel. And Valerie Lox, Kenneth Cornell, and Henry Lansman. We know the soldiers. What we want is the bankroll."

I could see that Vialet was concentrating on the names Lawless threw out.

"You seem to know more than I do," he said.

"Who is the man who has been traveling with Lamarr lately?" Archibald asked. "A white man in his forties. He has short hair, maybe graying, maybe not."

"Wayne Sacorliss," Vialet said without hesitation. "He's been around Lamarr for a few years. Just a toady as far as we can tell. He has an office on Lexington, just south of Forty-first."

"Who's the buyer?" Lawless asked.

"We think it's a Canadian named Rudolph Bickell. He's a very rich man and a collector of rare gems. He lives in Las Vegas half the year."

"How does he make his money?"

"Buying and selling," Vialet said. "Your

grain to bakeries, cotton to sweatshops in Asia, metal to gun makers and guns to the highest bidder."

"Weapons?"

"Anything," Vialet said. "He'd been making noise to Strangman about buying the gemstones until about three months ago. We figure that when he came up with the plan he stopped calling."

"How much?" Lawless asked.

"We'll go as high as three million. That's all the stones in perfect condition. No trouble to cover either."

"Will corroboration by the police about my central role in reclaiming the jewels be enough?" Lawless asked in flawless business contract style.

"Certainly," Vialet allowed.

"Come on, Felix," Archibald said.

We were out of the gray insurance building in less than five minutes.

16

"I thought that you were an anarchist," I was saying, "a political purist, a man of the people."

Lawless was sitting next to me in the back seat of Derek Chambers's limo, scanning the white pages.

"That sounds right to me," he said. "But mostly, Felix, like I told you before, I walk that line."

"So the three million means nothing to you?"

"That money will pay for a lot of walking, son. Slaves walking across borders, bound men dancing again—that's what it'll pay for, and more."

He gave Derek an address on Lexington.

Sacorliss ran an optical glass frame distribution business on the fourteenth floor. Many of the offices around him were empty. The reception room had been uninhabited for some while. There was dust on the blotter and no evidence that the phone was even plugged in. I wondered if Wayne Sacorliss had moved on to LensCrafters or some other larger optical business.

"Hello," I called.

There was a doorway beyond the reception desk leading to a passageway formed from opaque glass panels. This hallway was in the form of an L that one would suspect led to the main office.

"Who's there?" a mild mannered male voice inquired.

"Archibald Lawless," I said, "and his assistant." I couldn't get my tongue around the word scribe.

A man appeared in the glass angle. From the front he could have been the man I saw running from the death of Henry Lansman. Only this man wore a light brown suit instead of a red parka.

"Who?" he asked.

"We've come to ask you about Benny Lamarr," Lawless said.

Sacorliss had light blue eyes and a broad face. His eyes were elliptical in both shape and manner. His lips were so sensual they belonged on a younger man, or a slightly perverse demigod. His features were all that he showed. There wasn't even a glimmer of recognition for the man he assisted.

He didn't respond at all.

"Can we go into your office, Mr. Sacorliss?" I asked.

"Are you here to buy frames?"

"No."

"Then I don't see what we have to talk about."

"Henry Lansman for one thing," I said.

From the corner of my eye I saw Lawless swivel his head to regard me.

"I don't know who that is," Sacorliss was saying, "but if you must come in then follow me."

At the end of the L-shaped glass hall was a round room lined on one side by waist-high, old fashioned windows that were furbished with brown tinted glass. I could see people in offices not twenty feet away. Some were working and others talking. It was a pleasant proletariat view of the inner workings of a big city's commerce.

This room was also quite desolate. One maple desk with a square-cut oak chair, a telephone with a bare cord that ran across the room to find the jack in the opposite wall. There was a laptop computer on the floor and not one scrap of paper anywhere.

Sacorliss was a few inches taller than I and maybe twenty pounds more than he should have been. But he moved with grace and self-confidence. Once we were in the room he closed the door.

Lawless's eyes never left the smaller man. His wariness made me nervous but I didn't know what to do. So I perched myself on the edge of the maple desk while Wayne Sacorliss and Archibald faced each other.

"What is it you want from me?" Sacorliss asked the amber king before him.

"There's no need for trouble here, Wayne. I'm just interested in why the government wants to cover up Lansman's death, his and a few others whom you might or might not know."

Lawless's mouth turned up in a smile but his eyes were dull.

The baby finger of his left hand twitched.

Sacorliss moved a few inches to his right so that his back was turned fully toward me. Seeing his head from this position I was sure that he was the same man I saw fleeing the scene of Henry Lansman's death. I wanted to signal Lawless that we had what we needed but all of his attention was on the killer.

"I furnish frames for optical lenses, Mr., um, Lawless, wasn't it?"

"There's no need for conflict between us, Wayne," Lawless said in a uncharacteristically placating tone. "Felix here and I just want to know about who would want to hide the murders of international criminals. Especially when those murders were so well executed that no doctor would suspect foul play."

What happened next took me a few days to work out. Sacorliss lifted his right shoulder in a way that made me think he was about to deny any knowledge of Lawless's insinuations. Then Archibald took half a step backwards. Sacorliss moved the same distance forward by taking a step with his left foot. Then the assassin shouted and I felt a powerful impact against my chest. I flew backward over the desk, hit the floor and slid into the wall.

While I was still en route to the wall Sacorliss produced a very slender ten-inch blade from somewhere in his suit. He lunged at his anarchist inquisitor and stabbed him in the chest.

Lawless wasn't slow, however. He grabbed Sacorliss's arm at the elbow so that the tip of the blade went less than half an inch into his body.

I struggled to my feet coughing hard. The vision I saw was surreal: Before me the two men were struggling like the titans in Goya's black painting. Sacorliss's knife was still piercing Lawless's chest but the larger man was managing to impede the progress of the blade. Through the window two women were talking, a whole office full of workers were walking back and forth, there was even a man looking up from his keyboard staring dreamily toward the battle.

Sacorliss kicked Lawless in the thigh with a quick movement. He did this twice more and I knew that sooner or later the man I came in with would be dead. I tried the door but it was locked. I was still coughing and stunned from the roundhouse kick the killer had hit me with. I looked for something to hit him with. I tried to lift his oak chair but it was too heavy to get up over my head.

I was about to go for the laptop when Sacorliss tried another kick. Lawless moved his thigh and the assassin lost his balance. Lawless then lifted him up over his head. That's when the most amazing thing happened. Somehow Archibald managed to disarm Sacorliss so that when he slammed him down on the floor he also stabbed him through the chest.

Sacorliss kicked Lawless away and jumped to his feet. He looked at me and then at the computer. He took a step toward the laptop but his foot betrayed him and he went down on one knee. He looked at his killer then.

"Who are you?" I heard him ask. And then he fell face forward and I think he was dead.

Blood seeped toward the laptop.

Lawless turned Sacorliss over with a toe.

"Get the computer," he said to me.

While I did that, he wiped the haft of the knife clean of fingerprints.

People were still gabbing and working in the office building across the way.

On the way out, Lawless made sure that the doorknob was clean of prints. By the time we were back in Derek's limo, I was so cold that my teeth were chattering. Soon after that I lost consciousness.

17

When I woke up it was dark. I was still dressed and on my back on a bed that was fully made. There was a scented candle burning and mild recorder music wafting in from somewhere. I felt odd, both peaceful and numb. My hands were lying at my sides and I felt no need to move them. I remembered the death of Wayne Sacorliss and the bizarre witnesses from the windows across the way. I thought about the blood across the barren wood floor but none of that bothered me. I supposed that Lawless had given me some kind of sedative from his medical case; something to relax my nerves. I was grateful for whatever he'd done because I knew that unaided I would have been in the depths of anxious despair.

A feathery touch skimmed my brow. I turned to see a woman, somewhere near fifty but still very attractive, sitting at my side.

"You had quite a scare," she said.

"Where am I?"

"Have you ever been to Queens?" she asked with a smile.

"Kennedy Airport."

She was slight and pale with crystalline blue eyes and long fingers. She wore a cream colored dress. The bodice was raw silk and the rest was made from the more refined version of that material. It seemed as if her hair were platinum blond instead of white.

"Who are you?" I asked.

"A friend of Archibald," she said. "He's downstairs now. Would you like to see him?"

"I don't know if I can get up."

"Once you start moving it wears off," she said.

She took my hand and stood up, pulling me. She had no strength but I followed her lead. I worried that when I got to my feet I'd be dizzy but I wasn't. As a matter of fact I felt very good.

Outside the bedroom was a short hallway that shared space with a staircase leading down. Everything was covered in thick green carpeting and so our footsteps were silent.

On the first floor was a sitting room with two sofas and three stuffed chairs. Archibald Lawless, wearing a gold colored two-piece suit and an ochre shirt was sitting in one of the chairs with his feet up on a small stool.

"Felix. How are you, son?"

"You killed that man."

"I certainly did. Maybe if you hadn't told him about Lansman I could have kept him alive but—"

"You mean you blame your killing him on me?"

"As soon as you mentioned Lansman he was sure that we had identified him as the assassin. It was either us or him. I tried to tell him that I didn't care but he was a professional and he had to at least try and kill us."

I sat down on the corner of a sofa nearest to him.

"How can you be so cavalier about a murder?" I asked.

"I did not murder him," he replied. "I

saved our lives. That man was a stone cold killer. If I hadn't been keeping up with my tai chi he would have gutted me and then cut your throat."

I remembered the impact of his kick against my chest and the speed with which he attacked the seemingly unassailable Lawless.

"What about all those witnesses?"

"There were no witnesses."

"The people in the windows across the way. We were in plain sight of them."

"Oh no," Lawless said, shaking his spiky head. "Those windows were one-way panes. I've used the same brand myself."

"So no one saw?"

"No. And even if they did. He was trying to kill us. That was self-defense, Felix."

"Would either of you boys like to have some tea?" our hostess asked.

"I'd like some English Breakfast if you have it, ma'am," I said.

She smiled at me and said, "I like this one, Arch. You should hold on to him."

"He doesn't want to work for me, Red. Thinks that it's too dangerous."

She smiled again. "Green tea for you?"

Lawless nodded and she made her way out of the room.

"What did you call her?" I asked.

"Red."

"Red Tuesday?"

"Has she asked you if you were Catholic yet?"

For some reason I hadn't thought that Red Tuesday was a real person. At least not a beautiful middle-aged woman living in a standard working class home.

"If she does," Lawless continued, "Tell her that your parents are but that you have lapsed in your faith."

"Okay."

"Now," he said. "Let's talk about what we have to do tonight."

"Tonight? I'm not doing anything with you tonight or any other time. You killed that man."

"Did I have a choice?"

"*I* have a choice," I said. "The choice not to be in the same room with you."

"Yes," he said, nodding at me. "But this is a deep problem, Felix. You can see that even I'm in danger here. Sacorliss was an assassin. We certainly ran the danger of a violent confrontation with such a man. But now we're going to a sanitarium, to see a sick man. There's no danger involved."

"Why the hell do you need me in the first place?" I said. "You never even knew me before three days ago. How can I possibly help someone like you?"

"My kind of work is lonely, Felix. And maybe it's a little bit crazy. I've spent a whole lifetime trying to fix broken systems, making sure that justice is served. Lately I've been lagging a little. Slowing down, breaking down, making mistakes that could be fatal. Having you by me has given me a little bit of an edge, some confidence that I hadn't even known was eroded.

"All I ask is that you stick with me until we find the answer to why Sacorliss was activated. Just stick with me until the police believe they have the killer of Henry Lansman."

"I thought he had a heart attack?"

"No. He was accosted by an aerosol toxin. The autopsy showed that last night. And there's a warrant out for your arrest in connection with that killing."

"Me?"

"English Breakfast," Red Tuesday said as she came into the room. "And green tea for man who watches his health and the health of the enslaved world."

She carried the delicate teacups on a silver tray, proffering us our drinks.

"Felix?" she said.

"Yes, Ms. Tuesday?"

"Are you a Catholic by any chance?"

"My parents are, ma'am, but I never went after I was twelve."

Oberman's Sanitarium had only a small brass sign on the wall to identify itself. Otherwise you would have thought it was a residential prewar building like all its neighbors on the block.

It was twelve-fifteen by the time Derek dropped us off.

Lawless rang the bell and stood there in his gold suit, carrying his medical briefcase. He looked like a rattlesnake in a Sunday bonnet, a stick of dynamite with chocolate coating up to the fuse.

I was sickened by the events of the day but still I knew I had to stay with the anarchist because that was the only way for me to keep on top of what was happening. If I left then, even if I ran and went back to New Orleans, I would be vulnerable to dangerous people who could get at me without me ever knowing they were near. And there would still be a warrant out for my arrest.

The door was opened by a woman wearing all white. She was young, tall, and manlike in her demeanor and visage.

"Lawless?" she asked me.

"It's him," I said.

"Come quickly."

We hustled into the building.

She led us to an elevator made for two and took us to the sixth floor.

When we got out she said, "Do you have it?"

Lawless took out a large wallet from his front pocket and counted out five one-hundred-dollar bills. He handed these to the manly nurse.

"No funny stuff," she said as she folded the bills into her white apron.

"What room is he in?" Lawless responded.

"Seven."

18

I was surprised by the hominess of the room. Darkish yellow walls with a real wood-framed bed and knickknacks on the shelves and bureaus. On the wall with the largest expanse hung a framed picture that was at least six feet wide and almost that in height. The colors were buff and pale blue. It was a beach at first light. Almost devoid of details it seemed to me a commentary on the beginning of the world.

In a small padded chair next to the one window a thin white man sat looking out on the street. He wore a gray robe over striped blue and white pajamas. His elbows were on his knees, his small mustache was crooked.

"I, I, I thought you were here for me," he said softly.

The only clue that we were in some kind of medical facility was a metal tray-table at the foot of the bed. There was a medical form on a clipboard hanging from the side. Lawless unhooked the clipboard and began to read.

"Yes," he said to the patient. "I was told that you're suffering from a mild breakdown. I was called by Dr. Samson to administer Cronomicin."

"Wh-what's that?"

Lawless put his briefcase on the metal table and opened it. He took out a hypodermic needle that had already been filled with a pinkish fluid.

Gesturing at the needle, he said, "This will alleviate your anxiety and impose a feeling of calm that will allow you to sleep and wake up without a care in the world."

I wondered if he had given me some of the same juice.

"Why haven't they, why haven't they given it to me before?" Lionel Strangman asked.

"Cronomicin is very expensive. There was a hang-up with the insurance." Lawless's smile was almost benign.

"You don't look like a doctor." Strangman seemed to be speaking to someone behind the big amber liar.

"Catch me at office hours and I'll have on my smock just like everybody else."

"Maybe I should—" Strangman started.

"Give me your arm," Lawless commanded.

The thin white man did as he was told.

Lawless took a cotton swab and alcohol from his briefcase, cleaned a spot on Strangman's arm, and then began to search for a vein. I turned my back on them. I don't know why exactly. Maybe I thought if I didn't see the injection I couldn't bear witness in court.

I went to the picture on the wall. It wasn't a print, as I had at first thought, but an original oil painting. It was old too. From a few feet distant the beige sky and faint water looked to be seamless. But up close I could make out thousands of small brushstrokes composed of dozens of colors. I imagined some asylum patient of another century making this painting for the inmates of today.

"How are you feeling, Mr. Strangman?" Archibald Lawless was asking the man in the chair.

"Good," he said without hesitation. "Peaceful. Maybe I should lie down."

"In a minute. First I'd like to ask you a few questions."

"Okay."

"Dr. Samson told me that you had the collapse after a theft."

"Yes," he said. He looked down at his hands. "Funny, it doesn't seem so important now. They were beautiful, you know. Almost like rubies."

"They were stolen from a safe in your home?" Dr. Lawless asked.

"Yes." Strangman looked up. His eyes were beatific as if they were meant to be paired with that painting of the primordial first day. "I woke up and they were gone. They must have drugged me because the police said that they used an explosive on the safe."

He brought hands to lips as a reflex of grief but the sorrow was forgotten now with Lawless's elixir in his veins.

"Do you know Benny Lamarr?" Lawless asked.

"Why yes. How did you know that?"

"He called to ask how you were doing. Him and his friend Wayne Sacorliss."

"Wayne. To look at him you'd never think that he was from Lebanon, would you?"

"No," Lawless said carelessly. "It surprised me that he was a Moslem."

"Oh no," Strangman said in a high feminine voice. "Christian. Christian. His mother was from Armenia. But he's an American now."

"Did you work with him?"

"No. He works for Benny. Poor Benny."

"Why do you say that?" Lawless asked.

"He brought his fiancée to a party at my house. The next night she was in my bed." Even under the spell of the narcotic Strangman was a dog.

"Who are you?" I asked Archibald Lawless.

We were sitting in the window seat of a twenty-four-hour diner on the West Side Highway at 2:57 A.M.

"You're not questioning my name again, are you?"

"No. Not that. How did you get into that clinic? How did you know what drug to give Strangman? How did you know what that killer was thinking? No one man can do all these things."

"You're right."

"I thought so. Who do you work for? Really."

"You're a very intelligent young man, Felix. But intelligence alone doesn't help you rise above. You see clearly, more clearly, than most, but you don't apprehend.

"I am, everyone is, a potential sovereignty, a nation upon my own. I am responsible for every action taken in my name and for every step that I take—or that I don't take. When you get to the place that you can see yourself as a completely autonomous, self-governing entity then everything will come to you; everything that you will need."

A waiter brought us coffee then. I sat there drinking, thinking about the past few days. I had missed two seminars and a meeting with my advisor. I hadn't been home, though I doubted if my roommate would notice. I had been arrested for suspicion of my involvement in a murder, made love to by a woman I didn't really know, I had been an accessory to a killing, and party to the illegal impersonation of a doctor—in addition to the unlawful administration of contraband drugs. I was temporarily in the employ of a madman and involved in the investigation of the theft of millions of dollars in diamonds. And, even though I was aware of all those aspects of the past few days, I was still almost totally in the dark.

"What are we doing, Mr. Lawless? What are we involved in?"

He smiled at me. The swamp of his eyes grew to an endless, hopeless vista.

"Can't you put it together yet, Felix?"

"No sir."

He smiled and reached over to pat my forearm. There was something very calming about this gesture.

"To answer one of your questions," he said. "I once saved the life of the daughter of a man who is very influential at the St. Botolph Hospital."

"So?"

"Botolph funds Oberman's Sanitarium. I called this man and asked him to intervene. A price was set and there you are."

"I thought all you wanted me to do was take notes," I said, exhausted by the stretch of Lawless's reach.

"Tonight we'll go to a place I know across the river and tomorrow we'll come back to clear it all up." He reached in his pocket and came out with two dollar bills. "Oh. I seem to be a little short. Do you have any cash, son?"

"What about that big fat wallet you paid the nurse from?"

"I only had what I needed for the bribe. Don't you have some money left from that IOU you left me?"

I paid the bill and we left.

There was a motorboat waiting for us off a dilapidated pier across from the West Side Highway. Because there were no stairs we had to jump down onto the launch, which then took us upriver and deposited us at strange river inn on the Jersey side of the Hudson.

The inn had its own small dock. The boat captain, who was dark-skinned and utterly silent, let us off there. The key to the door was in a coffee can nailed to a wall. Lawless brought us in an area that was at least partially submerged in the river.

There was no one else in residence, at least no one there that I could see. The door Lawless opened led to a circular room that had four closed doors and led to an open hallway.

"Room two is yours," the anarchist told me. "Breakfast will be at the end of the hall when you wake up."

The bed was bunklike but very comfortable. Maybe the drug I'd been given before was still in effect but whatever the circumstance I was asleep as soon as I lay down.

19

The sunrise over Manhattan was magnificent. It sparkled on the water and shone brightly in my little cockleshell room. For almost the first full minute of consciousness I forgot my problems.

The respite was soon over, however. By the time I sat up anxiety was already clouding my mind. I dressed quickly. The hall outside my door led to a wide room under a low roof that was dominated by an irregularly shaped table—set for two.

"Good morning, Felix."

Archibald Lawless was eating scrambled

eggs. A small Asian woman sat on a small stool against the wall. When I entered the room she stood up and pulled out the seat next to the anarchist. She nodded for me to sit and when I did so she scuttled out of the room.

"Mr. Lawless."

"Don't look so sad, son. Today all of our problems will be solved."

"Where are we?" I asked.

"Oh," he said, half smiling, looking like the main deity of some lost Buddhist tribe that found itself marooned in Africa an eon ago. "This is a halfway house. One of many such places where certain unpopular foreign dignitaries and agents come when they have to do business in America."

"Like who?" I asked.

"Militants, dethroned dictators, communist sympathizers, even anarchists have stayed here. Presidents and kings unpopular with current American regimes have slept in the same bed that you have, waiting to meet with clandestine mediators or diplomats from the UN."

"But there's no security."

"None that you've seen," Lawless said, bearing that saintly mien. "But there's enough protection close at hand to fend off an NYPD SWAT team."

"You're joking," I said.

"All right," he replied. "Have it your way."

The small woman returned with a plate of eggs and herring, a small bowl of rice and a mug full of smoky flavored tea. After serving me she returned to her perch against the wall.

I ate for a while. Lawless looked out of the window at Manhattan.

"So at the office you look at New Jersey and here you look at New York."

He cackled and then laughed. He grabbed my neck with his powerful hand and said, "I like you, boy. You know how to make me laugh."

"Who do you plan to kill today?"

He laughed again.

"I talked to your girlfriend last night," he said.

"Who?" I wondered if he had somehow gotten in touch with Sharee.

"Lana," he said articulating her name as an opera singer might in preparation for singing it later on. "She and Mr. Lamarr practised being engaged before she seduced Strangman."

"Okay."

"He told her things."

"What things?"

"People he trusted . . . places where certain transactions were to transpire."

"And where might that be?" I asked, sucked into the rhythm of his improvisational operetta.

"Today we go to the Peninsula Hotel," he said. "There all of our problems will come to an end."

We exited the Refugee Inn (Lawless's term for it) by climbing a steep trail which led to a dirt path that became a paved lane after a quarter mile or so. There Derek was waiting for us. He drove off without asking for a destination.

On the way Lawless talked to me about my duties as his scribe. I was tired of arguing with him, and just a little frightened after seeing how easily he killed the assassin Wayne Sacorliss, and so I let him go on without contradiction.

A block away from the hotel I began to get nervous.

"What are we going to do here?" I asked.

"Have breakfast."

"We just had breakfast."

"The sacrifices we must make for the

movement," he said. "Sometimes you have to wallow with the fat cats and follow their lead. Here, put these on."

He handed me a pair of glasses that had thick black rims and a blond wig.

"What are these for?"

"You're going to be incognito."

I donned the glasses and wig because I had already learned that there was logic to every move that my would-be employer made. I also half believed that the outlandish getup would get us thrown out of the hotel.

We entered the restaurant at about ten-thirty. No one gave me a second look.

When Lawless introduced himself the maître d' guided us to a table in an isolated corner of the main dining room. Lawless put himself in a seat with his back to the rest of the room. I was seated in an alcove, hidden from view by the banquette.

He ordered salmon hash with shirred eggs and I had the Mascarpone pancakes with a side of apple smoked bacon.

After the breakfast was served I said, "I'm not going to work for you, you know."

"I know that you don't expect to take the job but the day is young."

"No. I'm not working for you under any condition. I don't even know what we're doing now. How can I take a job where I don't even know where I'll wake up in the morning?"

"You'd rather have a job where you'll know where you'll be every day for the rest of your life?" he asked.

"No. Of course not, but, I mean I don't want to be involved with criminals and dirty politics."

"You're the one who said that he always pays his taxes, Felix," he said. "That makes you a part of an elite criminal and political class. If you buy gasoline or knitted sweaters or even bananas then you belong to the greatest crime family on Earth."

I don't know why I argued with him. I had been around people like him ever since college. *Politico dingbats* is what my father calls them. People who see conspiracies in our economic system, people who believe America is actually set against the notion of liberty.

I talked about the Constitution. He talked about the millions dead in Africa, Cambodia, Vietnam, and Nagasaki. I talked about the freedom of speech. He came back with the millions of dark-skinned men and women who spend most of their lives in prison. I talked about international terrorism. He brushed that off and concentrated on the embargos imposed on Iraq, Iran, Cuba, and North Korea.

I was about to bring out the big guns: the American peoples and the part they played in World War Two. But just then a familiar man came up and sat down at our table.

"Right on time, Ray," Archibald Lawless said.

Our guest was dressed in a dark blue suit with a white shirt held together at the cuffs by sapphire studs. *Raymond,* I supposed his first name was. The only title I knew him by was Captain Delgado.

"Archie," he said. "Felix. What's up?"

The way he said my name was respectful, as if I deserved a place at the table. As much as I wanted to deny it, I liked that feeling.

"Two tables over to your right," Lawless told the police captain. "A man and a woman talking over caviar and scrambled eggs."

I leaned over and slanted my eyes to see them. Through the clear glass frames of my disguise I recognized Valerie Lox, the Madison Avenue real estate agent. The whole time we had been talking she was there meeting with a man who was unknown to me.

She was wearing a red Chanel suit and an orange scarf. I'd never seen the man she was with. He was porcine and yet handsome. His movements were self-assured to the degree where he almost seemed careless.

"You were recently made aware of a diamond theft, were you not, Captain Delgado?" Lawless asked.

"Are you telling me or digging?" the cop asked back.

"Red diamonds," Lawless replied. "Millions of dollars' worth. A syndicate represented by Lionel Strangman reported it to their insurance company."

"You have my attention."

"Is Felix still being sought in connection with the murder of Henry Lansman?"

"Until we find another candidate."

"Wait," I said. "Why would you even think of me?"

Delgado shrugged but said nothing.

"The boy has a right to know why he's being sought," Archibald said.

"The gems," the police captain said as if it

were patently obvious. "A special unit started investigating Lamarr as soon as the theft was reported. They had Lansman, Brexel, Cornell, and Ms. Lox over there under surveillance. There was a tap on her phone. When she called Cornell we picked up your name. Then when you were photographed at the scene of Lansman's murder you became a suspect."

"Why not Sacorliss?" I asked.

"He's out of bounds," Delgado said. "Works as an informant for the FBI."

"Regardless," Lawless said. "Sacorliss is your killer."

"Who does he work for?" Delgado asked.

"As you indicated," Lawless said with a sense of the dramatic in his tone, "the same people that you work for. He also killed Benny Lamarr and Kenneth Cornell. If you look into the records of those deaths you will find that they have disappeared. Gone to Arizona, I hear."

"Fuckin' meatheads," Delgado muttered.

"I agree," Lawless said. "You have another problem, however."

"What's that?"

"The man sitting with Ms. Lox is Rudolph Bickell, one of the richest men in Canada.

She is passing the diamonds to him. She may have already done so."

"You want me to arrest the richest man in Canada on your say-so?"

"It's a toss-up, my friend. Take the plunge and maybe you'll lose everything. Don't take it and pass up the chance of a lifetime."

Lawless gestured for the bill and then said to Delgado, "You can pay for our meal, officer. Because even just the arrest of Wayne Sacorliss will keep you in good standing with your superiors.

"Come on, Felix," he said then.

And he left without paying another bill.

20

Even *The Wall Street Journal* covered the arrest of the billionaire Rudolph Bickell. They also asked how the mysterious entrepreneur was able to make bail and flee the country within three hours of his arrest at the posh Peninsula Hotel in New York City. Bickell's spokesperson in Toronto told reporters that the industrialist had no knowledge that the diamonds he was purchasing were stolen; that there was no law against acquiring the gemstones from the legal representative of a diamond dealer. Valerie Lox, who *was* in jail, was working for a man named Benny Lamarr who had died in an unrelated auto accident.

The *Journal* didn't cover the murder of optical materials dealer Wayne Sacorliss. I had to read about that in the Metro Section of *The New York Times.* The police had no motive for the crime but they had not ruled out theft. It seemed that Sacorliss was known to carry large sums of cash.

No one connected Sacorliss with Lamarr.

There were no policemen waiting at my door either.

The next morning at five-fifty I was at the front desk of the Tessla building marveling bleary eyed at the saintliness of Joan of Arc.

"Mr. Orlean," a young red-headed guard said.

"How do you know my name?"

"Mr. Lawless gave us a picture of you so that we'd know to let you in even if you came in after five fifty-five."

He answered the door before I knocked. That morning he wore white overalls and a bloodred shirt. At his gesture I went into his office and sat on the tree trunk I'd used a few days before.

"What was it all about?" I asked him.

"That why you're here, Felix?"

"Yes sir."

"You want to know why," he said with a smile. "It bothers you to sit alone in your room thinking that the papers might have gotten it wrong, that the police might be covering up a crime. It's troubling that you can be exonerated from suspicion in a murder case with a few words over an expensive breakfast in midtown Manhattan. That's not the world you thought you were living in."

If I were superstitious I might have believed that he was a mind reader. As it was, I thought that he had incredible logical and intuitive faculties.

"Yes," I said, "but there's something else."

"First," he said, "let me tell you what I know."

He sat back in his chair and brought his hands together in front of his face as if in Christian prayer.

"There was, in the works of Agineau Armaments, a shipment being readied for delivery in Ecuador at the end of next month. The company slated to receive the shipment is a dummy corporation owned by a conservative plantation owner in Venezuela. It's not hard to see where the shipment is bound for and who will use the guns."

"So Bickell is funding conservative guerrillas in Venezuela?" I asked.

"Bickell wanted the diamonds. Sacorliss wanted to fund the revolution."

"Why?"

"That, my friend, is an argument that we will have over and over again. For my money Sacorliss is a well-trained operative of the United States government. His job was to plan a robbery set to fund our clandestine interests in South America. You probably believe that it isn't such a far-reaching conspiratorial act. Only time, and blood, will tell."

"What about Valerie Lox and Lana Drexel?"

"Lox was released from jail. She claimed that she knew nothing about stolen gems, that Lamarr had always been a reputable dealer. The prosecutors decided to believe her which makes me believe that she is also a government operative. I sent Drexel her money. She's moving to Hollywood. I've been trying to decipher the code of Sacorliss's computer. One day I'll succeed and prove to you that I'm right. All we have to discuss now are the final terms of your employment."

"What do you mean?" I asked. "You don't expect that I'm going to come work for you after what I've been through."

"Sure I do."

"Why?"

"Because of your aunt, of course. You'll agree to work for me for a specified amount of time and I will agree to do what your father refused to do, free your aunt from jail."

The hairs on the back of my neck rose up then. I hadn't even considered this option until the middle of the night before. My face must have exposed my surprise.

"I need you, Felix," Lawless said. "You complete a faulty circuit in my head. You give me the three years that your aunt has left on her sentence and I will make sure that she's out of the joint by Sunday next."

"I still won't be involved in any crimes," I said.

"Agreed. I won't knowingly put you in the position of breaking the law. You will write down everything of import that I say, regardless of your own opinions. I in turn will open your eyes to a whole new world. As a journalist you will learn more from me than from a thousand seminars."

There was no reason for me to argue.

"Okay," I said. "But I have two needs and one question."

"And what might those be?"

"First is salary."

"Forty-two thousand dollars a year payable from a fund set up by Auchschlous, Anterbe, and Grenell, the world's largest insurers of rare gems. They prepared the account at my behest."

"Two," I said, "is that you agree not to lie to me. If I ask you a question you answer to the best of your ability."

"Agreed," Lawless replied, "depending upon circumstances. It might be that the truth would be giving away someone else's secret and that I have no right to do."

"Okay. Fine. Then I agree. Three years terminable if you decide I can't do the job or if you break your word to me. All of course contingent upon the release of my aunt Alberta."

"You had a question," Lawless reminded me.

"Oh. Yeah. It didn't have to do with our contract."

"Ask anyway."

"Who was the woman who came to your apartment door, the one in Harlem? I think she said her name was Maddie."

"Oh. No one. She had nothing to do with our business."

"But who was she?" I asked.

"My fiancée," he said. "She's been looking for me for a couple of years now."

I'm still in school, still out of contact with my parents. My aunt Alberta was freed from jail on a technicality that a colleague of my father turned up. She's coming to live in New York.

I work for the anarchist at least four days a week. We argue almost every day I'm there. I still think he's crazy but I've learned that doesn't always mean he's wrong.

Ed McBain

The word "prolific" had been used to describe Ed McBain many times, but there's no denying that McBain—a.k.a. Evan Hunter (1926–2005)—had also amassed a body of work that stuns the senses when one sits down to reckon with it. That so much of it is excellent, that some of it is possessed of true genius, and that every single piece of it makes for enjoyable reading is a testament to the man's amazing prowess as an author. Reading his work is like watching a world-class boxer at his peak; he knows all the moves. Because of such bestsellers as *The Blackboard Jungle* and *A Matter of Conviction*, his early fame was for his mainstream novels. But over the years he became better known for the 87th Precinct series. It's impossible to choose the "best" of the 87th books—there are just too many good ones—but one might suggest a peek at *He Who Hesitates, Blood Relatives, Long Time No See*, and *The Big Bad City*. He wrote the screenplay of *The Birds* for Alfred Hitchcock and his powerful novel *Last Summer* became one of the seminal films of the seventies. Still writing every day until the very end, his last 87th Precinct novel was *Fiddlers*, along with his non-fiction memoir *Let's Talk*, and the reissued pulp novel *The Gutter and the Grave*, which, along with his enormous body of work, will be read well into the twenty-second century and beyond.

MERELY HATE

Ed McBain

A blue Star of David had been spray-painted on the windshield of the dead driver's taxi.

"This is pretty unusual," Monoghan said.

"The blue star?" Monroe asked.

"Well, that, too," Monoghan agreed.

The two homicide detectives flanked Carella like a pair of bookends. They were each wearing black suits, white shirts, and black ties, and they looked somewhat like morticians, which was not a far cry from their actual calling. In this city, detectives from Homicide Division were overseers of death, expected to serve in an advisory and supervisory capacity. The actual murder investigation was handled by the precinct that caught the squeal—in this case, the Eight-Seven.

"But I was referring to a cabbie getting killed," Monoghan explained. "Since they started using them plastic partitions . . . what, four, five years ago? . . . yellow-cab homicides have gone down to practically zip."

Except for tonight, Carella thought.

Tall and slender, standing in an easy slouch, Steve Carella looked like an athlete, which he wasn't. The blue star bothered him. It bothered his partner, too. Meyer was hoping the blue star wasn't the start of something. In this city—in this world—things started too fast and took too long to end.

"Trip sheet looks routine," Monroe said, looking at the clipboard he'd recovered from the cab, glancing over the times and locations handwritten on the sheet. "Came on at midnight, last fare was dropped off at one-forty. When did you guys catch the squeal?"

Car four, in the Eight-Seven's Adam Sector, had discovered the cab parked at the curb on Ainsley Avenue at two-thirty in the morning. The driver was slumped over the wheel, a bullet hole at the base of his skull. Blood was running down the back of his neck, into his collar. Blue paint was running down his windshield. The uniforms had phoned the detective squadroom some five minutes later.

"We got to the scene at a quarter to three," Carella said.

"Here's the ME, looks like," Monoghan said.

Carl Blaney was getting out of a black sedan marked with the seal of the Medical Examiner's Office. Blaney was the only person Carella knew who had violet eyes. Then again, he didn't know Liz Taylor.

"What's this I see?" he asked, indicating the clipboard in Monroe's hand. "You been compromising the crime scene?"

"Told you," Monoghan said knowingly.

"It was in plain sight," Monroe explained.

"This the vic?" Blaney asked, striding over to the cab and looking in through the open window on the driver's side. It was a mild night at the beginning of May. Spectators who'd gathered on the sidewalk beyond the yellow CRIME SCENE tapes were in their shirt sleeves. The detectives in sport jackets and ties, Blaney and the homicide dicks in suits and ties, all looked particularly formal, as if they'd come to the wrong street party.

"MCU been here yet?" Blaney asked.

"We're waiting," Carella said.

Blaney was referring to the Mobile Crime Unit, which was called the CSI in some cities. Before they sanctified the scene, not even the ME was supposed to touch anything. Monroe felt this was another personal jab, just because he'd lifted the goddamn clipboard from the front seat. But he'd never liked Blaney, so fuck him.

"Why don't we tarry over a cup of coffee?" Blaney suggested, and without waiting for company, started walking toward an all-night diner across the street. This was a black neighborhood, and this stretch of turf was largely retail, with all of the shops closed at three-fifteen in the morning. The diner was the only place ablaze with illumination, although lights had come on in many of the tenements above the shuttered shops.

The sidewalk crowd parted to let Blaney through, as if he were a visiting dignitary come to restore order in Baghdad. Carella and Meyer ambled along after him. Monoghan and Monroe lingered near the taxi, where three or four blues stood around scratching their asses. Casually, Monroe tossed the clipboard through the open window and onto the front seat on the passenger side.

There were maybe half a dozen patrons

in the diner when Blaney and the two detectives walked in. A man and a woman sitting in one of the booths were both black. The girl was wearing a purple silk dress and strappy high-heeled sandals. The man was wearing a beige linen suit with wide lapels. Carella and Meyer each figured them for a hooker and her pimp, which was profiling because for all they knew, the pair could have been a gainfully employed, happily married couple coming home from a late party. Everyone sitting on stools at the counter was black, too. So was the man behind it. They all knew this was the Law here, and the Law frequently spelled trouble in the hood, so they all fell silent when the three men took stools at the counter and ordered coffee.

"So how's the world treating you these days?" Blaney asked the detectives.

"Fine," Carella said briefly. He had come on at midnight, and it had already been a long night.

The counterman brought their coffees.

Bald and burly and blue-eyed, Meyer picked up his coffee cup, smiled across the counter, and asked, "How you doing?"

"Okay," the counterman said warily.

"When did you come to work tonight?"

"Midnight."

"Me, too," Meyer said. "Were you here an hour or so ago?"

"I was here, yessir."

"Did you see anything going down across the street?"

"Nossir."

"Hear a shot?"

"Nossir."

"See anyone approaching the cab there?"

"Nossir."

"Or getting out of the cab?"

"I was busy in here," the man said.

"What's your name?" Meyer asked.

"Whut's my name got to do with who got aced outside?"

"Nothing," Meyer said. "I have to ask."

"Deaven Brown," the counterman said.

"We've got a detective named Arthur Brown up the Eight-Seven," Meyer said, still smiling pleasantly.

"That right?" Brown said indifferently.

"Here's Mobile," Carella said, and all three men hastily downed their coffees and went outside again.

The chief tech was a Detective/First named Carlie . . .

"For Charles," he explained.

. . . Epworth. He didn't ask if anyone had touched anything, and Monroe didn't volunteer the information either. The MCU team went over the vehicle and the pavement surrounding it, dusting for prints, vacuuming for fibers and hair. On the cab's dashboard, there was a little black holder with three miniature American flags stuck in it like an open fan. In a plastic holder on the partition facing the back seat, there was the driver's pink hack license. The name to the right of the photograph was Khalid Aslam. It was almost four A.M. when Epworth said it would be okay to examine the corpse.

Blaney was thorough and swift.

Pending a more thorough examination at the morgue, he proclaimed cause of death to be a gunshot wound to the head—

Big surprise, Monroe thought, but did not say.

—and told the assembled detectives that they would have his written report by the end of the day. Epworth promised likewise, and one of the MCU team drove the taxi off to the police garage where it would be sealed as evidence. An ambulance carried off the stiff. The blues took down the CRIME

SCENE tapes, and told everybody to go home, nothing to see here anymore, folks.

Meyer and Carella still had four hours to go before their shift ended.

"Khalid Aslam, Khalid Aslam," the man behind the computer said. "Must be a Muslim, don't you think?"

The offices of the License Bureau at the Taxi and Limousine Commission occupied two large rooms on the eighth floor of the old brick building on Emory Street all the way downtown. At five in the morning, there were only two people on duty, one of them a woman at another computer across the room. Lacking population, the place seemed cavernous.

"Most of the drivers nowadays are Muslims," the man said. His name was Lou Foderman, and he seemed to be close to retirement age, somewhere in his mid-sixties, Meyer guessed.

"Khalid Aslam, Khalid Aslam," he said again, still searching. "The names these people have. You know how many licensed yellow-cab drivers we have in this city?" he asked, not turning from the computer screen. "Forty-two thousand," he said, nodding. "Khalid Aslam, where are you hiding, Khalid Aslam? Ninety percent of them are immigrants, seventy percent from India, Pakistan, and Bangladesh. You want to bet Mr. Aslam here is from one of those countries? How much you wanna bet?"

Carella looked up at the wall clock.

It was five minutes past five.

"Back when *I* was driving a cab," Foderman said, "this was during the time of the Roman Empire, most of your cabbies were Jewish or Irish or Italian. We still got a couple of Jewish drivers around, but they're mostly from Israel or Russia. Irish and Italian, forget about it. You get in a cab nowadays, the driver's talking Farsi to some other guy on his cell phone, you think they're planning a terrorist attack. I wouldn't be surprised Mr. Aslam was talking on the phone to one of his pals, and the passenger shot him because he couldn't take it anymore, you said he was shot, correct?"

"He was shot, yes," Meyer said.

He looked up at the clock, too.

"Because he was babbling on the phone, I'll bet," Foderman said. "These camel jockeys think a taxi is a private phone booth, never mind the passenger. You ask them to please stop talking on the phone, they get insulted. We get more complaints here about drivers talking on the phone than anything else. Well, maybe playing the radio. They play their radios with all this string music from the Middle East, sitars, whatever they call them. Passengers are trying to have a decent conversation, the driver's either playing the radio or talking on the phone. You tell him please lower the radio, he gives you a look could kill you on the spot. Some of them even wear turbans and carry little daggers in their boots, Sikhs, they call themselves. 'All Singhs are Sikhs,'" Foderman quoted, "'but not all Sikhs are Singhs,' that's an expression they have. Singhs is a family name. Or the other way around, I forget which. Maybe it's 'All Sikhs are Singhs,' who knows? Khalid Aslam, here he is. What do you want to know about him?"

Like more than thousands of other Muslim cab drivers in this city, Khalid Aslam was born in Bangladesh. Twelve years ago, he came to America with his wife and one child. According to his updated computer file, he now had three children and lived with his family at 3712 Locust Avenue in Majesta, a neighborhood that once—like the city's cab drivers—was almost exclusively Jewish, but which now was predominately Muslim.

Eastern Daylight Savings Time had gone into effect three weeks ago. This morning, the sun came up at six minutes to six. There was already heavy early-morning rush-hour traffic on the Majesta Bridge. Meyer was driving. Carella was riding shotgun.

"You detect a little bit of anti-Arab sentiment there?" Meyer asked.

"From Foderman, you mean?"

"Yeah. It bothers me to hear another Jew talk that way."

"Well, it bothers me, too," Carella said.

"Yeah, but you're not Jewish."

Someone behind them honked a horn.

"What's with him?" Meyer asked.

Carella turned to look.

"Truck in a hurry," he said.

"I have to tell you," Meyer said, "that blue star on the windshield bothers me. Aslam being Muslim. A bullet in the back of his head, and a Star of David on the windshield, that bothers me."

The truck driver honked again.

Meyer rolled down the window and threw him a finger. The truck driver honked again, a prolonged angry blast this time.

"Shall we give him a ticket?" Meyer asked jokingly.

"I think we should," Carella said.

"Why not? Violation of Section Two Twenty-One, Chapter Two, Subchapter Four, Noise Control."

"Maximum fine, eight hundred and seventy-five smackers," Carella said, nodding, enjoying this.

"Teach him to honk at cops," Meyer said.

The driver behind them kept honking his horn.

"So much hate in this city," Meyer said softly. "So much hate."

Shalah Aslam opened the door for them only after they had both held up their shields and ID cards to the three inches of space allowed by the night chain. She was wearing a blue woolen robe over a long white cotton nightgown. There was a puzzled look on her pale face. This was six-thirty in the morning, she had to know that two detectives on her doorstep at this hour meant something terrible had happened.

There was no diplomatic way to tell a woman that her husband had been murdered.

Standing in a hallway redolent of cooking smells, Carella told Shalah that someone had shot and killed her husband, and they would appreciate it if she could answer a few questions that might help them find whoever had done it. She asked them to come in. The apartment was very still. In contrast to the night before, the day had dawned far too cold for May. There was a bleak chill to the Aslam dwelling.

They followed her through the kitchen and into a small living room where the detectives sat on an upholstered sofa that probably had been made in the mountains of North Carolina. The blue robe Shalah Aslam was wearing most likely had been purchased at the Gap. But here on the mantel was a clock shaped in the form of a mosque, and there were beaded curtains leading to another part of the apartment, and there were the aromas of strange foods from other parts of the building, and the sounds of strange languages wafting up from the street through the open windows. They could have been somewhere in downtown Dhakar.

"The children are still asleep," Shalah explained. "Benazir is only six months old. The two other girls don't catch their school bus until eight-fifteen. I usually wake them at seven."

She had not yet cried. Her pale narrow face seemed entirely placid, her dark brown eyes vacant. The shock had registered, but the emotions hadn't yet caught up.

"Khalid was worried that something like this might happen," she said. "Ever since 9/11. That's why he had those American flags in his taxi. To let passengers know he's American. He got his citizenship five years ago. He's American, same as you. We're all Americans."

They had not yet told her about the Star of David painted on her husband's windshield.

"Seven Bangladesh people died in the towers, you know," she said. "It is not as if we were not victims, too. Because we are Muslim, that does not make us terrorists. The terrorists on those planes were Saudi, you know. Not people from Bangladesh."

"Mrs. Aslam, when you say he was worried, did he ever say specifically . . . ?"

"Yes, because of what happened to some other drivers at Regal."

"Regal?"

"That's the company he works for. A Regal taxi was set on fire in Riverhead the very day the Americans went into Afghanistan. And another one parked in Calm's Point was vandalized the week after we invaded Iraq. So he was afraid something might happen to him as well."

"But he'd never received a specific death threat, had he? Or . . ."

"No."

". . . a threat of violence?"

"No, but the fear was always there. He has had rocks thrown at his taxi. He told me he was thinking of draping a small American flag over his hack license, to hide his picture and name. When passengers ask if he's Arab, he tells them he's from Bangladesh."

She was still talking about him in the present tense. It still hadn't sunk in.

"Most people don't even know where Bangladesh is. Do you know where Bangladesh is?" she asked Meyer.

"No, ma'am, I don't," Meyer said.

"Do you?" she asked Carella.

"No," Carella admitted.

"But they know to shoot my husband because he is from Bangladesh," she said, and burst into tears.

The two detectives sat opposite her clumsily, saying nothing.

"I'm sorry," she said.

She took a tiny, crochet-trimmed handkerchief from the pocket of the robe, dabbed at her eyes with it.

"Khalid was always so careful," she said. "He never picked up anyone wearing a ski cap," drying her cheeks now. "If he got sleepy, he parked in front of a twenty-four-hour gas station or a police precinct. He never picked up anyone who didn't look right. He didn't care what color a person was. If that person looked threatening, he wouldn't pick him up. He hid his money in his shoes, or in an ashtray, or in the pouch on the driver-side door. He kept only a few dollars in his wallet. He was a very careful man."

Meyer bit the bullet.

"Did your husband know any Jewish people?" he asked.

"No," she said. "Why?"

"Mama?" a child's voice asked.

A little girl in a white nightgown, six, seven years old, was standing in the doorway to one of the other rooms. Her dark eyes were big and round in a puzzled face Meyer had seen a thousand times on television these past several years. Straight black hair.

A slight frown on the face now. Wondering who these strange men were in their living room at close to seven in the morning.

"Where's Daddy?" she asked.

"Daddy's working," Shalah said, and lifted her daughter onto her lap. "Say hello to these nice men."

"Hello," the little girl said.

"This is Sabeen," Shalah said. "Sabeen is in the first grade, aren't you, Sabeen?"

"Uh-huh," Sabeen said.

"Hello, Sabeen," Meyer said.

"Hello," she said again.

"Sweetie, go read one of your books for a while, okay?" Shalah said. "I have to finish here."

"I have to go to school," Sabeen said.

"I know, darling. I'll just be a few minutes."

Sabeen gave the detectives a long look, and then went out of the room, closing the door behind her.

"Did a Jew kill my husband?" Shalah asked.

"We don't know that," Carella said.

"Then why did you ask if he knew any Jews?"

"Because the possibility exists that this might have been a hate crime," Meyer said.

"My husband was not a Palestinian," Shalah said. "Why would a Jew wish to kill him?"

"We don't know for a fact . . ."

"But you must at least *suspect* it was a Jew, isn't that so? Otherwise, why would you ask such a question? Bangladesh is on the Bay of Bengal, next door to India. It is nowhere near Israel. So why would a Jew . . . ?"

"Ma'am, a Star of David was painted on his windshield," Meyer said.

The room went silent.

"Then it *was* a Jew," she said, and clasped her hands in her lap.

She was silent for perhaps twenty seconds.

Then she said, "The rotten bastards."

"I shouldn't have told her," Meyer said.

"Be all over the papers, anyway," Carella said. "Probably make the front page of the afternoon tabloid."

It was ten minutes past seven, and they were on their way across the bridge again, to where Regal Taxi had its garage on Abingdon and Hale. The traffic was even heavier than it had been on the way out. The day was warming up a little, but not much. This had been the worst damn winter Carella could ever remember. He'd been cold since October. And every time it seemed to be warming up a little, it either started snowing or raining or sleeting or some damn thing to dampen the spirits and crush all hope. Worst damn shitty winter ever.

"What?" Meyer said.

"Nothing."

"You were frowning."

Carella merely nodded.

"When do you think she'll tell the kids?" Meyer asked.

"I think she made a mistake saying he was working. She's got to tell them sooner or later."

"Hard call to make."

"Well, she's not gonna send them to school today, is she?"

"I don't know."

"Be all over the papers," Carella said again.

"I don't know what I'd do in a similar situation."

"When my father got killed, I told my kids that same day," Carella said.

"They're older," Meyer said.

"Even so."

He was silent for a moment.

"They really loved him," he said.

Meyer figured he was talking about himself.

There are times in this city when it is impossible to catch a taxi. Stand on any street corner between three-fifteen and four o'clock and you can wave your hand at any passing blur of yellow, and—forget about it. That's the forty-five minutes when every cabbie is racing back to the garage to turn in his trip sheet and make arrangements for tomorrow's tour of duty. It was the same with cops. The so-called night shift started at four P.M. and ended at midnight. For the criminally inclined, the shift change was a good time for them to do their evil thing because that's when all was confusion.

Confusion was the order of the day at the Regal garage when Meyer and Carella got there at seven-thirty that morning. Cabs were rolling in, cabs were rolling out. Assistant managers were making arrangements for tomorrow's short-terms, and dispatchers were sending newly gassed taxis on their way through the big open rolling doors. This was the busiest time of the day. Even busier than the pre-theater hours. Nobody had time for two flatfoots investigating a homicide.

Carella and Meyer waited.

Their own shift would end in—what was it now?—ten minutes, and they were bone-weary and drained of all energy, but they waited patiently because a man had been killed and Carella had been First Man Up when he answered the phone. It was twelve minutes after eight before the manager, a man named Dennis Ryan, could talk to them. Tall, and red-headed, and fortyish, harried-looking even though all of his cabs were on their way now, he kept nodding impatiently as they told him what had happened to Khalid Aslam.

"So where's my cab?" he asked.

"Police garage on Courtney," Meyer told him.

"When do I get it back? That cab is money on the hoof."

"Yes, but a man was killed in it," Carella said.

"When I saw Kal didn't show up this morning . . ."

Kal, Carella thought. Yankee Doodle Dandy.

". . . I figured he stopped to say one of his bullshit prayers."

Both detectives looked at him.

"They're supposed to pray five times a day,

you know, can you beat it? Five times! Sunrise, early afternoon, late afternoon, sunset, and then before they go to bed. Five friggin times! And two *optional* ones if they're *really* holy. Most of them recognize they have a job to do here, they don't go flopping all over the sidewalk five times a day. Some of them pull over to a mosque on their way back in, for the late afternoon prayer. Some of them just do the one before they come to work, and the sunset one if they're home in time, and then the one before they go to bed. I can tell you anything you need to know about these people, we got enough of them working here, believe me."

"What kind of a worker was Aslam?" Carella asked.

"I guess he made a living."

"Meaning?"

"Meaning, it costs eighty-two bucks a shift to lease the cab. Say the driver averages a hundred above that in fares and tips. Gasoline costs him, say, fifteen, sixteen bucks? So he ends up taking home seventy-five, eighty bucks for an eight-hour shift. That ain't bad, is it?"

"Comes to around twenty grand a year," Meyer said.

"Twenty, twenty-five. That ain't bad," Ryan said again.

"Did he get along with the other drivers?" Carella asked.

"Oh, sure. These friggin Arabs are thick as thieves."

"How about your non-Arab drivers? Did he get along with them?"

"What non-Arab drivers? Why? You think one of my drivers done him?"

"Did he ever have any trouble with one of the other drivers?"

"I don't think so."

"Ever hear him arguing with one of them?"

"Who the hell knows? They babble in Bangla, Urdu, Sindi, Farsi, who the hell knows what else? They all sound the same to me. And they *always* sound like they're arguing. Even when they got smiles on their faces."

"Have you got any Jewish drivers?" Meyer asked.

"Ancient history," Ryan said. "I ain't *ever* seen a Jewish driver at Regal."

"How about anyone who might be sympathetic to the Jewish cause?"

"Which cause is that?" Ryan asked.

"Anyone who might have expressed pro-Israel sympathies?"

"Around here? You've got to be kidding."

"Did you ever hear Aslam say anything *against* Israel? Or the Jewish people?"

"No. Why? Did a Jew kill him?"

"What time did he go to work last night?"

"The boneyard shift goes out around eleven-thirty, quarter to twelve, comes in around seven, seven-thirty—well, you saw. I guess he must've gone out as usual. Why? What time was he killed?"

"Around two, two-thirty."

"Where?"

"Up on Ainsley and Twelfth."

"Way up there, huh?" Ryan said. "You think a nigger did it?"

"We don't know if who did it was white, purple, or black, was the word you meant, right?" Carella said, and looked Ryan dead in the eye.

And fuck you, too, Ryan thought, but said only, "Good luck catching him," making it sound like a curse.

Meyer and Carella went back to the squadroom to type up their interim report on the case.

It was almost a quarter to nine when they finally went home.

The day shift had already been there for half an hour.

Detectives Arthur Brown and Bert Kling made a good salt-and-pepper pair.

Big and heavyset and the color of his surname, Brown looked somewhat angry even when he wasn't. A scowl from him was usually enough to cause a perp to turn to Kling for sympathy and redemption. A few inches shorter than his partner—*everybody* was a few inches shorter than Brown—blond and hazel-eyed, Kling looked like a broad-shouldered farm boy who'd just come in off the fields after working since sunup. Good Cop–Bad Cop had been invented for Kling and Brown.

It was Brown who took the call from Ballistics at 10:27 that Friday morning.

"You handling this cabbie kill?" the voice said.

Brown immediately recognized the caller as a brother.

"I've been briefed on it," he said.

"This is Carlyle, Ballistics. We worked that evidence bullet the ME's office sent over, you want to take this down for whoever's running the case?"

"Shoot," Brown said, and moved a pad into place.

"Nice clean bullet, no deformities, must've lodged in the brain matter, ME's report didn't say exactly where they'd recovered it. Not that it matters. First thing we did here, bro . . ."

He had recognized Brown's voice as well.

". . . was compare a rolled impression of the evidence bullet against our specimen cards. Once we got a first-sight match, we did a microscopic examination of the actual bullet against the best sample bullet in our file. Way we determine the make of an unknown firearm is by examining the grooves on the bullet and the right or left direction of twist—but you don't want to hear all that shit, do you?"

Brown had heard it only ten thousand times before.

"Make a long story short," Carlyle said, "what we got here is a bullet fired from a .38-caliber Colt revolver, which is why you didn't find an ejected shell in the taxi, the gun being a revolver and all. Incidentally, there are probably a hundred thousand unregistered, illegal .38-caliber Colts in this city, so the odds against you finding it are probably eighty to one. End of story."

"Thanks," Brown said. "I'll pass it on."

"You see today's paper?" Carlyle asked.

"No, not yet."

"Case made the front page. Makes it sound like the Israeli army invaded Majesta with tanks, one lousy Arab. Is this true about a Jewish star on the windshield?"

"That's what our guys found."

"Gonna be trouble, bro," Carlyle said.

He didn't know the half of it.

While Carella and Meyer slept like hibernating grizzlies, Kling and Brown read their typed report, noted that the dead driver's widow had told them the Aslams' place of worship was called Majid Hazrat-i-Shabazz, and went out at eleven that morning to visit the mosque.

If either of them had expected glistening white minarets, arches, and domes, they were sorely disappointed. There were more than a hundred mosques in this city, but only a handful of them had been originally designed as such. The remainder had been converted to places of worship from private homes, warehouses, storefront buildings, and lofts. There were, in fact, only three requirements for any building that now called itself a mosque: that males and females be separated during prayer; that there be no images of animate objects inside the building; and that the *quibla*—the orientation of prayer in the direction of the Kabba in Mecca—be established.

A light rain began falling as they got out of the unmarked police sedan and began walking toward a yellow brick building that had once been a small supermarket on the corner of Lowell and Franks. Metal shutters were now in place where earlier there'd been plate glass display windows. Graffiti decorated the yellow brick and the green shutters. An ornately hand-lettered sign hung above the entrance doors, white on a black field, announcing the name of the mosque: Majid Hazrat-i-Shabazz. Men in flowing white garments and embroidered prayer caps, other men in dark business suits and pillbox hats milled about on the sidewalk with young men in team jackets, their baseball caps turned backward. Friday was the start of the Muslim sabbath, and now the faithful were being called to prayer.

On one side of the building, the detectives could see women entering through a separate door.

"My mother knows this Muslim lady up in Diamondback," Brown said, "she goes to this mosque up there—lots of blacks are Muslims, you know . . ."

"I know," Kling said.

"And where she goes to pray, they got no space for this separation stuff. So the men and women all pray together in the same open hall. But the women sit *behind* the men. So this fat ole sister gets there late one Friday, and the hall is already filled with men, and they tell her there's no room for her. Man, she takes a fit! Starts yelling, 'This is America, I'm as good a Muslim as any man here, so how come they's only room for *brothers* to pray?' Well, the imam—that's the man in charge, he's like the preacher—he quotes scripture and verse that says only men are *required* to come to Friday prayer, whereas women are not. So they have to let the men in first. It's as simple as that. So she quotes right back at him that in Islam, women are *spose* to be highly respected and revered, so how come he's dissing her this way? And she walked away from that mosque and never went back. From that time on, she prayed at home. That's a true story," Brown said.

"I believe it," Kling said.

The imam's address that Friday was about the dead cab driver. He spoke first in Arabic—which, of course, neither Kling nor Brown understood—and then he translated his words into English, perhaps for their benefit, perhaps in deference to the younger worshippers in the large drafty hall. The male worshippers knelt at the front of the hall. Behind a translucent, moveable screen, Brown and Kling could perceive a small number of veiled female worshippers.

The imam said he prayed that the strife in the Middle East was not now coming to this city that had known so much tragedy already. He said he prayed that an innocent and hard-working servant of Allah had not paid with his life for the acts of a faraway people bent only on destruction—

The detectives guessed he meant the Israelis.

—prayed that the signature star on the windshield of the murdered man's taxi was not a promise of further violence to come.

"It is foolish to grieve for our losses," he said, "since all is ordained by Allah. Only by working for the larger nation of Islam can we understand the true meaning of life."

Men's foreheads touched the cement floor.

Behind the screen, the women bowed their heads as well.

The imam's name was Muhammad Adham Akbar.

"What we're trying to find out," Brown said, "is whether or not Mr. Aslam had any enemies that you know of."

"Why do you even ask such a question?" Akbar said.

"He was a worshipper at your mosque," Kling said. "We thought you might know."

"Why would he have enemies here?"

"Men have enemies everywhere," Brown said.

"Not in a house of prayer. If you want to know who Khalid's enemy was, you need only look at his windshield."

"Well, we have to investigate every possibility," Kling said.

"The star on his windshield says it all," Akbar said, and shrugged. "A Jew killed him. That would seem obvious to anyone."

"Well, a Jew may have committed those murders," Kling agreed. "But . . ."

"May," the imam said, and nodded cynically.

"But until we catch him, we won't know for sure, will we?" Kling said.

Akbar looked at him.

Then he said, "The slain man had no enemies that I know of."

Just about when Carella and Meyer were each and separately waking up from eight hours of sleep, more or less, the city's swarm of taxis rolled onto the streets for the four-to-midnight shift. And as the detectives sat down to late afternoon meals which for each of them were really hearty breakfasts, many of the city's more privileged women were coming out into the streets to start looking for taxis to whisk them homeward. Here was a carefully coiffed woman who'd just enjoyed afternoon tea, chatting with another equally stylish woman as they strolled together out of a midtown hotel. And here was a woman who came out of a department store carrying a shopping bag in each hand, shifting one of the bags to the other hand, freeing it so she could hail a taxi. And here was a woman coming out of a Korean nail shop, wearing paper sandals to protect her freshly painted toenails. And another coming out of a deli, clutching a bag with baguettes showing, raising one hand to signal a cab. At a little before five, the streets were suddenly alive with the leisured women of this city, the most beautiful women in all the world, all of them ready to kill if another woman grabbed a taxi that had just been hailed.

This was a busy time for the city's cabbies. Not ten minutes later, the office buildings would begin spilling out men and women who'd been working since nine this morning, coming out onto the pavements now and sucking in great breaths of welcome spring air. The rain had stopped, and the sidewalk and pavements glistened, and there was the strange aroma of freshness on the air. This had been one hell of a winter.

The hands went up again, typists' hands, and file clerks' hands, and the hands of lawyers and editors and agents and producers and exporters and thieves, yes, even thieves took taxis—though obvious criminal types were avoided by these cabbies steering their vehicles recklessly toward the curb in a relentless pursuit of passengers. These men had paid eighty-two dollars to lease their taxis. These men had paid fifteen, twenty bucks to gas their buggies and get them on the road. They were already a hundred bucks in the hole before they put foot to pedal. Time was money. And there were hungry mouths to feed. For the most part, these men were Muslims, these men were gentle strangers in a strange land.

But someone had killed one of them last night.

And he was not yet finished.

Salim Nazir and his widowed mother left Afghanistan in 1994, when it became apparent that the Taliban were about to take over the entire country. His father had been one of the mujahideen killed fighting the Russian occupation; Salim's mother did not wish the wrath of "God's Students" to fall upon their heads if and when a new regime came to power.

Salim was now twenty-seven years old, his mother fifty-five. Both had been American citizens for three years now, but neither approved of what America had done to their native land, the evil Taliban notwithstanding. For that matter they did not appreciate what America had done to Iraq in its search for imaginary weapons of mass destruction. (Salim called them "weapons of mass deception.") In fact, Salim totally disapproved of the mess America had made in what once was his part of the world, but he rarely expressed these views out loud, except when he was among other Muslims who lived—as he and his mother did now—in a ghettolike section of Calm's Point.

Salim knew what it was like to be an outsider in George W. Bush's America, no matter how many speeches the president made about Islam being a peaceful religion. With all his heart, Salim knew this to be true, but he doubted very much that Mr. Bush believed what he was saying.

Just before sundown that Friday, Salim pulled his yellow taxi into the curb in front of a little shop on a busy street in Majesta. Here in Ikram Hassan's store, devout Muslims could purchase whatever food and drink was considered *halal*—lawful or permitted for consumption as described in the Holy Koran.

The Koran decreed, "Eat of that over which the name of Allah hath been mentioned, if ye are believers in His revelations." Among the acceptable foods were milk (from cows, sheep, camels, or goats), honey, fish, plants that were not intoxicant, fresh or naturally frozen vegetables, fresh or dried fruits, legumes (like peanuts, cashews, hazelnuts, and walnuts), and grains such as wheat, rice, barley, and oats.

Many animals, large and small, were considered *halal* as well, but they had to be slaughtered according to Islamic ritual. Ikram Hassan was about to slay a chicken just as his friend Salim came into the shop. He looked up when a small bell over his door sounded.

"Hey there, Salim," he said in English.

There were two major languages in Afghanistan, both of them imported from Iran, but Pushto was the official language the two men had learned as boys growing up in Kandahar, and this was the language they spoke now.

Salim fidgeted and fussed as his friend hunched over the chicken; he did not want to be late for the sunset prayer. Using a very sharp knife, and making certain that he cut the main blood vessels without completely severing the throat, Ikram intoned "*Bismillah Allah-u-Albar*" and completed the ritual slaughter.

Each of the men then washed his hands to the wrists, and cleansed the mouth and the nostrils with water, and washed the face and the right arm and left arm to the elbow, and washed to the ankle first the right foot and then the left, and at last wiped the top of the head with wet hands, the three middle fingers of each hand joined together.

Salim consulted his watch yet another time.

Both men donned little pillbox hats.

Ikram locked the front door to his store, and together they walked to the mosque four blocks away.

The sun had already set.

It was ten minutes to seven.

Among other worshippers, Salim and Ikram stood facing Mecca, their hands raised to their ears, and they uttered the words, "*Allahu Akbar*," which meant "Allah is the greatest of all." Then they placed the right hand just below the breast and recited in unison the prayer called *istiftah.*

"Surely I have turned myself, being upright holy to Him Who originated the heavens and the earth and I am not of the polytheists. Surely my prayer and my sacrifice and my life and my death are for Allah, the Lord of the worlds, no associate has He; and this I am commanded and I am one of those who submit. Glory to Thee, O Allah, and Thine is the praise, and blessed is Thy name, and exalted is Thy majesty, and there is none to be served besides Thee."

A'udhu bi-llahi minash-shaitani-r-rajim.

"I seek the refuge of Allah from the accursed devil."

Six hours later, Salim Nazir would be dead.

In this city, all the plays, concerts, and musicals let out around eleven, eleven-thirty, the cabarets around one, one-thirty. The night clubs wouldn't break till all hours of the night. It was Salim's habit during the brief early-morning lull to visit a Muslim friend who was a short-order cook at a deli on Culver Avenue, a mile and a half distant from all the midtown glitter. He went into the deli at one-thirty, enjoyed a cup of coffee and a chat with his friend, and left twenty minutes later. Crossing the street to where he'd parked his taxi, he got in behind the wheel, and was just about to start the engine when he realized someone was sitting in the dark in the back seat.

Startled, he was about to ask what the hell, when the man fired a bullet through the plastic divider and into his skull.

The two Midtown South detectives who responded to the call immediately knew this killing was related to the one that had taken place uptown the night before; a blue Star of David had been spray-painted on the windshield. Nonetheless, they called their lieutenant from the scene, and he informed them that this was a clear case of First Man Up, and advised them to wait right there while he contacted the Eight-Seven, which had caught the original squeal. The detectives were still at the scene when Carella and Meyer got there at twenty minutes to three.

Midtown South told Carella that both MCU and the ME had already been there and gone, the corpse and the vehicle carried off respectively to the morgue and the PD garage to be respectively dissected and impounded. They told the Eight-Seven dicks that they'd talked to the short-order cook in the deli across the street, who informed them that he was a friend of the dead man, and that he'd been in there for a cup of coffee shortly before he got killed. The vic's name was Salim Nazir, and the cab company he worked for was called City Transport. They assumed the case was now the Eight-Seven's and that Carella and Meyer would do all the paper shit and send them dupes. Carella assured them that they would.

"We told you about the blue star, right?" one of the Midtown dicks said.

"You told us," Meyer said.

"Here's the evidence bullet we recovered," he said, and handed Meyer a sealed manila envelope. "Chain of Custody tag on it, you sign next. Looks like you maybe caught an epidemic."

"Or maybe a copycat," Carella said.

"Either way, good luck," the other Midtown dick said.

Carella and Meyer crossed the street to the deli.

Like his good friend, Salim, the short-order cook was from Afghanistan, having arrived here in the city seven years ago. He offered at once to show the detectives his green card, which made each of them think he was probably an illegal with a counterfeit card, but they had bigger fish to fry and Ajmal Khan was possibly a man who could help them do just that.

Ajmal meant "good-looking" in his native

tongue, a singularly contradictory description for the man who now told them he had heard a shot outside some five minutes after Salim finished his coffee. Dark eyes bulging with excitement, black mustache bristling, bulbous nose twitching like a rabbit's, Ajmal reported that he had rushed out of the shop the instant he heard the shot, and had seen a man across the street getting out of Salim's taxi on the driver's side, and leaning over the windshield with a can of some sort in his hand. Ajmal didn't know what he was doing at the time but he now understood the man was spray-painting a Jewish star on the windshield.

"Can you describe this man?" Carella asked.

"Is that what he was doing? Painting a Star of David on the windshield?"

"Apparently," Meyer said.

"That's bad," Ajmal said.

The detectives agreed with him. That was bad. They did not believe this was a copycat. This was someone specifically targeting Muslim cab drivers. But they went through the routine anyway, asking the questions they always asked whenever someone was murdered: Did he have any enemies that you know of, did he mention any specific death threats, did he say he was being followed or harassed, was he in debt to anyone, was he using drugs?

Ajmal told them that his good friend Salim was loved and respected by everyone. This was what friends and relatives always said about the vic. He was a kind and gentle person. He had a wonderful sense of humor. He was thoughtful and generous. He was devout. Ajmal could not imagine why anyone would have done this to a marvelous person like his good friend Salim Nazir.

"He was always laughing and friendly, a very warm and outgoing man. Especially with the ladies," Ajmal said.

"What do you mean?" Carella asked.

"He was quite a ladies' man, Salim. It is written that men may have as many as four wives, but they must be treated equally in every way. That is to say, emotionally, sexually, and materially. If Salim had been a wealthy man, I am certain he would have enjoyed the company of many wives."

"How many wives did he actually *have*?" Meyer asked.

"Well, none," Ajmal said. "He was single. He lived with his mother."

"Do you know where?"

"Oh yes. We were very good friends. I have been to his house many times."

"Can you give us his address?"

"His phone number, too," Ajmal said. "His mother's name is Gulalai. It means 'flower' in my country."

"You say he was quite a ladies' man, is that right?" Carella asked.

"Well, yes. The ladies liked him."

"More than one lady?" Carella said.

"Well, yes, more than one."

"Did he ever mention any jealousy among these various ladies?"

"I don't even know who they were. He was a discreet man."

"No reason any of these ladies might have wanted to shoot him?" Carella said.

"Not that I know of."

"But he *did* say he was seeing several women, is that it?"

"In conversation, yes."

"He said he was in *conversation* with several women?"

"No, he said to *me* in conversation that he was enjoying the company of several women, yes. As I said, he was quite a ladies' man."

"But he didn't mention the names of these women."

"No, he did not. Besides, it was a man I saw getting out of his taxi. A very tall man."

"Could it have been a very tall woman?"

"No, this was very definitely a man."

"Can you describe him?"

"Tall. Wide shoulders. Wearing a black raincoat and a black hat." Ajmal paused. "The kind rabbis wear," he said.

Which brought them right back to that Star of David on the windshield.

Two windshields.

This was not good at all.

This was a mixed lower-class neighborhood—white, black, Hispanic. These people had troubles of their own, they didn't much care about a couple of dead Arabs. Matter of fact, many of them had sons or husbands who'd fought in the Iraqi war. Lots of the people Carella and Meyer spoke to early that morning had an "Army of One," was what it was called nowadays, who'd gone to war right here from the hood. Some of these young men had never come back home except in a box.

You never saw nobody dying on television. All them reporters embedded with the troops, all you saw was armor racing across the desert. You never saw somebody taking a sniper bullet between the eyes, blood spattering. You never saw an artillery attack with arms and legs flying in the air. You could see more people getting killed right here in the hood than you saw getting killed in the entire Iraqi war. It was an absolute miracle, all them embedded newspeople out there reporting, and not a single person getting killed for the cameras. Maybe none of them had a camera handy when somebody from the hood got killed. So who gave a damn around here about a few dead Arabs more or less?

One of the black women they interviewed explained that people were asleep, anyway, at two in the morning, wun't that so? So why go axin a dumb question like did you hear a shot that time of night? A Hispanic man they interviewed told them there were *always* shots in the barrio; nobody ever paid attention no more. A white woman told them she'd got up to go pee around that time, and thought she heard something but figured it was a backfire.

At 4:30 A.M., Meyer and Carella spoke to a black man who'd been blinded in Iraq. He was in pajamas and a bathrobe, and he was wearing dark glasses. A white cane stood angled against his chair. He could remember President Bush making a little speech to a handful of veterans like himself at the hospital where he was recovering, his eyes still bandaged. He could remember Bush saying something folksy like, "I'll bet those Iraqi soldiers weren't happy to meet *you* fellas!" He could remember thinking, I wun't so happy to meet *them*, either. I'm goan be blind the ress of my life, Mr. Pres'dunt, how you feel about *that*?

"I heerd a shot," he told the detectives.

Travon Nelson was his name. He worked as a dishwasher in a restaurant all the way downtown. They stopped serving at eleven, he was usually out by a little before one, took the number 17 bus uptown, got home here around two. He had just got off the bus, and was walking toward his building, his white cane tapping the sidewalk ahead of him . . .

He had once thought he'd like to become a Major League ballplayer.

. . . when he heard the sharp crack of a small-arms weapon, and then heard a car door slamming, and then a hissing sound, he didn't know what it was . . .

The spray paint, Meyer thought.

. . . and then a man yelling.

"Yelling at *you?*" Carella asked.

"No, sir. Must've been some girl."

"What makes you think that?"

"Cause whut he yelled was 'You *whore*!' An' then I think he must've hit her, cause she screamed an' kepp right on screamin an' screamin."

"Then what?" Meyer asked.

"He run off. She run off, too. I heerd her heels clickin away. High heels. When you blind . . ."

His voice caught.

They could not see his eyes behind the dark glasses.

". . . you compensate with yo' other senses. They was the sound of the man's shoes runnin off and then the click of the girl's high heels."

He was silent for a moment, remembering again what high heels on a sidewalk sounded like.

"Then evy'thin went still again," he said.

Years of living in war-torn Afghanistan had left their mark on Gulalai Nazir's wrinkled face and stooped posture; she looked more like a woman in her late sixties than the fifty-five-year-old mother of Salim. The detectives had called ahead first, and several grieving relatives were already in her apartment when they got there at six that Saturday morning. Gulalai—although now an American citizen—spoke very little English. Her nephew—a man who at the age of sixteen had fought with the mujahideen against the Russians—translated for the detectives.

Gulalai told them what they had already heard from the short-order cook.

Her son was loved and respected by everyone. He was a kind and gentle person. A loving son. He had a wonderful sense of humor. He was thoughtful and generous. He was devout. Gulalai could not imagine why anyone would have done this to him.

"Unless it was that Jew," she said.

The nephew translated.

"Which Jew?" Carella asked at once.

"The one who killed that other Muslim cab driver uptown," the nephew translated.

Gulalai wrung her hands and burst into uncontrollable sobbing. The other women began wailing with her.

The nephew took the detectives aside.

His name was Osman, he told them, which was Turkish in origin, but here in

America everyone called him either Ozzie or Oz.

"Oz Kiraz," he said, and extended his hand. His grip was firm and strong. He was a big man, possibly thirty-two, thirty-three years old, with curly black hair and an open face with sincere brown eyes. Carella could visualize him killing Russian soldiers with his bare hands. He would not have enjoyed being one of them.

"Do you think you're going to get this guy?" he asked.

"We're trying," Carella said.

"Or is it going to be the same song and dance?"

"Which song and dance is that, sir?" Meyer said.

"Come on, this city is run by Jews. If a Jew killed my cousin, it'll be totally ignored."

"We're trying to make sure that doesn't happen," Carella said.

"I'll bet," Oz said.

"You'd win," Meyer said.

The call from Detective Carlyle in Ballistics came at a quarter to seven that Saturday morning.

"You the man I spoke to yesterday?" he asked.

"No, this is Carella."

"You workin this Arab shit?"

"Yep."

"It's the same gun," Carlyle said. "This doesn't mean it was the same *guy*, it coulda been his cousin or his uncle or his brother pulled the trigger. But it was the same .38-caliber Colt that fired the bullet."

"That it?"

"Ain't that enough?"

"More than enough," Carella said. "Thanks, pal."

"Buy me a beer sometime," Carlyle said, and hung up.

At 8:15 that morning, just as Carella and Meyer were briefing Brown and Kling on what had happened the night before, an attractive young black woman in her mid twenties walked into the squadroom. She introduced herself as Wandalyn Holmes, and told the detectives that she'd been heading home from baby-sitting her sister's daughter last night—walking to the corner to catch the number 17 bus downtown, in fact—when she saw this taxi sitting at the curb, and a man dressed all in black spraying paint on the windshield.

"When he saw I was looking at him, he pointed a finger at me . . ."

"Pointed . . . ?"

"Like this, yes," Wandalyn said, and showed them how the man had pointed his finger. "And he yelled 'You! Whore!' and I screamed and he came running after me."

" 'You whore'?"

"No, two words. First 'You!' and *then* 'Whore!' "

"Did you know this man?"

"Never saw him in my life."

"But he pointed his finger at you and called you a whore."

"Yes. And when I ran, he came after me and caught me by the back of the coat, you know what I'm saying? The collar of my coat? And pulled me over, right off my feet."

"What time was this, Miss Holmes?" Carella asked.

"About two in the morning, a little after."

"What happened then?"

"He kicked me. While I was laying on the ground. He seemed mad as hell. I thought at first he was gonna rape me. I kept screaming, though, and he ran off."

"What'd you do then?" Brown asked.

"I got up and ran off, too. Over to my sister's place. I was scared he might come back."

"Did you get a good look at him?"

"Oh yes."

"Tell us what he looked like," Meyer said.

"Like I said, he was all in black. Black hat, black raincoat, black everything."

"Was he himself black?" Kling asked.

"Oh no, he was a white man."

"Did you see his face?"

"I did."

"Describe him."

"Dark eyes. Angry. Very angry eyes."

"Beard? Mustache?"

"No."

"Notice any scars or tattoos?"

"No."

"Did he say anything to you?"

"Well, yes, I told you. He called me a whore."

"*After* that."

"No. Nothing. Just pulled me over backward, and started kicking me when I was down. I thought he was gonna rape me, I was scared to death." Wandalyn paused a moment. The detectives caught the hesitation.

"Yes?" Carella said. "Something else?"

"I'm sorry I didn't come here right away

last night, but I was too scared," Wandalyn said. "He was very angry. *So* angry. I was scared he might come after me if I told the police anything."

"You're here now," Carella said. "And we thank you."

"He *won't* come after me, right?" Wandalyn asked.

"I'm sure he won't," Carella said. "It's not you he's angry with."

Wandalyn nodded. But still looked skeptical.

"You'll be okay, don't worry," Brown said, and led her to the gate in the slatted wooden railing that divided the squadroom from the corridor outside.

At his desk, Carella began typing up their Detective Division report. He was still typing when Brown came over and said, "You know what time it is?"

Carella nodded and kept typing.

It was 9:33 A.M. when he finally printed up the report and carried it over to Brown's desk.

"Go home," Brown advised, scowling.

They had worked important homicides before, and these had also necessitated throwing the schedule out the window. What was new this time around—

Well, no, there was also a murder that had almost started a race riot, this must've been two, three years back, they hadn't got much sleep that time, either. This was similar, but different. This was two Muslim cabbies who'd been shot to death by someone, obviously a Jew, eager to take credit for both murders.

Meyer didn't know whether he dreamt it, or whether it was a brilliant idea he'd had before he fell asleep at nine that morning. Dream or brilliant idea, the first thing he did when the alarm clock rang at three that afternoon was find a fat felt-tipped pen and a sheet of paper and draw a big blue Star of David on it.

He kept staring at the star and wondering if the department's handwriting experts could tell them anything about the man or men who had spray-painted similar stars on the windshields of those two cabs.

He was almost eager to get to work.

Six hours of sleep wasn't bad for what both detectives considered a transitional period, similar to the decompression a deep-sea diver experienced while coming up to the surface in stages. Actually, they were moving back from the midnight shift to the night shift, a passage that normally took place over a period of days, but which given the exigency of the situation occurred in the very same day. Remarkably, both men felt refreshed and—in Meyer's case at least—raring to go.

"I had a great idea last night," he told Carella. "Or maybe it was just a dream. Take a look at this," he said, and showed Carella the Star of David he'd drawn.

"Okay," Carella said.

"I'm right-handed," Meyer said. "So what I did . . ."

"So am I," Carella said.

"What I did," Meyer said, "was start the

first triangle here at the northernmost point of the star . . . there are six points, you know, and they mean something or other, I'm not really sure what. I am not your ideal Jew."

"I never would have guessed."

"But religious Jews know what the six points stand for."

"So what's your big idea?"

"Well, I was starting to tell you. I began the first triangle at the very top, and drew one side down to this point here," he said, indicating the point on the bottom right . . .

". . . and then I drew a line across to the left . . ."

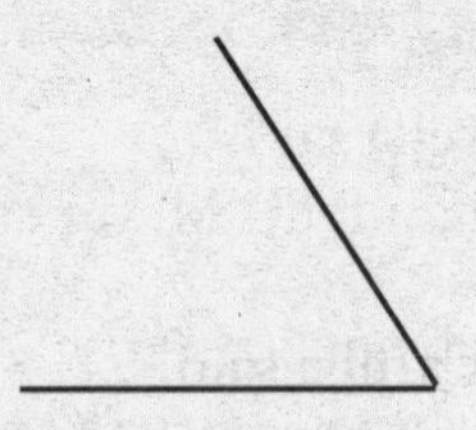

"... and another line up to the northern point again, completing the first triangle."

"Okay," Carella said, and picked up a pen and drew a triangle in exactly the same way.

"Then I started the second triangle at the western point—the one here on the left—and drew a line over to the east here ..."

"... and then down on an angle to the south ..."

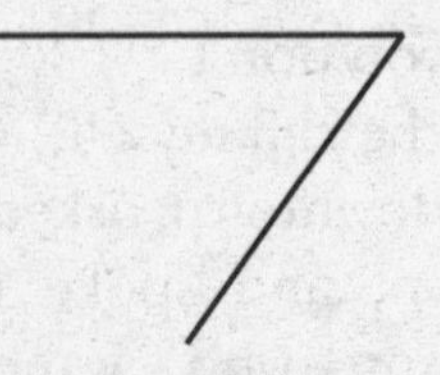

"... and back up again to ... northwest, I guess it is ... where I started."

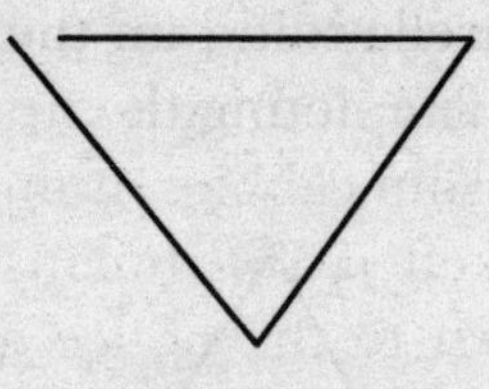

Carella did the same thing.

"That's right," he said. "That's how you do it."

"Yes, but we're both right-handed."

"So?"

"I think a left-handed person might do it differently."

"Ah," Carella said, nodding.

"So I think we should call Documents and get them to look at both those cabs. See if the same guy painted those two stars, and find out if he was right-handed or left-handed."

"I think that's brilliant," Carella said.

"You don't."

"I do."

"I can tell you don't."

"I'll make the call myself," Carella said.

He called downtown, asked for the Documents Section, and spoke to a detective named Jackson who agreed that there would be a distinct difference between left- and right-handed handwriting, even if the writing instrument—so to speak—was a spray can. Carella told him they were investigating a double homicide . . .

"Those Muslim cabbies, huh?"

. . . and asked if Documents could send someone down to the police garage to examine the spray-painting on the windshields of the two impounded taxis. Jackson said it would have to wait till tomorrow morning, they were a little short-handed today.

"While I have you," Carella said, "can you switch me over to the lab?"

The lab technician he spoke to reported that the paint scrapings from the windshields of both cabs matched laboratory samples of a product called Redi-Spray, which was manufactured in Milwaukee, Wisconsin, distributed nationwide, and sold in virtually every hardware store and supermarket in this city. Carella thanked him and hung up.

He was telling Meyer what he'd just learned, when Rabbi Avi Cohen walked into the squadroom.

"I think I may be able to help you with the recent cab driver murders," the rabbi said.

Carella offered him a chair alongside his desk.

"If I may," the rabbi said, "I would like to go back to the beginning."

Would you be a rabbi otherwise? Meyer thought.

"The beginning was last month," the rabbi said, "just before Passover. Today is the sixteenth day of the Omer, which is one week and nine days from the second day of Passover, so this would have been before Passover. Around the tenth of April, a Thursday I seem to recall it was."

As the rabbi remembers it . . .

This young man came to him seeking guidance and assistance. Was the rabbi familiar with a seventeen-year-old girl named Rebecca Schwartz, who was a member of the rabbi's own congregation? Well, yes, of course, Rabbi Cohen knew the girl well. He had, in fact, officiated at her *bat mitzvah* five years ago. Was there some problem?

The problem was that the young man was in love with young Rebecca, but he was not of the Jewish faith—which, by the way, had been evident to the rabbi at once, the boy's olive complexion, his dark brooding eyes. It seemed that Rebecca's parents had forbidden her from seeing the boy ever again, and this was why he was here in the synagogue today, to ask the rabbi if he could speak to Mr. Schwartz and convince him to change his mind.

Well.

The rabbi explained that this was an Orthodox congregation and that anyway there was a solemn prohibition in Jewish religious law against a Jew marrying anyone but another Jew. He went on to explain that this ban against intermarriage was especially pertinent to our times, when statistics indicated that an alarming incidence of intermarriage threatened the very future of American Jewry.

"In short," Rabbi Cohen said, "I told him I was terribly sorry, but I could never approach Samuel Schwartz with a view toward encouraging a relationship between his daughter and a boy of another faith. Do you know what he said to me?"

"What?" Carella asked.

" 'Thanks for nothing!' He made it sound like a threat."

Carella nodded. So did Meyer.

"And then the e-mails started," the rabbi said. "Three of them all together. Each with the same message. 'Death to all Jews.' And just at sundown last night . . ."

"When was this?" Meyer asked. "The e-mails?"

"Last week. All of them last week."

"What happened last night?" Carella asked.

"Someone threw a bottle of whiskey with a lighted wick through the open front door of the synagogue."

The two detectives nodded again.

"And you think this boy . . . the one who's in love with Rebecca . . . ?"

"Yes," the rabbi said.

"You think he might be the one responsible for the e-mails and the Molotov . . ."

"Yes. But not only that. I think he's the one who killed those cab drivers."

"I don't understand," Carella said. "Why would a Muslim want to kill *other* Mus . . . ?"

"But he's *not* Muslim. Did I say he was Muslim?"

"You said this was related to the . . ."

"Catholic. He's a Catholic."

The detectives looked at each other.

"Let me understand this," Carella said. "You think this kid . . . how old is he, anyway?"

"Eighteen, I would guess. Nineteen."

"You think he got angry because you wouldn't go to Rebecca's father on his behalf . . ."

"That's right."

"So he sent you three e-mails, and tried to fire-bomb your temple . . ."

"Exactly."

". . . and also killed two Muslim cab drivers?"

"Yes."

"Why? The Muslims, I mean."

"To get even."

"With?"

"With me. And with Samuel Schwartz. And Rebecca. With the entire Jewish population of this city."

"How would killing two . . . ?"

"The *magen David*," the rabbi said.

"The Star of David," Meyer explained.

"Painted on the windshields," the rabbi said. "To let people think a Jew was responsible. To enflame the Muslim community against Jews. To cause trouble between us. To cause more killing. That is why."

The detectives let this sink in.

"Did this kid happen to give you a name?" Meyer asked.

Anthony Inverni told the detectives he didn't wish to be called Tony.

"Makes me sound like a wop," he said. "My grandparents were born here, my parents were born here, my sister and I were both born here, we're Americans. You call me Tony, I'm automatically *Italian*. Well, the way I look at it, Italians are people who are born in Italy and live in Italy, not Americans who were born here and live here. And we're not *Italian*-Americans, either, by the way, because *Italian*-Americans are people who came here from Italy and *became* American citizens. So don't call me Tony, okay?"

He was nineteen years old, with curly black hair, and an olive complexion, and dark brown eyes. Sitting at sunset on the front steps of his building on Merchant Street, all the way downtown near Ramsey University, his arms hugging his knees, he could have been any Biblical Jew squatting outside a baked-mud dwelling in an ancient world. But Rabbi Cohen had spotted him for a *goy* first crack out of the box.

"Gee, who called you Tony?" Carella wanted to know.

"You were about to. I could feel it coming."

Calling a suspect by his first name was an old cop trick, but actually Carella hadn't been about to use it on the Inverni kid here. In fact, he agreed with him about all these proliferating hyphenated Americans in a nation that broadcast the words "United We Stand" as if they were a newly minted advertising slogan. But his father's name had been Anthony. And his father had called himself Tony.

"What would you like us to call you?" he asked.

"Anthony. Anthony could be British. In fact, soon as I graduate, I'm gonna change my last name to Winters. Anthony Winters. I could be the prime minister of England, Anthony Winters. That's what Inverni means anyway, in Italian. Winters."

"Where do you go to school, Anthony?" Carella asked.

"Right here," he said, nodding toward the towers in the near distance. "Ramsey U."

"You studying to be a prime minister?" Meyer asked.

"A writer. Anthony Winters. How does that sound for a writer?"

"Very good," Meyer said, trying the name, "Anthony Winters, excellent. We'll look for your books."

"Meanwhile," Carella said, "tell us about your little run-in with Rabbi Cohen."

"What run-in?"

"He seems to think he pissed you off."

"Well, he did. I mean, why *wouldn't* he go to Becky's father and put in a good word for me? I'm a straight-A student, I'm on the dean's list, am I some kind of pariah? You know what that means, 'pariah'?"

Meyer figured this was a rhetorical question.

"I'm not even *Catholic*, no less pariah," Anthony said, gathering steam. "I gave up the church the minute I tipped to what they were selling. I mean, am I supposed to believe a *virgin* gave birth? To the son of *God*, no less? That goes back to the ancient Greeks, doesn't it? All their Gods messing in the affairs of humans? I mean, give me a break, man."

"Just how pissed off were you?" Carella asked.

"Enough," Anthony said. "But you should've seen *Becky*! When I told her what the rabbi said, she wanted to go right over there and kill him."

"Then you're still seeing her, is that it?"

"Of course I'm still seeing her! We're gonna get married, what do you think? You think her bigoted father's gonna stop us? You think Rabbi Cohen's gonna stop us? We're in *love*!"

Good for you, Meyer thought. And *mazel-tov*. But did you kill those two cabbies, as the good *rov* seems to think?

"Are you on the internet?" he asked.

"Sure."

"Do you send e-mails?"

"That's the main way Becky and I communicate. I can't phone her because her father hangs up the minute he hears my voice. Her mother's a little better, she at least lets me talk to her."

"Ever send an e-mail to Rabbi Cohen?"

"No. Why? An e-mail? Why would . . . ?"

"Three of them, in fact."

"No. What kind of e-mails?"

" 'Death to all Jews,' " Meyer quoted.

"Don't be ridiculous," Anthony said. "I love a Jewish *girl*! I'm gonna *marry* a Jewish girl!"

"Were you anywhere near Rabbi Cohen's synagogue last night?" Carella asked.

"No. Why?"

"You didn't throw a fire-bomb into that synagogue last night, did you?"

"No, I did not!"

"Sundown last night? You didn't . . . ?"

"Not at sundown and not at *any* time! I was with *Becky* at sundown. We were walking in the park outside school at sundown. We were trying to figure out our next *move*."

"You may love a Jewish girl," Meyer said, "but how do you feel about *Jews*?"

"I don't know what that means."

"It means how do you feel about all these *Jews* who are trying to keep you from marrying this Jewish *girl* you love?"

"I did not throw a fucking fire-bomb . . ."

"Did you kill two Muslim cabbies . . . ?"

"What!"

". . . and paint Jewish stars on their windshields?"

"Holy shit, is *that* what this is about?"

"Did you?"

"Who said I did?" Anthony wanted to know. "Did the rabbi say I did such a thing?"

"Did you?"

"No. Why would . . . ?"

"Because you were pissed off," Meyer said. "And you wanted to get even. So you killed two Muslims and made it look like a Jew did it. So Muslims would start throwing fire-bombs into . . ."

"I don't give a damn about Muslims or Jews *or* their fucking problems," Anthony said. "All I care about is Becky. All I care about is marrying Becky. The rest is all bullshit. I did not send any e-mails to that jackass rabbi. I did not throw a fire-bomb into his dumb temple, which by the way won't let women sit with men. I did not kill any Muslim cab drivers who go to stupid temples of their own, where *their* women aren't allowed to sit with men, either. That's a nice little plot you've cooked up there, and I'll use it one day, when I'm Anthony Winters the best-selling writer. But right now, I'm still just Tony Inverni, right? And that's the only thing that's keeping me from marrying the girl I love, and that is a shame, gentlemen, that is a fucking crying shame. So if you'll excuse me, I really don't give a damn about *your* little problem, because Becky and I have a major problem of our own."

He raised his right hand, touched it to his temple in a mock salute, and went back into his building.

At nine the next morning, Detective Wilbur Jackson of the Documents Section called to say they'd checked out the graffiti—

He called the Jewish stars graffiti.

—on the windshields of those two evidence cabs and they were now able to report that the handwriting was identical in both instances and that the writer was right-handed.

"Like ninety percent of the people in this city," he added.

That night, the third Muslim cabbie was killed.

"Let's hear it," Lieutenant Byrnes said.

He was not feeling too terribly sanguine this Monday morning. He did not like this at all. First off, he did not like murder epidemics. And next, he did not like murder epidemics that could lead to full-scale riots. White-haired and scowling, eyes an icy-cold blue, he glowered across his desk as though the eight detectives gathered in his corner office had themselves committed the murders.

Hal Willis and Eileen Burke had been riding the midnight horse when the call came in about the third dead cabbie. At five-eight, Willis had barely cleared the minimum height requirement in effect before women were generously allowed to become police officers, at which time five-foot-two-eyes-of-blue became threatening when one was carrying a nine-millimeter Glock on her hip. That's exactly what Eileen was carrying this morning. Not on her hip, but in a tote bag slung over her shoulder. At five-nine, she topped Willis by an inch. Red-headed and green-eyed, she provided Irish-setter contrast to his dark, curly-haired, brown-eyed, cocker-spaniel look. Byrnes was glaring at both of them. Willis deferred to the lady.

"His name is Ali Al-Barak," Eileen said. "He's a Saudi. Married with three . . ."

"That's the most common Arabic name," Andy Parker said. He was slumped in one of the chairs near the windows. Unshaven and unkempt, he looked as if he'd just come off a plant as a homeless wino. Actually, he'd come straight to the squadroom from home, where he'd dressed hastily, annoyed because he wasn't supposed to come in until four, and now another fuckin Muslim had been aced.

"Al-Barak?" Brown asked.

"No, Ali," Parker said. "More than five million men in the Arab world are named Ali."

"How do you know that?" Kling asked.

"I know such things," Parker said.

"And what's it got to do with the goddamn price of fish?" Byrnes asked.

"In case you run into a lot of Alis," Parker explained, "you'll know it ain't a phenomenon, it's just a fact."

"Let me hear it," Byrnes said sourly, and nodded to Eileen.

"Three children," she said, picking up where she'd left off. "Lived in a Saudi neighborhood in Riverhead. No apparent connection to either of the two other vics. All three even worshipped at different mosques. Shot at the back of the head, same as the other two. Blue star on the windshield . . ."

"The other two were the same handwriting," Meyer said.

"Right-handed writer," Carella said.

"Anything from Ballistics yet?" Byrnes asked Eileen.

"Slug went to them, too soon to expect anything."

"Two to one, it'll be the same," Richard Genero said.

He was the newest detective on the squad and rarely ventured comments at these clambakes. Taller than Willis—hell, *everybody* was taller than Willis—he nonetheless looked like a relative, what with the same dark hair and eyes. Once, in fact, a perp had asked them if they were brothers. Willis, offended, had answered, "I'll give you brothers."

"Which'll mean the same guy killed all three," Byrnes said.

Genero felt rewarded. He smiled in acknowledgment.

"Or the same gun, anyway," Carella said.

"Widow been informed?"

"We went there directly from the scene," Willis said.

"What've we got on the paint?"

"Brand name sold everywhere," Meyer said.

"What's with this Inverni kid?"

"He's worth another visit."

"Why?"

"He has a thing about religion."

"What kind of thing?"

"He thinks it's all bullshit."

"Doesn't everyone?" Parker said.

"I don't," Genero said.

"That doesn't mean he's going around killing Muslims," Byrnes said. "But talk to him again. Find out where he was last night at . . . Hal? What time did the cabbie catch it?"

"Twenty past two."

"Be nice if Inverni's our man," Brown said.

"Yes, that would be very nice."

"In your dreams," Parker said.

"You got a better idea?"

Parker thought this over.

"You're such an expert on Arabian first names . . ."

"Arabic."

". . . I thought maybe you might have a better idea," Byrnes said.

"How about we put undercovers in the cabs?"

"Brilliant," Byrnes said. "You know any Muslim cops?"

"Come to think of it," Parker said, and shrugged again.

"Where'd this last one take place?"

"Booker and Lowell. In Riverhead," Eileen said. "Six blocks from the stadium."

"He's ranging all over the place."

"Got to be random," Brown said.

"Let's scour the hood," Kling suggested. "Must be somebody heard a shot at two in the morning."

"Two-twenty," Parker corrected.

"I'm going to triple-team this," Byrnes said. "Anybody not on vacation or out sick, I want him on this case. I'm surprised the commissioner himself hasn't called yet. Something like this . . ."

The phone on his desk rang.

"Let's get this son of a bitch," Byrnes said, and waved the detectives out of his office.

His phone was still ringing.

He rolled his eyes heavenward and picked up the receiver.

THIRD HATE KILLING

MUSLIM MURDERS MOUNT

All over the city, busy citizens picked up the afternoon tabloid, and read its headline, and then turned to the story on page three.

Unless the police were withholding vital information, they still did not have a single clue. This made people nervous. They did not want these stupid killings to escalate into the sort of situation that was a daily occurrence in Israel. They did not want retaliation to follow retaliation. They did not want hate begetting more hate.

But they were about to get it.

The first of what the police hoped would be the last of the bombings took place that very afternoon, the fifth day of May.

Parker—who knew such things—could have told the other detectives on the squad that the fifth of May was a date of vast importance in Mexican and Chicano communities, of which there were not a few in this sprawling city. *Cinco de Mayo*, as it was called in Spanish, celebrated the victory of the Mexican Army over the French in 1862. Hardly anyone today—except Parker maybe—knew that *La Batalla de Puebla* had been fought and won by Mestizo and Zapotec Indians. Nowadays, many of the Spanish-speaking people in this city thought the date commemorated Mexican independence, which Parker could have told you was September 16, 1810, and not May 5, 1862. Some people suspected Parker was an idiot savant, but this was only half true. He merely read a lot.

On that splendid, sunny, fifth day of May, as the city's Chicano population prepared for an evening of folklorico dancing and mariachi music and margaritas, and as the weary detectives of the Eight-Seven spread out into the three sections of the city that had so far been stricken with what even the staid morning newspaper labeled "The Muslim Murders," a man carrying a narrow Gucci dispatch case walked into a movie theater that was playing a foreign film about a Japanese prostitute who aspires to become an internationally famous violinist, took a seat in the center of the theater's twelfth row, watched the commercials for furniture stores and local restaurants and antique shops, and then watched the coming attractions, and finally, at 1:37 P.M.—just as the feature film was about to start—got up to go to the men's room.

He left the Gucci dispatch case under the seat.

There was enough explosive material in

that sleek leather case to blow up at least seven rows of seats in the orchestra. There was also a ticking clock set to trigger a spark at 3:48 P.M., just about when the Japanese prostitute would be accepted at Juilliard.

Spring break had ended not too long ago, and most of the students at Ramsey U still sported tans they'd picked up in Mexico or Florida. There was an air of bustling activity on the downtown campus as Meyer and Carella made their way through crowded corridors to the Registrar's Office, where they hoped to acquire a program for Anthony Inverni. This turned out to be not as simple as they'd hoped. Each and separately they had to show first their shields and next their ID cards, and still had to invoke the sacred words "Homicide investigation," before the yellow-haired lady with a bun would reveal the whereabouts of Anthony Inverni on this so-far eventless Cinco de Mayo.

The time was 1:45 P.M.

They found Inverni already seated in the front row of a class his program listed as

"Shakespearean Morality." He was chatting with a girl wearing a blue scarf around her head and covering her forehead. The detectives assumed she was Muslim, though this was probably profiling. They asked Inverni if he would mind stepping outside for a moment, and he said to the girl, "Excuse me, Halima," which more or less confirmed their surmise, but which did little to reinforce the profile of a hate criminal.

"So what's up?" he asked.

"Where were you at two this morning?" Meyer asked, going straight for the jugular.

"That, huh?"

"That," Carella said.

"It's all over the papers," Inverni said. "But you're still barking up the wrong tree."

"So where were you?"

"With someone."

"Who?"

"Someone."

"The someone wouldn't be Rebecca Schwartz, would it? Because as an alibi . . ."

"Are you kidding? You think old Sam would let her out of his sight at two in the morning?"

"Then who's this 'someone' we're talking about?"

"I'd rather not get her involved."

"Oh? Really? We've got three dead cabbies here. You'd better start worrying about *them* and not about getting *someone* involved. Who is she? Who's your alibi?"

Anthony turned to look over his shoulder, into the classroom. For a moment, the detectives thought he was going to name the girl with the blue scarf. Hanima, was it? Halifa? He turned back to them again. Lowering his voice, he said, "Judy Manzetti."

"Was with you at two this morning?"

"Yes."

His voice still a whisper. His eyes darting.

"Where?"

"My place."

"Doing what?"

"Well . . . you know."

"Spell it out."

"We were in bed together."

"Give us her address and phone number," Carella said.

"Hey, come on. I told you I didn't want to get her involved."

"She's already involved," Carella said. His notebook was in his hand.

Inverni gave him her address and phone number.

"Is that it?" he asked. "Cause class is about to start."

"I thought you planned to marry Becky," Meyer said.

"Of *course* I'm marrying Becky!" Inverni said. "But meanwhile . . ."—and here he smiled conspiratorially—". . . I'm fucking Judy."

No, Meyer thought. It's Becky who's getting fucked.

The time was two P.M.

As if to confirm Parker's fact-finding acumen, the two witnesses who'd heard the shot last night were both named Ali. They'd been coming home from a party at the time, and each of them had been a little drunk. They explained at once that this was not a habit of theirs. They fully understood that the imbibing of alcoholic beverages was strictly forbidden in the Koran.

"*Haram*," the first Ali said, shaking his head. "Most definitely *haram*."

"Oh yes, unacceptable," the second Ali agreed, shaking his head as well. "Forbidden. Prohibited. In the Koran, it is written, 'They ask thee concerning wine and gambling. In them is great sin, and some profit, for men; but the sin is greater than the profit.' "

"But our friend was celebrating his birthday," the first Ali said, and smiled apologetically.

"It was a party," the second Ali explained.

"Where?" Eileen asked.

The two Alis looked at each other.

At last, they admitted that the party had taken place at a club named Buffers, which Eileen and Willis both knew was a topless joint, but the Alis claimed that no one in their party had gone back to the club's so-called private room but had instead merely enjoyed the young ladies dancing around their poles.

Eileen wondered *whose* poles?

The young ladies' poles?

Or the poles of Ali and Company?

She guessed she maybe had a dirty mind.

At any rate, the two Alis were staggering out of Buffers at two o'clock in the morning when they spotted a yellow cab parked at the curb up the block. They were planning on taking the subway home, but one never argued with divine providence so they decided on the spot to take a taxi instead. As they tottered and swayed toward the idling cab—the first Ali raising his hand to hail it, the second Ali breaking into a trot toward it and almost tripping—they heard a single shot from inside the cab. They both stopped dead still in the middle of the pavement.

"A man jumped out," the first Ali said now, his eyes wide with the excitement of recall.

"What'd he look like?" Eileen asked.

"A tall man," the second Ali said. "Dressed all in black."

"Black suit, black coat, black hat."

"Was he bearded or clean-shaven?"

"No beard. No."

"You're sure it was a man?"

"Oh yes, positive," the second Ali said.

"What'd he do after he got out of the cab?"

"Went to the windshield."

"Sprayed the windshield."

"You saw him spraying the windshield?"

"Yes."

"Oh yes."

"Then what?"

"He ran away."

"Up the street."

"Toward the subway."

"There's an entrance there."

"For the subway."

Which could have taken him anywhere in the city, Eileen thought.

"Thanks," Willis said.

It was 2:15 P.M.

Parker and Genero were the two detectives who spoke once again to Ozzie Kiraz, the cousin of the second dead cabbie.

Kiraz was just leaving for work when they got there at a quarter past three that afternoon. He introduced them to his wife, a diminutive woman who seemed half his size, and who immediately went into the kitchen of their tiny apartment to prepare tea for the men. Fine-featured, dark-haired and dark-eyed, Badria Kiraz was a woman in her late twenties, Parker guessed. Exotic features aside, she looked very American to him, sporting lipstick and eye shadow, displaying a nice ass in beige tailored slacks, and good tits in a white cotton blouse.

Kiraz explained that he and his wife both worked night shifts at different places in different parts of the city. He worked at a pharmacy in Majesta, where he was manager of the store. Badria worked as a cashier in a supermarket in Calm's Point. They both started work at four, and got off at midnight. Kiraz told them that in Afghanistan he'd once hoped to become a schoolteacher. That was before he started fighting the Russians. Now, here in America, he was the manager of a drugstore.

"Land of the free, right?" he said, and grinned.

Genero didn't know if he was being a wise guy or not.

"So tell us a little more about your cousin," he said.

"What would you like to know?"

"One of the men interviewed by our colleagues . . ."

Genero liked using the word "colleagues." Made him sound like a university professor. He consulted his notebook, which made him feel even more professorial.

"Man named Ajmal, is that how you pronounce it?"

"Yes," Kiraz said.

"Ajmal Khan, a short-order cook at a deli named Max's in Midtown South. Do you know him?"

"No, I don't."

"Friend of your cousin's," Parker said.

He was eyeing Kiraz's wife, who was carrying a tray in from the kitchen. She set it down on the low table in front of the sofa, smiled, and said, "We drink it sweet, but I didn't add sugar. It's there if you want it. Cream and lemon, too. Oz," she said, "do you know what time it is?"

"I'm watching it, Badria, don't worry. Maybe you should leave."

"Would that be all right?" she asked the detectives.

"Yes, sure," Genero said, and both detectives rose politely. Kiraz kissed his wife on the cheek. She smiled again and left the room. They heard the front door to the apartment closing. The men sat again. Through the open windows, they could heard the loud-speakered cry of the muezzin calling the faithful to prayer.

"The third prayer of the day," Kiraz explained. "The *Salat al-'Asr*," and added almost regretfully, "I never pray anymore. It's too difficult here in America. If you want to be American, you follow American ways, am I right? You do what Americans do."

"Oh sure," Parker agreed, even though he'd never had any problem following American ways or doing what Americans do.

"Anyway," Genero said, squeezing a little lemon into one of the tea glasses, and then picking it up, "this guy at the deli told our colleagues your cousin was dating quite a few girls . . ."

"That's news to me," Kiraz said.

"Well, that's what we wanted to talk to you about," Parker said. "We thought you might be able to help us with their names."

"The names of these girls," Genero said.

"Because this guy in the deli didn't know who they might be," Parker said.

"I don't know, either," Kiraz said, and looked at his watch.

Parker looked at his watch, too.

It was twenty minutes past three.

"Ever *talk* to you about any of these girls?" Genero asked.

"Never. We were not that close, you know. He was single, I'm married. We have our own friends, Badria and I. This is America. There are different customs, different ways. When you live here, you do what Americans do, right?"

He grinned again.

Again, Genero didn't know if he was getting smart with them.

"You wouldn't know if any of these girls were Jewish, would you?" Parker asked.

"Because of the blue star, you mean?"

"Well . . . yes."

"I would sincerely doubt that my cousin was dating any Jewish girls."

"Because sometimes . . ."

"Oh sure," Kiraz said. "Sometimes things aren't as simple as they appear. You're thinking this wasn't a simple hate crime. You're thinking this wasn't a mere matter of a Jew killing a Muslim simply because he *was* a Muslim. You're looking for complications. Was Salim involved with a Jewish girl? Did the Jewish girl's father or brother become enraged by the very *thought* of such a relationship? Was Salim killed as a warning to any other Muslim with interfaith aspirations? Is that why the Jewish star was painted on the windshield? Stay away! Keep off!"

"Well, we weren't thinking *exactly* that," Parker said, "but, yes, that's a possibility."

"But you're forgetting the *other* two Muslims, aren't you?" Kiraz said, and smiled in what Genero felt was a superior manner, fuckin guy thought he was Chief of Detectives here.

"No, we're not forgetting them," Parker said. "We're just trying to consider all the possibilities."

"A mistake," Kiraz said. "I sometimes talk to this doctor who comes into the pharmacy.

He tells me, 'Oz, if it has stripes like a zebra, don't look for a horse.' Because people come in asking me what I've got for this or that ailment, you know? Who knows why?" he said, and shrugged, but he seemed pleased by his position of importance in the workplace. "I'm only the manager of the store, I'm not a pharmacist, but they ask me," he said, and shrugged again. "What's good for a headache, or a cough, or the sniffles, or this or that? They ask me all the time. And I remember what my friend the doctor told me," he said, and smiled, seemingly pleased by this, too, the fact that his friend was a doctor. "If it has the symptoms of a common cold, don't go looking for SARS. Period." He opened his hands to them, palms up, explaining the utter simplicity of it all. "Stop looking for zebras," he said, and smiled again. "Just find the fucking Jew who shot my cousin in the head, hmm?"

The time was 3:27 P.M.

In the movies these days, it was not unusual for a working girl to become a princess overnight, like the chambermaid who not only gets the hero onscreen but in real life as well, talk about Cinderella stories! In other movies of this stripe, you saw common working-class girls who aspired to become college students. Or soccer players. It was a popular theme nowadays. America was the land of opportunity. So was Japan, apparently, although Ruriko—the prostitute in the film all these people were waiting on line to see— was a "working girl" in the truest sense, and she didn't even want to become a princess, just a concert violinist. She was about to become just that in about three minutes.

The two girls standing on line outside the theater box office also happened to be true working girls, which was why they were here to catch the four o'clock screening of the Japanese film. They had each separately seen *Pretty Woman*, another Working Girl Becomes Princess film, and did not for a moment believe that Julia Roberts had ever blown anybody for fifty bucks, but maybe it would be different with this Japanese actress, whatever her name was. Maybe this time, they'd believe that these One in a Million fairy tales could really happen to girls who actually did this sort of thing for a living.

The two girls, Heidi and Roseanne, looked and dressed just like any secretary who'd got out of work early today . . .

It was now 3:46 P.M.

. . . and even sounded somewhat like girls with junior college educations. As the line inched closer to the box office, they began talking about what Heidi was going to do to celebrate her birthday tonight. Heidi was nineteen years old today. She'd been hooking for two years now. The closest she'd got to becoming a princess was when one of her old-fart regulars asked her to come to London with him on a weekend trip. He rescinded the offer when he learned she was expecting her period, worse luck.

"You doing anything special tonight?" Roseanne asked.

"Jimmy's taking me out to dinner," Heidi said.

Jimmy was a cop she dated. He knew what profession she was in.

"That's nice."

"Yeah."

In about fifteen seconds, it would be 3:48 P.M.

"I still can't get over it," Roseanne said.

"What's that, hon?"

"The *coincidence*!" Roseanne said, amazed. "Does your birthday *always* fall on Cinco de Mayo?"

A couple sitting in the seats just behind the one under which the Gucci dispatch case had been left were seriously necking when the bomb exploded.

The boy had his hand under the girl's skirt, and she had her hand inside his unzippered fly, their fitful manual activity covered by the raincoat he had thrown over both their laps. Neither of them really gave a damn about whether or not Ruriko passed muster with the judges at Juilliard, or went back instead to a life of hopeless despair in the slums of Yokohama. All that mattered to them was achieving mutual orgasm here in the flickering darkness of the theater while the soulful strains of Aram Khachaturian's *Spartacus* flowed from Ruriko's violin under the expert coaxing of her talented fingers.

When the bomb exploded, they both thought for the tiniest tick of an instant that they'd died and gone to heaven.

Fortunately for the Eight-Seven, the movie-theater bombing occurred in the Two-One downtown. Since there was no immediate connection between this new outburst of violence and the Muslim Murders, nobody from the Two-One called uptown in an attempt to unload the case there. Instead, because this was an obvious act of terrorism, they called the Joint Terrorist Task Force at One Federal Square further downtown, and dumped the entire matter into their laps. This did not, however, stop the talking heads on television from linking the movie bombing to the murders of the three cabbies.

The liberal TV commentators noisily insisted that the total mess we'd made in Iraq was directly responsible for this new wave of violence here in the United States. The conservative commentators wagged their heads in tolerant understanding of their colleagues' supreme ignorance, and then sagely suggested that if the police in this city would only learn how to handle the problems manifest in a gloriously diverse population, there wouldn't be any civic violence at all.

It took no more than an hour and a half before all of the cable channels were demanding immediate arrests in what was now perceived as a single case. On the six-thirty network news broadcasts, the movie-theater bombing was the headline story, and without fail the bombing was linked to the cab-driver killings, the blue Star of David on the windshields televised over and over again as the unifying leitmotif.

Ali Al-Barak, the third Muslim victim, had worked for a company that called itself simply Cabco. Its garage was located in the shadow of the Calm's Point Bridge, not too distant from the market under the massive stone supporting pillars on the Isola side of the bridge. The market was closed and shuttered when Meyer and Carella drove past it at a quarter to seven that evening. They had trouble finding Cabco's garage and drove around the block several times, getting entangled in bridge traffic. At one point, Carella suggested that they hit the hammer, but Meyer felt use of the siren might be excessive.

They finally located the garage tucked between two massive apartment buildings. It could have been the underground garage for either of them, but a discreet sign identified it as Cabco. They drove down the ramp, found the dispatcher's office, identified themselves, and explained why they were there.

"Yeah," the dispatcher said, and nodded.

His name was Hazhir Demirkol. He explained that like Al-Barak, he too was a Muslim, though not a Saudi. "I'm a Kurd," he told them. "I came to this country ten years ago."

"What can you tell us about Al-Barak?" Meyer asked.

"I knew someone would kill him sooner or later," Demirkol said. "The way he was shooting up his mouth all the time."

Shooting *off*, Carella thought, but didn't correct him.

"In what way?" he asked.

"He kept complaining that Israel was responsible for all the trouble in the Arab world. If there was no Israel, there would have been no Iraqi war. There would be no terrorism. There would be no 9/11. Well, he's a Saudi, you know. His countrymen were the ones who *bombed* the World Trade Center! But he was being foolish. It doesn't matter how you feel about Jews. I feel the same way. But in this city, I have learned to keep my thoughts to myself."

"Why's that?" Meyer asked.

Demirkol turned to him, looked him over. One eyebrow arched. Sudden recognition crossed his face. This man was a Jew. This detective was a Jew.

"It doesn't matter why," he said. "Look what happened to Ali. *That* is why."

"You think a Jew killed him, is that it?"

"No, an angel from Paradise painted that blue star on his windshield."

"Who might've heard him when he was airing all these complaints?" Carella asked.

"Who knows? Ali talked freely, *too* freely, you ask me. This is a democracy, no? Like the one America brought to Iraq, no?" Demirkol asked sarcastically. "He talked everywhere. He talked here in the garage with his friends, he talked to his passengers, I'm sure he talked at the mosque, too, when he went to prayer. Freedom of speech, correct? Even if it gets you killed."

"You think he expressed his views to the wrong person, is that it?" Meyer asked. "The wrong *Jew*."

"The *same* Jew who killed the other drivers," Demirkol said, and nodded emphatically, looking Meyer dead in the eye, challenging him.

"This mosque you mentioned," Carella said. "Would you know . . . ?"

"Majid At-Abu," Demirkol said at once. "Close by here," he said, and gestured vaguely uptown.

Now *this* was a mosque.

This was what one conjured when the very word was uttered. This was straight out of *Arabian Nights*, minarets and domes, blue tile and gold leaf. This was the real McCoy.

Opulent and imposing, Majid At-Abu was not as "close by" as Demirkol had suggested, it was in fact a good mile and a half uptown. When the detectives got there at a little past eight that night, the faithful were already gathered inside for the sunset prayer. The sky beyond the mosque's single glittering dome was streaked with the last red-purple streaks of a dying sun. The minaret from which the muezzin called worshippers to prayer stood tall and stately to the right of the arched entrance doors. Meyer and Carella stood on the sidewalk outside, listening to the prayers intoned within, waiting for an opportune time to enter.

Across the street, some Arabic-looking boys in T-shirts and jeans were cracking themselves up. Meyer wondered what they were saying. Carella wondered why they weren't inside praying.

"Ivan Sikimiavuçlyor!" one of the kids

shouted, and the others all burst out laughing.

"How about Alexandr Siksallandr?" one of the other kids suggested, and again they all laughed.

"Or Madame Döllemer," another boy said.

More laughter. Carella was surprised they didn't all fall to the sidewalk clutching their bellies. It took both of the detectives a moment to realize that these were *names* the boys were bandying about. They had no idea that in Turkish "Ivan Sikimiavuçlyor" meant "Ivan Holding My Cock," or that "Alexandr Siksallandr" meant "Alexander Who Swings a Cock," or that poor "Madame Döllemer" was just a lady "Sucking Sperm." Like the dirty names Meyer and Carella had attached to fictitious book titles when they themselves were kids . . .

The Open Robe by Seymour Hare.

The Russian Revenge by Ivana Kutchakokoff.

The Chinese Curse by Wan Hong Lo.

Hawaiian Paradise by A'wana Leia Oo'aa.

. . . these Arab teenagers growing up here in America were now making puns on their parents' native tongue.

"Fenasi Kerim!" one of the boys shouted finally and triumphantly, and whereas neither of the detectives knew that this invented name meant "I Fuck You Bad," the boys' ensuing exuberant laughter caused them to laugh as well.

The sunset prayer had ended.

They took off their shoes and placed them outside in the foyer—alongside the loafers and sandals and jogging shoes and boots and laced brogans parked there like autos in a used-car lot—and went inside to find the imam.

"I never heard Ali Al-Barak utter a single threatening word about the Jewish people, or the Jewish state, or any Jew in particular," Mohammad Talal Awad said.

They were standing in the vast open hall of the mosque proper, a white space the size of a ballroom, with arched windows and tiled floors and an overhead clerestory through which the detectives could see the beginnings of a starry night. The imam was wearing white baggy trousers and a flowing white tunic and a little while pillbox hat. He had a long black beard, a narrow nose and eyes almost black, and he directed his every word to Meyer.

"Nor is there anything in the Koran that

directs Muslims to kill anyone," he said. "Not Jews, not anyone. There is nothing there. Search the Koran. You will find not a word about murdering in the name of Allah."

"We understand Al-Barak made remarks some people might have found inflammatory," Carella said.

"Political observations. They had nothing to do with Islam. He was young, he was brash, perhaps he was foolish to express his opinions so openly. But this is America, and one may speak freely, isn't that so? Isn't that what democracy is all about?"

Here we go again, Meyer thought.

"But if you think Ali's murder had anything to do with the bombing downtown . . ."

Oh? Carella thought.

". . . you are mistaken. Ali was a pious young man who lived with another man his own age, recently arrived from Saudi Arabia. In their native land, they were both students. Here, one drove a taxi and the other bags groceries in a supermarket. If you think Ali's friend, in revenge for his murder, bombed that theater downtown . . ."

Oh? Carella thought again.

". . . you are very sadly mistaken."

"We're not investigating that bombing,"

Meyer said. "We're investigating Ali's murder. And the murder of two other Muslim cab drivers. If you can think of anyone who might possibly . . ."

"I know no Jews," the imam said.

You know one now, Meyer thought.

"This friend he lived with," Carella said. "What's his name, and where can we find him?"

The music coming from behind the door to the third-floor apartment was very definitely rap. The singers were very definitely black, and the lyrics were in English. But the words weren't telling young kids to do dope or knock women around or even up. As they listened at the wood, the lyrics the detectives heard spoke of intentions alone not being sufficient to bring reward . . .

When help is needed, prayer to Allah is the answer . . .

Allah alone can assist in . . .

Meyer knocked on the door.

"Yes?" a voice yelled.

"Police," Carella said.

The music continued to blare.

"Hello?" Carella said. "Mind if we ask you some questions?"

No answer.

"Hello?" he said again.

He looked at Meyer.

Meyer shrugged. Over the blare of the music, he yelled, "Hello in there!"

Still no answer.

"This is the police!" he yelled. "Would you mind coming to the door, please?"

The door opened a crack, held by a night chain.

They saw part of a narrow face. Part of a mustache. Part of a mouth. A single brown eye.

"Mr. Rajab?"

"Yes?"

Wariness in the voice and in the single eye they could see.

"Mind if we come in? Few questions we'd like to ask you."

"What about?"

"You a friend of Ali Al-Barak?"

"Yes?"

"Do you know he was murdered last . . . ?"

The door slammed shut.

They heard the sudden click of a bolt turning.

Carella backed off across the hall. His gun was already in his right hand, his knee coming up for a jackknife kick. The sole of his shoe collided with the door, just below the lock. The lock held.

"The yard!" he yelled, and Meyer flew off down the stairs.

Carella kicked at the lock again. This time, it sprang. He followed the splintered door into the room. The black rap group was still singing praise to Allah. The window across the room was open, a curtain fluttering in the mild evening breeze. He ran across the room, followed his gun hand out the window and onto a fire escape. He could hear footsteps clattering down the iron rungs to the second floor.

"Stop!" he yelled. "Police!"

Nobody stopped.

He came out onto the fire escape, took a quick look below, and started down.

From below, he heard Meyer racketing into the backyard. They had Rajab sandwiched.

"Hold it right there!" Meyer yelled.

Carella came down to the first-floor fire escape, out of breath, and handcuffed Rajab's hands behind his back.

They listened in total amazement as Ishak Rajab told them all about how he had plotted instant revenge for the murder of his friend and roommate, Ali Al-Barak. They listened as he told them how he had constructed the suitcase bomb . . .

He called the Gucci dispatch case a suitcase.

. . . and then had carefully chosen a movie theater showing so-called art films because he knew Jews pretended to culture, and there would most likely be many Jews in the audience. Jews had to be taught that Arabs could not wantonly be killed without reprisal.

"Ali was killed by a Jew," Rajab said. "And so it was fitting and just that Jews be killed in return."

Meyer called the JTTF at Fed Square and told them they'd accidentally lucked into catching the guy who did their movie-theater bombing.

Ungrateful humps didn't even say thanks.

It was almost ten o'clock when he and Carella left the squadroom for home. As they passed the swing room downstairs, they looked in through the open door to where a uniformed cop was half-dozing on one of the couches, watching television. One of cable's most vociferous talking heads was demanding to know when a terrorist was *not* a terrorist.

"Here's the story," he said, and glared out of the screen. "A green-card Saudi Arabian named Ishak Rajab was arrested and charged with the wanton slaying of sixteen movie patrons and the wounding of twelve others. Our own police and the Joint Terrorist Task Force are to be highly commended for their swift actions in this case. It is now to be hoped that a trial and conviction will be equally swift.

"However . . .

"Rajab's attorneys are already indicating they'll be entering a plea of insanity. Their reasoning seems to be that a man who *deliberately* leaves a bomb in a public place is not a terrorist—have you got that? *Not* a terrorist! Then what is he, huh, guys? Well, according to his attorneys, he was merely a man blinded by rage and seeking retaliation. The rationale for Rajab's behavior would seem to be his close friendship with Ali Al-Barak, the third victim in the wave of taxi-driver slayings that have swept the city since last Friday: Rajab was Al-Barak's roommate.

"Well, neither I nor any right-minded citizen would condone the senseless murder of Muslim cab drivers. That goes without saying. But to invoke a surely inappropriate Biblical—*Biblical,* mind you—'eye for an eye' defense by labeling premeditated mass murder 'insanity' is in itself insanity. A terrorist is a terrorist, and this was an act of terrorism, pure and simple. Anything less than the death penalty would be gross injustice in the case of Ishak Rajab. That's my opinion, now let's hear yours. You can e-mail me at . . ."

The detectives walked out of the building and into the night.

In four hours, another Muslim cabbie would be killed.

The police knew at once that this wasn't their man.

To begin with, none of the other victims had been robbed.

This one was.

All of the other victims had been shot only once, at the base of the skull.

This one was shot three times through the open driver-side window of his cab, two of the bullets entering his face at the left temple and just below the cheek, the third passing through his neck and lodging in the opposite door panel.

Shell casings were found on the street outside the cab, indicating that the murder weapon had been an automatic, and not the revolver that had been used in the previous three murders. Ballistics confirmed this. The bullets and casings were consistent with samples fired from a Colt .45 automatic.

Moreover, two witnesses had seen a man leaning into the cab window moments before they heard shots, and he was definitely not a tall white man dressed entirely in black.

There were only two similarities in all four murders. The drivers were all Muslims, and a blue star had been spray-painted onto each of their windshields.

But the Star of David had six points, and this new one had only five, and it was turned on end like the inverted pentagram used by devil-worshippers.

They hoped to hell yet *another* religion wasn't intruding its beliefs into this case.

But they knew for sure this wasn't their man.

This was a copycat.

CABBIE SHOT AND KILLED
FOURTH MUSLIM MURDER

So read the headline in the Metro Section of the city's staid morning newspaper. The story under it was largely put together from details supplied in a Police Department press release. The flak that had gone out from the Public Relations Office on the previous three murders had significantly withheld any information about the killer himself or his MO. None of the reporters—print, radio, or television—had been informed that the killer had been dressed in black from head to toe, or that he'd fired just a single shot into his separate victims' heads. They were hoping the killer himself—if ever they caught him—would reveal this information, thereby incriminating himself.

But this time around, because the police knew this was a copycat, the PR release was a bit more generous, stating that the cabbie had been shot three times, that he'd been robbed of his night's receipts, and that his assailant, as described by two eyewitnesses, was a black man in his early twenties, about five feet seven inches tall, weighing some hundred and sixty pounds and wearing blue jeans, white sneakers, a brown leather jacket, and a black ski cap pulled low on his forehead.

The man who'd murdered the previous three cabbies must have laughed himself silly.

Especially when another bombing took place that Tuesday afternoon.

The city's Joint Terrorist Task Force was an odd mix of elite city detectives, FBI Special Agents, Homeland Security people, and a handful of CIA spooks. Special Agent in Charge Brian Hooper and a team of four other Task Force officers arrived at The Merrie Coffee Bean at three that afternoon, not half an hour after a suicide bomber had killed himself and a dozen patrons sitting at tables on the sidewalk outside. Seven wounded people had already been carried by ambulance to the closest hospital, Abingdon Memorial, on the river at Condon Street.

The coffee shop was a shambles.

Wrought iron tables and chairs had been twisted into surreal and smoldering bits of modern sculpture. Glass shards lay all over the sidewalk and inside the shop gutted and flooded by the Fire Department.

A dazed and dazzled waitress, wide-eyed and smoke-smudged but remarkably unharmed otherwise, told Hooper that she was at the cappuccino machine picking up an order when she heard someone yelling outside. She thought at first it was one of the customers, sometimes they got into arguments over choice tables. She turned from the counter to look outside, and saw this slight man running toward the door of the shop, yelling at the top of his lungs . . .

"What was he yelling, miss, do you remember?" Hooper asked.

Hooper was polite and soft-spoken, wearing a blue suit, a white shirt, a blue tie, and polished black shoes. Two detectives from the Five-Oh had also responded. Casually, dressed in sport jackets, slacks, and shirts open at the throat, they looked like bums in contrast. They stood by trying to look interested and significant while Hooper conducted the questioning.

"Something about Jews," the waitress said. "He had a foreign accent, you know, so it was hard to understand him to begin with. And this was like a rant, so that made it even more difficult. Besides, it all happened so fast. He was running from the open sidewalk down this, like, *space* we have between the tables? Like an *aisle* that leads to the front of the shop? And he was yelling Jews-this, Jews-that, and waving his arms in the air like some kind of nut? Then all at once there was this terrific explosion, it almost knocked *me* off my feet, and I was all the way inside the shop, near the cap machine. And I saw . . . there was like sunshine outside, you know? Like shining through the windows? And all of a sudden I saw all body parts flying in the air in the sunshine. Like in silhouette. All these people getting blown apart. It was, like, awesome."

Hooper and his men went picking through the rubble.

The two detectives from the Five-Oh were thinking this was very bad shit here.

If I've already realized what I hoped to accomplish, why press my luck, as they say? The thing has escalated beyond my wildest expectations. So leave it well enough alone, he told himself.

But that idiot last night has surely complicated matters. The police aren't fools, they'll recognize at once that last night's murder couldn't possibly be linked to the other three. So perhaps another one *was* in order, after all. To nail it to the wall. Four would round it off, wouldn't it?

To the Navajo Indians—well, Native Americans, as they say—the number four was sacred. Four different times of day, four sacred mountains, four sacred plants, four different directions. East was symbolic of Positive Thinking. South was for Planning. West for Life itself. North for Hope and Strength. They believed all this, the Navajo people. Religions were so peculiar. The things people believed. The things he himself had once believed, long ago, so very long ago.

Of course the number four wasn't *truly* sacred, that was just something the Navajos believed. The way Christians believed that the number 666 was the mark of the beast, who was the Antichrist and who—well, of course, what else?—had to be Jewish, right? There were even people who believed that the internet acronym "www" for "World Wide Web" really transliterated into the Hebrew letter "*vav*" repeated three times, *vav, vav, vav,* the numerical equivalent of 666, the mark of the beast. *Let him that hath understanding count the number of the beast: for it is the number of a man; and his number is six hundred threescore and six,* Revelations 13. Oh yes, I've read the Bible, thank you, *and* the

Koran, *and* the teachings of Buddha, and they're all total bullshit, as they say. But there are people who believe in a matrix, too, and not all of them are in padded rooms wearing straitjackets.

So, yes, I think there should be another one tonight, a tip of the hat, as they say, to the Navajo's sacred number four, and that will be the end of it. The last one. The same signature mark of the beast, the six-pointed star of the Antichrist. Then let them go searching the synagogues for me. Let them try to find the murdering Jew. After tonight, I will be finished!

Tonight, he thought.

Yes.

Abbas Miandad was a Muslim cab driver, and no fool.

Four Muslim cabbies had already been killed since Friday night, and he didn't want to be number five. He did not own a pistol—carrying a pistol would be exceedingly stupid in a city already so enflamed against people of the Islamic faith—nor did he own a dagger or a sword, but his wife's kitchen was well stocked with utensils and before he set out on his midnight shift he took a huge bread knife from the rack . . .

"Where are you going with that?" his wife asked.

She was watching television.

They were reporting that there'd been a suicide bombing that afternoon. They were saying the bomber had not been identified as yet.

"Never mind," he told her, and wrapped a dishtowel around the knife and packed it in a small tote bag that had BARNES & NOBLE lettered on it.

He had unwrapped the knife the moment he drove out of the garage. At three that Wednesday morning, it was still in the pouch on the driver's side of the cab. He had locked the cab when he stopped for a coffee break. Now, he walked up the street to where he'd parked the cab near the corner, and saw a man dressed all in black, bending to look into the backseat. He walked to him swiftly.

"Help you, sir?" he asked.

The man straightened up.

"I thought you might be napping in there," he said, and smiled.

"No, sir," he said. "Did you need a taxi?"

"Is this your cab?"

"It is."

"Can you take me to Majesta?" he said.

"Where are you going, sir?"

"The Boulevard and a Hundred Twelfth."

"Raleigh Boulevard?"

"Yes."

Abbas knew the neighborhood. It was residential and safe, even at this hour. He would not drive anyone to neighborhoods that he knew to be dangerous. He would not pick up black men, even if they were accompanied by women. Nowadays, he would not pick up anyone who looked Jewish. If you asked him how he knew whether a person was Jewish or not, he would tell you he just knew. This man dressed all in black did not look Jewish.

"Let me open it," he said, and took his keys from the right-hand pocket of his trousers. He turned the key in the door lock and was opening the door when, from the corner of his eye, he caught a glint of metal. Without turning, he reached for the bread knife tucked into the door's pouch.

He was too late.

The man in black fired two shots directly into his face, killing him at once.

Then he ran off into the night.

"Changed his MO," Byrnes said. "The others were shot from the back seat, single bullet to the base of the skull . . ."

"Not the one Tuesday night," Parker said.

"Tuesday was a copycat," Genero said.

"Maybe this one was, too," Willis suggested.

"Not if Ballistics comes back with a match," Meyer said.

The detectives fell silent.

They were each and separately hoping this newest murder would not trigger another suicide bombing someplace. The Task Force downtown still hadn't been able to get a positive ID from the smoldering remains of the Merrie Coffee Bean bomber.

"Anybody see anything?" Byrnes asked.

"Patrons in the diner heard shots, but didn't see the shooter."

"Didn't see him painting that blue star again?"

"I think they were afraid to go outside," Carella said. "Nobody wants to get shot, Pete."

"Gee, no kidding?" Byrnes said sourly.

"Also, the cab was parked all the way up the street, near the corner, some six cars back from the diner, on the same side of the street. The killer had to be standing on the passenger side . . ."

"Where he could see the driver's hack license . . ." Eileen said.

"Arab name on it," Kling said.

"Bingo, he had his victim."

"Point is," Carella said, "standing where he was, the people in the diner couldn't have seen him."

"Or just didn't *want* to see him."

"Well, sure."

"Cause they *could've* seen him while he was painting the star," Parker said.

"That's right," Byrnes said. "He had to've come around to the windshield."

"They could've at least seen his back."

"Tell us whether he was short, tall, what he was wearing . . ."

"But they didn't."

"Talk to them again."

"We talked them deaf, dumb, and blind," Meyer said.

"Talk to them *again*," Byrnes said. "And talk to anybody who was in those coffee shops, diners, delis, whatever, at the scenes of the other murders. These cabbies stop for coffee breaks, two, three in the morning, they go back to their cabs and get shot. That's no coincidence. Our man knows their habits. And he's a night-crawler. What's with the Inverni kid? Did his alibi stand up?"

"Yeah, he was in bed with her," Carella said.

"In bed with who?" Parker asked, interested.

"Judy Manzetti. It checked out."

"Okay, so talk to everybody *else* again," Byrnes said. "See who might've been lurking about, hanging around, casing these various sites *before* the murders were committed."

"We *did* talk to everybody again," Genero said.

"Talk to them *again* again!"

"They all say the same thing," Meyer said. "It was a Jew who killed those drivers, all we have to do is look for a goddamn Jew."

"You're too fucking sensitive," Parker said.

"I'm telling you what we're getting. Anybody we talk to thinks it's an open-and-shut case. All we have to do is round up every Jew in the city . . ."

"Take forever," Parker said.

"What does that mean?"

"It means there are millions of Jews in this city."

"And what does *that* mean?"

"It means you're too fucking sensitive."

"Knock it off," Byrnes said.

"Anyway, Meyer's right," Genero said. "That's what we got, too. You know that, Andy."

"What do I know?" Parker said, glaring at Meyer.

"They keep telling us all we have to do is find the Jew who shot those guys in the head."

"Who told you that?" Carella said at once.

Genero looked startled.

"Who told you they got shot in the head?"

"Well . . . they *all* did."

"No," Parker said. "It was just the cousin, whatever the fuck his name was."

"What cousin?"

"The second vic. His cousin."

"Salim Nazir? *His* cousin?"

"Yeah, Ozzie something."

"Osman," Carella said. "Osman Kiraz."

"That's the one."

"And he said these cabbies were shot in the *head*?"

"Said his cousin was."

"Told us to stop looking for zebras."

"What the hell is that supposed to mean?" Byrnes asked.

"Told us to just find the Jew who shot his cousin in the head."

"The *fucking* Jew," Parker said.

Meyer looked at him.

"Were his exact words," Parker said, and shrugged.

"How did he know?" Carella asked.

"Go get him," Byrnes said.

Ozzie Kiraz was asleep when they knocked on his door at nine-fifteen that Wednesday morning. Bleary-eyed and unshaven, he came to the door in pajamas over which he had thrown a shaggy blue robe, and explained that he worked at the pharmacy until midnight each night and did not get home until one, one-thirty, so he normally slept late each morning.

"May we come in?" Carella asked.

"Yes, sure," Kiraz said, "but we'll have to be quiet, please. My wife is still asleep."

They went into a small kitchen and sat at a wooden table painted green.

"So what's up?" Kiraz asked.

"Few more questions we'd like to ask you."

"Again?" Kiraz said. "I told those other two . . . what were their names?"

"Genero and Parker."

"I told them I didn't know any of my cousin's girlfriends. Or even their names."

"This doesn't have anything to do with his girlfriends," Carella said.

"Oh? Something new then? Is there some new development?"

"Yes. Another cab driver was killed last night."

"Oh?"

"You didn't know that."

"No."

"It's already on television."

"I've been asleep."

"Of course."

"Was he a Muslim?"

"Yes."

"And was there another . . . ?"

"Yes, another Jewish star on the windshield."

"This is bad," Kiraz said. "These killings, the bombings . . ."

"Mr. Kiraz," Meyer said, "can you tell us where you were at three o'clock this morning?"

"Is that when it happened?"

"Yes, that's exactly when it happened."

"Where?"

"You tell us," Carella said.

Kiraz looked at them.

"What is this?" he asked.

"How'd you know your cousin was shot in the head?" Meyer asked.

"Was he?"

"That's what you told Genero and Parker. You told them a Jew shot your cousin in the head. How did you . . . ?"

"And did a Jew also shoot this man last night?" Kiraz asked. "In the head?"

"Twice in the face," Carella said.

"I asked you a question," Meyer said. "How'd you know . . . ?"

"I saw his body."

"You saw your cousin's . . ."

"I went with my aunt to pick up Salim's corpse at the morgue. After the people there were finished with him."

"When was this?" Meyer asked.

"The day after he was killed."

"That would've been . . ."

"Whenever. I accompanied my aunt to the morgue, and an ambulance took us to the mosque where they bathed the body according to Islamic law . . . they have rules, you know. Religious Muslims. They have many rules."

"I take it you're not religious."

"I'm American now," Kiraz said. "I don't believe in the old ways anymore."

"Then what were you doing in a mosque, washing your cousin's . . . ?"

"My aunt asked me to come. You saw her. You saw how distraught she was. I went as a family duty."

"I thought you didn't believe in the old ways anymore," Carella said.

"I don't believe in any of the *religious* bullshit," Kiraz said. "I went with her to help her. She's an old woman. She's alone now that her only son was killed. I went to help her."

"So you washed the body . . ."

"No, the *imam* washed the body."

"But you were there when he washed the body."

"I was there. He washed it three times. That's because it's written that when the daughter of Muhammad died, he instructed his followers to wash her three times, or more than that if necessary. Five times, seven, whatever. But always an *odd* number of times. Never an *even* number. That's what I mean about all the religious *bullshit.* Like having to wrap the body in *three* white sheets. That's because when Muhammad died, he himself was wrapped in three white sheets. From Yemen. That's what's written. So God forbid you should wrap a Muslim corpse in *four* sheets! Oh no! It has to be three. But you have to use *four* ropes to tie the sheets, not *three*, it has to be four. And the ropes each have to be seven feet long. Not three, or four, but *seven*! Do you see what I mean? All mumbo-jumbo bullshit."

"So you're saying you saw your cousin's body . . ."

"Yes."

". . . while he was being washed."

"Yes."

"And that's how you knew he was shot in the head."

"Yes. I saw the bullet wound at the base of his skull. Anyway, where *else* would he have been shot? If his murderer was sitting behind him in the taxi . . ."

"How do you know that?"

"What?"

"How do you know his murderer was inside the taxi?"

"Well, if Salim was shot at the back of the head, his murderer *had* to be sitting . . ."

"Oz?"

She was standing in the doorway to the kitchen, a diminutive woman with large brown eyes, her long ebony hair trailing down the back of the yellow silk robe she wore over a long white nightgown.

"Badria, good morning," Kiraz said. "My wife, gentlemen. I'm sorry, I've forgotten your names."

"Detective Carella."

"Detective Meyer."

"How do you do?" Badria said. "Have you offered them coffee?" she asked her husband.

"I'm sorry, no."

"Gentlemen? Some coffee?"

"None for me, thanks," Carella said.

Meyer shook his head.

"Oz? Would you like some coffee?"

"Please," he said. There was a faint amused smile on his face now. "As an illustration," he said, "witness my wife."

The detectives didn't know what he was talking about.

"The wearing of silk is expressly forbidden in Islamic law," he said. " 'Do not wear silk, for one who wears it in the world will not wear it in the Hereafter.' That's what's written. You're not allowed to wear yellow clothing, either, because 'these are the clothes usually worn by nonbelievers,' quote unquote. But here's my beautiful wife wearing a yellow silk robe, oh shame unto her," Kiraz said, and suddenly began laughing.

Badria did not laugh with him.

Her back to the detectives, she stood before a four-burner stove, preparing her husband's coffee in a small brass pot with a tin lining.

" 'A man was wearing clothes dyed in saffron,' " Kiraz said, apparently quoting again, his laughter trailing, his face becoming serious again. " 'And finding that Muhammad disapproved of them, he promised to wash them. But the Prophet said, *Burn* them!' " That's written, too. So tell me, Badria. Should we burn your pretty yellow silk robe? What do you think, Badria?"

Badria said nothing.

The aroma of strong Turkish coffee filled the small kitchen.

"You haven't answered our very first question," Meyer said.

"And what was that? I'm afraid I've forgotten it."

"Where were you at three o'clock this morning?"

"I was here," Kiraz said. "Asleep. In bed with my beautiful wife. Isn't that so, Badria?"

Standing at the stove in her yellow silk robe, Badria said nothing.

"Badria? Tell the gentlemen where I was at three o'clock this morning."

She did not turn from the stove.

Her back still to them, her voice very low, Badria Kiraz said, "I don't know where you were, Oz."

The aroma of the coffee was overpowering now.

"But you weren't here in bed with me," she said.

Nellie Brand left the District Attorney's Office at eleven that Wednesday morning and was uptown at the Eight-Seven by a little before noon. She had cancelled an important lunch date, and even before the detectives filled her in, she warned them that this better be real meat here.

Osman Kiraz had already been read his rights and had insisted on an attorney before he answered any questions. Nellie wasn't familiar with the man he chose. Gulbuddin Amin was wearing a dark-brown business suit, with a tie and vest. Nellie was wearing a suit, too. Hers was a Versace, and it was a deep shade of green that complimented her blue eyes and sand-colored hair. Amin had a tidy little mustache and he wore eyeglasses. His English was impeccable, with a faint Middle

Eastern accent. Nellie guessed he might originally have come from Afghanistan, as had his client. She guessed he was somewhere in his mid fifties. She herself was thirty-two.

The police clerk's fingers were poised over the stenotab machine. Nellie was about to begin the questioning when Amin said, "I hope this was not a frivolous arrest, Mrs. Brand."

"No, counselor . . ."

". . . because that would be a serious mistake in a city already fraught with Jewish-Arab tensions."

"I would not use the word frivolous to describe this arrest," Nellie said.

"In any case, I've already advised my client to remain silent."

"Then we have nothing more to do here," Nellie said, briskly dusting the palm of one hand against the other. "Easy come, easy go. Take him away, boys, he's all yours."

"Why are you afraid of her?" Kiraz asked his lawyer.

Amin responded in what Nellie assumed was Arabic.

"Let's stick to English, shall we?" she said. "What'd you just say, counselor?"

"My comment was privileged."

"Not while your man's under oath, it isn't."

Amin sighed heavily.

"I told him I'm afraid of no woman."

"Bravo!" Nellie said, applauding, and then looked Kiraz dead in the eye. "How about you?" she asked. "Are *you* afraid of me?"

"Of course not!"

"So would you like to answer some questions?"

"I have nothing to hide."

"Yes or no? It's your call. I haven't got all day here."

"I would like to answer her questions," Kiraz told his lawyer.

Amin said something else in Arabic.

"Let us in on it," Nellie said.

"I told him it's his own funeral," Amin said.

Q: Mr. Kiraz, would you like to tell us where you were at three this morning?

A: I was at home in bed with my wife.

Q: You wife seems to think otherwise.

A: My wife is mistaken.

Q: Well, she'll be subpoenaed before the grand jury, you know, and she'll have to tell them under oath whether you were in bed with her or somewhere else.

A: I was home. She was in bed with me.

Q: You yourself are under oath right this minute, you realize that, don't you?

A: I realize it.

Q: You swore on the Koran, did you not? You placed your left hand on the Koran and raised your right hand . . .

A: I know what I did.

Q: Or does that mean anything to you?

Q: Mr. Kiraz?

Q: Mr. Kiraz, does that mean anything to you? Placing your hand on the Islamic holy book . . .

A: I heard you.

Q: May I have your answer, please?

A: My word is my bond. It doesn't matter whether I swore on the Koran or not.

Q: Well, good, I'm happy to hear that. So tell me, Mr. Kiraz, where were you on these *other* dates at around two in the morning? Friday, May second . . . Saturday, May third . . . and Monday, May fifth. All at around two in the morning, where were you, Mr. Kiraz?

A: Home asleep. I work late. I get home around one, one-fifteen. I go directly to bed.

Q: Do you know what those dates signify?

A: I have no idea.

Q: You don't read the papers, is that it?

A: I read the papers. But those dates . . .

Q: Or watch television? You don't watch television?

A: I work from four to midnight. I rarely watch television.

Q: Then you don't know about these Muslim cab drivers who were shot and killed, is that it?

A: I know about them. Is that what those dates are? Is that when they were killed?

Q: How about Saturday, May third? Does that date hold any particular significance for you?

A: Not any more than the other dates.

Q: Do you know who was killed on that date?

A: No.

Q: Your cousin. Salim Nazir.

A: Yes.

Q: Yes what?

A: Yes. Now I recall that was the date.

Q: Because the detectives spoke to you that morning, isn't that so? In your aunt's apartment? Gulalai Nazir, right? Your aunt? You spoke to the detectives at six that morning, didn't you?

A: I don't remember the exact time, but yes, I spoke to them.

Q: And told them a Jew had killed your cousin, isn't that so?

A: Yes. Because of the blue star.

Q: Oh, is that why?

A: Yes.

Q: And you spoke to Detective Genero and Parker, did you not, after a third Muslim cab driver was killed? This would have been on Monday, May fifth, at around three in the afternoon, when you spoke to them. And at that time you said, correct me if I'm wrong, you said, "Just find the fucking Jew who shot my cousin in the head," is that correct?

A: Yes, I said that. And I've already explained how I knew he was shot in the head. I was there when the imam washed him. I saw the bullet wound . . .

Q: Did you know any of these other cab drivers?

A: No.

Q: Khalid Aslam . . .

A: No.

Q: Ali Al-Barak?

A: No.

Q: Or the one who was killed last night, Abbas Miandad, did you know any of these drivers?

A: I told you no.

Q: So the only one you knew was your cousin, Salim Nazir.

A: Of course I knew my cousin.

Q: And you also knew he was shot in the head.

A: Yes. I told you . . .

Q: Like all the other drivers.

A: I don't know how the other drivers were killed. I didn't see the other drivers.

Q: But you saw your cousin while he was being washed, is that correct?

A: That is correct.

Q: Would you remember the name of the imam who washed him?

A: No, I'm sorry.

Q: Would it have been Ahmed Nur Kabir?

A: It could have. I had never seen him before.

Q: If I told you his name was Ahmed Nur Kabir, and that the name of the mosque where your cousin's body was prepared for burial is Masjid Al-Barbrak, would you accept that?

A: If you say that's where . . .

Q: Yes, I say so.

A: Then, of course, I would accept it.

Q: Would it surprise you to learn that the detectives here—Detectives Carella and Meyer—spoke to the imam at Masjid Al-Barbrak?

A: I would have no way of knowing whether or not they . . .

Q: Will you accept my word that they spoke to him?

A: I would accept it.

Q: They spoke to him and he told them he was alone when he washed your cousin's body, alone when he wrapped the body in its shrouds. There was no one in the room with him. He was alone, Mr. Kiraz.

A: I don't accept that. I was with him.

Q: He says you were waiting outside with your aunt. He says he was alone with the corpse.

A: He's mistaken.

Q: If he was, in fact, alone with your cousin's body . . . ?

A: I told you he's mistaken.

Q: You think he's lying?

A: I don't know what . . .

Q: You think a holy man would lie?

A: *Holy* man! *Please*!

Q: If he was alone with the body, how do you explain seeing a bullet wound at the back of your cousin's head?

Q: Mr. Kiraz?

Q: Mr. Kiraz, how did you know your cousin was shot in the head? None of the newspaper or television reports . . .

Q: Mr. Kiraz? Would you answer my question, please?

Q: Mr. Kiraz?

A: Any man would have done the same thing.

Q: What would any man . . . ?

A: She is not one of his *whores*! She is my *wife*!

I knew, of course, that Salim was seeing a lot of women. That's okay, he was young, he was good-looking, the Koran says a man can take as many as four wives, so long as he can support them emotionally and financially. Salim wasn't even married, so there's nothing wrong with dating a lot of girls, four, five, a dozen, who cares? This is America, Salim was American, we're all Americans, right? You watch television, the bachelor has to choose from *fifteen* girls, isn't that so? This is America. So there was nothing wrong with Salim dating all these girls.

But not my wife.

Not Badria.

I don't know when it started with her. I don't know when it started between them. I know one night I called the supermarket where she works. This was around ten o'clock one night, I was at the pharmacy. I manage a pharmacy, you know. People ask me all sorts of questions about what they should do for various ailments. I'm not a pharmacist, but they ask me questions. I know a lot of doctors. Also, I read a lot. I have time during the day, I don't start work till four in the afternoon. So I read a lot. I wanted to be a teacher, you know.

They told me she had gone home early.

I said, Gone home? Why?

I was alarmed.

Was Badria sick?

The person I spoke to said my wife had a headache. So she went home.

I didn't know what to think.

I immediately called the house. There was no answer. Now I became really worried. Was she seriously ill? Why wasn't she answering the phone? Had she fainted? So I went home, too. I'm the manager, I can go home if I like. This is America. A manager can go home if he likes. I told my assistant I thought my wife might be sick.

I was just approaching my building when I saw them. This was now close to eleven o'clock that night. It was dark, I didn't recognize them at first. I thought it was just a young couple. Another young couple. Only that. Coming up the street together. Arm in arm. Heads close. She turned to kiss him. Lifted her head to his. Offered him her lips. It was Badria. My wife. Kissing Salim. My cousin.

Well, they knew each other, of course. They had met at parties, they had met at family gatherings, this was my *cousin*! "Beware of getting into houses and meeting women," the Prophet said. "But what about the husband's brother?" someone asked, and the Prophet replied, "The husband's brother is like death." He often talked in riddles, the Prophet, it's all such bullshit. The Prophet believed that the influence of an evil eye is *fact.* Fact, mind you. The evil eye. The Prophet believed that he himself had once been put under a spell by a Jew and his daughters. The Prophet believed that the fever associated with plague was due to the intense heat of Hell. The Prophet once said, "Filling the belly of a person with pus is better than stuffing his brain with poetry." Can you believe that? I *read* poetry! I read a lot. The Prophet believed that if you had a bad dream, you should spit three times on your left side. That's what Jews do when they want to take the curse off something, you know, they spit on their fingers, ptui, ptui, ptui. I've seen elderly Jews doing that on the street. It's the same thing, am I right? It's all bullshit, all of it. Jesus turning water into wine, Jesus raising the dead! I mean, come on! Raising the *dead*? Moses parting the Red Sea? I'd love to see that one!

It all goes back to the time of the dinosaurs, when men huddled in caves in fear of thunder and lightning. It all goes back to God-fearing men arguing violently about which son of Abraham was the true descendant of the one true God, and whether or not Jesus was, in fact, the Messiah. As if a one *true* God, if there *is* a God at all, doesn't know who the hell he himself is! All of them killing each other! Well, it's no different today, is it? It's all about killing each other in the name of God, isn't it?

In the White House, we've got a born-again Christian who doesn't even realize he's fighting a holy war. An angry dry-drunk, as they say, full of hate, thirsting for white wine, and killing Arabs wherever he can find them. And in the sand out there, on their baggy-pantsed knees, we've got a zillion Muslim fanatics, full of hate, bowing to Mecca and vowing to drive the infidel from the Holy Land. Killing each other. All of them killing each other in the name of a one true God.

In my homeland, in my village, the tribal elders would have appointed a council to rape my wife as punishment for her transgression. And then the villagers would have stoned her to death.

But this is America.

I'm an American.

I knew I had to kill Salim, yes, that is what an American male would do, protect his wife, protect the sanctity of his home, kill the intruder. But I also knew I had to get away with it, as they say, I had to kill the violator and still be free to enjoy the pleasures of my wife, my position, I'm the manager of a pharmacy!

I bought the spray paint, two cans, at a hardware store near the pharmacy. I thought that was a good idea, the Star of David. Such symbolism! The six points of the star symbolizing God's rule over the universe in all six directions, north, south, east, west, up and down. Such bullshit! I didn't kill Salim until the second night, to make it seem as if he wasn't the true target, this was merely hate, these were hate crimes. I should have left it at three. Three would have been convincing enough, weren't you convinced after three? Especially with the bombings that followed? Weren't you convinced? But I had to go for four. Insurance. The Navajos think four is a sacred number, you know. Again, it has to do with religion, with the four directions. They're all related, these religions. Jews, Christians, Muslims, they're all related. And they're all the same bullshit.

Salim shouldn't have gone after my wife.

He had enough whores already.

My wife is not a whore.

I did the right thing.

I did the American thing.

They came out through the back door of the station house—a Catholic who hadn't been to church since he was twelve, and a Jew who put up a tree each and every Christmas—and walked to where they'd parked their cars early this morning. It was a lovely bright afternoon. They both turned their faces up to the sun and lingered a moment. They seemed almost reluctant to go home. It was often that way after they cracked a tough one. They wanted to savor it a bit.

"I've got a question," Meyer said.

"Mm?"

"Do you think I'm too sensitive?"

"No. You're not sensitive at all."

"You mean that?"

"I mean it."

"You'll make me cry."

"I just changed my mind."

Meyer burst out laughing.

"I'll tell you one thing," he said. "I'm sure glad this didn't turn out to be what it looked like at first. I'm glad it wasn't hate."

"Maybe it was," Carella said.

They got into their separate cars and drove toward the open gate in the cyclone fence, one car behind the other. Carella honked "Shave-and-a-hair-cut," and Meyer honked back "Two-bits!" As Carella made his turn, he waved so long. Meyer tooted the horn again.

Both men were smiling.